NUTCRACKER

French: Casse-noisette(s)
English: Nutcracker(s)

NUTCRACKER

John Rhodes

iUniverse, Inc.
New York Lincoln Shanghai

Nutcracker

iUniverse, Inc.

For information address:
iUniverse, Inc.
2021 Pine Lake Road, Suite 100
Lincoln, NE 68512
www.iuniverse.com

ISBN: 0-595-31863-0 (pbk)

ISBN: 0-595-66436-9 (cloth)

Printed in the United States of America

For Kim, Dave, Chris, Kate, Will, Rich, Jamie, Shep, Cathy, and especially Carole, for putting up with me

Prologue

"This can't be right." Jeannette Bois muttered to herself, and checked her computer records again. But it was right, and it stayed right however often she checked it.

Ninety-nine point nine-nine-nine percent of the world's population finds the arcane processes of inter-bank accounting acutely boring. Jeannette Bois was one of the tiny handfuls of people who do not. She was a middle-aged woman with plain features and limited social skills and, denied other outlets for her emotions, she focused her love on her job and her cats.

She worked at a large bank in Paris, in a group with a name as convoluted and tedious as the job it did—the 'International Correspondent Banking Institutional Nostro Reconciliation Department'. Their task was to track the flow of funds between large international organizations which had accounts at the bank.

It was after seven in the evening, but she called her friend Inge in a small Swiss bank, betting that she, too, would still be at her desk. After exchanging pleasantries about the health of their respective animals, Jeannette said, "I think I have a bunch of misapplied funds I need to reverse." She read off the SWIFT numbers which identified the transactions between the two banks through the international funds transfer system.

"No, I have them too, they're correct" responded Inge. "I'll e-mail you the details."

Jeannette printed off the details of the incredible accounting entries and Inge's e-mail with no clear purpose in mind, although she felt she should tell *someone* about it; she just wasn't sure who to tell. Inge was a nice woman—they often spent their vacations together—but she was a bit dense, to tell the truth.

In the end Jeannette told her sister, who told her husband, and the very next day Jeannette was mugged on the metro and died of her stab wounds. Inge did not attend her good friend's funeral, for she died less than twenty-four hours later.

PART I

Squeeze

CHAPTER 1

We will place the balls of the American President in a nutcracker, and then we will squeeze.

—Jean Luc Lafarge

The man who called himself Kamal parked his panel van on a quiet street in Jerusalem. The vehicle had a sliding panel in the roof and he retracted it, letting in the cool evening air and the busy hum of the city. A spring-loaded U-shaped metal frame was bolted to the floor in the rear of the vehicle. The device was part of a plumber's work bench used for cutting domestic water pipes. Several lengths of metal and polystyrene piping lay on the floor of the van, together with an extensive array of welding equipment and battered tools of the trade.

Kamal opened a metal toolbox and took out a hand grenade. He released the safety pin and placed it into a concave depression in the U-frame. He pulled a release lever and the U-frame jerked violently upward, acting as a slingshot. The grenade flew silently into the night sky.

The apparatus could hurl a one-pound grenade a maximum range of two hundred and fifty yards. Kamal engaged an electric motor which lifted the U-frame against the tension of the springs. He loaded a second grenade just as he heard a muffled explosion in the distance. At the top of the U-frame's arc, a cam disengaged and the frame jerked forward again. The second grenade was projected in the wake of the first; then the motor re-engaged and began to lift the mechanism again.

He had spent several weeks of testing and modification in perfecting the slingshot mechanism and the technique of lobbing a grenade in a high parabolic trajectory so that it would fly over the buildings that separate one street from the next.

At the end of its hurling arc the U-frame struck heavy rubber stoppers that reduced the noise of its release to a deep '*thunk*' rather than a loud bang, and the interior of the van was lined with sheets of plastic foam insulation which further muffled the thud. The CD player was playing *California Girls* by the Beach Boys, and the mechanism was timed so that the release of the slingshot coincided with the heavy rhythm. At ten paces a passerby could not distinguish the sound of the slingshot from the thump of the drums in the rock song. The van's suspension had been stiffened and it scarcely moved in recoil. The dull gray grenades were virtually invisible against the night sky, unless someone with exceptional night vision stood directly behind the van and knew exactly where to look.

Kamal fired a total of five grenades in thirty seconds, and then disengaged the motor, closed the roof hatch, and climbed back into the driver's seat. His face was expressionless as he looked carefully around, but there were no pedestrians who might have seen something.

He had no way of knowing if his aim had been accurate. He had calculated the precise angle at which to park the van so it was aligned at the target street intersection using satellite imagery, and he knew the exact distance involved. Even so, he could expect an accuracy of no better than a circle with a diameter of thirty meters. A grenade is simply a small explosive charge inside a metal case which shatters into fragments when the charge is detonated. In contrast to depictions in innumerable movies, almost all the damage is caused by the jagged fragments of casing rather than the force of the explosion itself.

In addition, a grenade has the ballistic qualities of a brick. At the range Kamal was attempting, the grenades would wobble and flutter in their arcs of flight like a knuckleball, so that hitting the exact center of the target would be a matter of luck, but he was unconcerned with great accuracy. He was simply trying to create shock and horror.

Kamal's aim had been remarkably true for a first effort and his grenades had fallen into the busy intersection at which he had been aiming. The first landed in the roadway at the center of the crossing and exploded with a sharp crack, causing the driver of a passing car to lose control of his vehicle, which veered violently to its right and crashed through the window of a small bakery. The owner of the store was killed instantly by flying plate glass and the driver bled to death before the paramedics could save him.

The second grenade landed within yards of the first. The spray of shrapnel struck a grandmother and granddaughter waiting to cross the intersection. The woman had just collected the child from tap dancing lessons, and the six-year-old was proudly exhibiting her newly acquired impression of Shirley Temple—they'd played an old movie in class—when flying metal severed both her feet.

The third grenade landed in an open convertible. The occupants were a young man who had recently returned from college in the United States and his girlfriend. They had been out together on six dates in the last two weeks and she had decided not to keep him waiting any longer. They were on their way to her apartment. The grenade landed between the young man's feet and the explosion tore his lower body to pieces.

Shards of heated flying metal from the casing passed through his thighs and abdomen and ripped open the gasoline tank. The car exploded into a fireball. The shrapnel had miraculously missed the young woman and she was uninjured until the fire consumed her. She screamed and sucked burning petroleum vapor into her lungs. She would have screamed again but her vocal cords were no longer functional. She remained conscious for some thirty seconds; even more than agony, her principal sensation was one of acute loneliness, isolated inside the volcano of fire with the rest of the world on the outside.

The fourth grenade passed clear across the intersection and exploded on a roof, tearing up several tiles but causing little structural damage. The fifth and final grenade struck in almost the same spot as the first, in the center of the intersection, peppering the area with shrapnel and striking the grandmother for a second time as she bent over her granddaughter in horrified disbelief. She grunted and collapsed across the shrieking child.

Two thousand miles to the west the murmurs of conversation died away around a Parisian dinner table and the guests turned politely to their host. Dinner had been excellent and the conversation had been interesting and enjoyable, but they all knew they had not been invited simply out of hospitality or friendship. Jean Luc Lafarge never did anything without a purpose.

"Gentlemen, I do not believe that any of you are pleased with the progress of world events. It is my intention to redirect them." He spoke without drama or emphasis but his voice projected power. "The objective is very simple: to reverse the long and steady decline of France as a world power. I am inviting you to join me."

His guests, a group of middle-aged men dressed in quiet business suits, absorbed this opening. Their conservatism seemed to emphasize the gilt splendor of the ornate rococo dining room in which they sat. A central candelabrum sent flickering shadows to the mirrored recesses of the room. Jean Luc's tastes were traditional, and his townhouse in the heart of Paris was an impeccably preserved example of the Second Empire. Cognac was served with their coffee and the air was pungent with the heavy smoke of Cuban cigars.

"Let me begin by asking our old friend Francois Diderot to give his assessment of the current geopolitical situation."

"Thank you, Jean Luc." Professor Diderot was a man whose professional success depended upon succinct and forceful arguments, and his acerbic tongue had made him a frequent guest on late night intellectual talk shows. His broad knowledge of international affairs and pedantic style had often been compared with those of Henry Kissinger. He was dressed as conservatively as any of them, but he left his thin graying hair un-brushed and tousled to create the impression of academic independence.

"Gentlemen, it is my thesis that France has made a series of decisions which, while they may have seemed prudent at the time, even clever and incisive, have had very unfortunate long-term effects. I believe these mistakes fall into three categories."

He raised a pudgy finger. "The first mistake has been our military strategy. Let us begin my account at the end of World War II, when the Americans generously, and foolishly, granted us the status of victors, as if we were still a great power. Since then our military experience has been one long chapter of disasters: our defeats in Suez, Indo-China, and Algeria; our attempts to weaken NATO; our absurd and completely irrelevant insistence on having our own nuclear deterrent....

"In light of these repeated failures, we decided to take advantage of the generosity of the American taxpayer. Since the United States was prepared to guarantee our defense, we reasoned, why bother to pay for it ourselves? As a consequence of this decision, the reality is that over the past twenty years we have effectively disarmed ourselves, with a few minor exceptions."

He shook his head sadly. "We have saved a great deal of money, but France has no ability to take independent military action, and we have therefore excluded ourselves from decisive influence over any course of action involving force. Whenever a crisis occurs, in the Balkans or the Middle East, for example, we must always insist on a diplomatic solution, because we have no military option of our own. We cannot shape events of military consequence and our best military efforts are trivial."

"I think your judgment is a little harsh, Professor," said an elegant silver-haired gentleman, seated at the far end of the table. Michel Leclerc was Jean Luc's oldest and closest friend.

"I wish it were, Michel, I wish it were...." Diderot shook his head a second time. "When we landed alongside the US Marines in Haiti when Aristide lost power, I wish we had not had to rent a school bus to carry our troops in the town, because we lack the ability to transport our own vehicles....

"But, if I may return to my thesis. In the First World War we had the largest army in the world and yet it took the British and the Americans to save us. At the beginning of World War II we had more tanks, and bigger tanks, than the Germans, and yet we collapsed completely within a few short weeks."

The professor shook his head ruefully again. "If permanent seats in the Security Council had been awarded based on military strengths and accomplishments, Canada would have a seat and we would not."

The silver-haired gentleman decided he would probably not win this argument, and the professor held up a second digit.

"The second mistake has been our social and economic policy. I speak not of its political principles, but of its practical effects. We decided, along with much of the rest of Europe, to build an economy dominated by the public sector. While we have had our successes with state supported enterprises—notably Airbus, for example—the fact is we have eliminated the kind of open entrepreneurial capitalism which leads to innovation and economic vitality."

There was a perceptible quiver around the table, for, although everyone knew the professor's analysis to be true, no one liked to hear it stated so baldly.

Diderot ploughed on, piling unpleasant fact upon unpleasant fact. "Instead, we have achieved a high standard of living when measured in terms of social security, the number of hours we work, long vacations, secure employment, and so forth, but a low standard of living when measured in disposable income and the ability to aggregate assets.

"I fear matters will get worse. As our population ages, the costs of our social structure will increase, while our productive resources will decrease. Less and less workers will support more and more retirees. The results will be ever-increasing taxes, decreasing social benefits, and emigration; already a third of the graduates of our major universities leave France."

Michel wondered if the professor took a particular pleasure in dissecting weakness. The man was on a roll and seemed unstoppable.

Diderot continued. "Our third mistake has been in our recent management—or perhaps I should say mismanagement—of European affairs. It was always our plan to dominate Europe in partnership with Germany, ceding them economic leadership in return for diplomatic leadership. With German support behind us, the British would not be able to compete. But, as we know, that did not turn out to be the case."

He paused long enough to take a sip of wine.

"To cut a very long and convoluted story short, the Iraqi debacle coincided with the expansion of Europe to include ten additional countries. Rather than uniting Europe behind our leadership in opposition to American imperialism, we found ourselves in a minority position. The eastern European countries, along with Italy and Britain, are solidly pro-US. Even the Madrid bombs didn't change the basic pattern: people had second thoughts about voting for governments which would be softer on terror when the ETA stepped up its campaign and the IRA resurfaced."

"Public opinion is highly anti-American all across Europe, even in…." Michel began again, but was interrupted.

"Public opinion is formed by the media." Diderot nodded down the table to a press baron, who grunted in acknowledgement. "As long as the media are anti-American, the public will believe what they are told, and they are told that America is out of control."

He shrugged and spread his arms as he reached his conclusions.

"But let me finish my thesis. The future is no more promising than the present. Our population is declining. The number of people in the world who speak French is declining—in sharp contrast to Spanish and English, I might add. Our culture is eroding. It is, in my opinion, inevitable that France will continue to decline. By the middle of the century, we will have no more influence than Portugal—and perhaps less, since the Brazilians speak Portuguese."

There was a gloomy silence around the table. One might nitpick at the professor's arguments, but one could not dispute his overall direction.

Kamal smoked a cigarette and waited thirty minutes until he estimated that the rescue and recovery process was well underway. The warm night air was strident with sirens and the stations on his radio were beginning to broadcast news of the attack. He was able to guess the broad outlines of the damage he had inflicted. The main point was that he had indeed struck the intersection at which he had been aiming.

The residential block on which he was parked was relatively quiet. The occasional emergency vehicle howled to or from the carnage. There were no police or soldiers in sight, although there were heads peering out of windows and a few of the residents had hurried from their homes to help the injured.

In his mind's eye Kamal contrasted the peaceful street in which he sat with the scene of carnage he had created a short distance away. The sudden and utterly unexpected attack would have frozen the victims with its extreme violence so that initially they were too shocked to respond. Once the grenades had stopped falling, hysteria would have set in. The shrieking of the wounded would have replaced the earsplitting cracks of the exploding grenades and competed with the screaming of those who had been spared.

Kamal had experienced combat and knew well that a sudden assault can incapacitate even trained soldiers: one simply cannot believe what is happening. The effect is even more traumatic for hapless civilians exposed to mayhem. After such an attack, autonomic physical reactions set in; unmanageable shaking, loss of control of one's bowel muscles, a tendency to unexpected bursts of weeping.

Kamal decided his risk of detection was low. He flipped his spent cigarette into the street where it lay glowing the darkness and restarted the Beach Boys track. He climbed back into the rear of the van, reopened the roof and launched five more grenades. Then he drove carefully away and in fifteen minutes he was parked safely back in his garage. He climbed the stairs to his apartment, exchanging words of horror at the breaking news with his neighbor, and turned on the television.

Evidently his second attack had been even more successful than the first, for several policemen and paramedics had been killed in the explosions, and a jumpy soldier had opened fire into an apartment window overlooking the intersection, killing a teenager who had been foolish enough to poke his head out.

Kamal stretched and worked his back and shoulders against the persistent ache in his neck, and then opened the fridge and took out a beer.

❧ ❧ ❧

"Thank you, Francois," said Jean Luc Lafarge when Professor Diderot finally sat back in his chair at the end of his lecture on the state of France's misfortunes. "You paint a bleak picture, but I believe it is absolutely necessary, gentlemen, to look at our situation objectively. As we all know, one cannot solve problems by pretending they simply don't exist."

He leaned forward to address his friends. In the urbane surroundings of his townhouse he might well have been addressing a board meeting.

"As I said, it is my intention to change this direction. But let me make myself very clear at the outset. Many of the actions I contemplate are criminal, and I am not discussing hiring pimply youths to trash McDonald's restaurants. It is likely that a significant number of innocent people will die.

"Therefore, I must ask each of you to make a decision, here and now, whether you wish to participate or not. If you choose to participate, it must be on the condition of absolute secrecy, and with the clear understanding that betrayal of our secrets will result in your death. There can be no half measures."

He shrugged and smiled. "Obviously, I am placing my life in your hands. You may simply leave now, and place a call to the appropriate authorities. But I trust you will not do so. If you choose not to participate I trust you will simply observe as events unfold. Now, enough melodrama! Please make your decisions."

"Jean Luc," said Michel Leclerc, "If I understand you correctly, you are proposing to form a conspiracy which will somehow advance the ability of France to influence world events by undermining the power of the United States. Your allusion to criminal acts suggests terrorism. Are you proposing that we finance a terrorist cell?"

"Perhaps, but I must have your decisions first, if you please. We are all men who understand risk. I simply wanted to point out the risk involved in this enterprise before you make your commitment, if that is what you decide to do."

The room grew silent as the men considered Jean Luc's proposal. They were all successful and wealthy; they were all highly intelligent; and they all believed passionately in the qualities which make France unique.

On the other hand, none of them were strongly anti-American. Their business enterprises depended on the strength of the American economy, as all global enterprises do; they all knew that France's security depended ultimately on American protection; they all knew that America's policies might be crass but were ultimately benign. They all knew that most anti-Americanism was pure hype, such as the fiction that genetically-improved foods are poisonous; they knew—to quote a trivial example—that Hollywood is simply better than the French film industry at making movies people want to watch.

Nonetheless, they all wished America was a little less...American. They were all prepared to accept, regretfully but realistically, that American policy would lead the world, but preferably only if there was a European, or specifically, a French stamp of approval on it.

Above all, they knew Jean Luc. Like them, he was smart, hardworking, successful, influential, rich, urbane, and ruthless when he needed to be. He came, like most of them, from a modest background, and had climbed the ladder of success in business and society through his own accomplishments.

Yet he was the most successful of them all, for he had a quality that all of them envied: he was *lucky*. He had the knack of being in the right place at the right time. He was the epitome of the old expression 'timing is everything'. He seemed to know with unerring instinct when a competitor was vulnerable, when a market would open up, when a stock would rise, when a woman was ready to be seduced.

Michel studied his old friend: his carefully brushed silver hair, his handsome face, his startlingly bright blue eyes, and his calm certainty.

"Jean Luc," he said, "You are asking us to take a significant risk toward an almost impossible goal. We could all agree with your objectives, but chose to stay out of your enterprise simply because of the difficulties involved. You are also giving us no time to consider. 'Take it or leave it,' the negotiating stance for which you are famous."

He chuckled to remove the offense.

"However, I don't believe any of us believes great objectives can be obtained without taking risks, and so I, for one, will join your enterprise." He looked around the table. "Gentlemen, I appeal to you in the spirit of Alexander Dumas—'All for one and one for all'."

Michel's commitment changed the dynamic around the table. Michel was known for his prudence and his utter dependability. By joining Jean Luc, the enterprise ceased to be simply a quixotic proposal by Jean Luc to tilt at the transatlantic windmill, but a practical enterprise planned by two of France's most powerful and successful commercial leaders.

"Gentlemen," said Diderot, "I lack your financial resources, but, with respect, I am not without influence and I am not bereft of ideas on how to damage America's hegemony. I have studied history all my life, which means that I have studied power all my life: its acquisition, its retention, and its loss. I must say that my goal is not simply to wipe off Uncle Sam's arrogant smile with a well-timed slap or two: my goal is also to save Europe from itself.

"Do we really want a Union of bickering equals," he asked theatrically. "A Europe in which the Spanish and, God save us, the *Poles* have as much influence as France? Or do we want a powerful, unified Europe, led by French realism and ingenuity?

"Not only is France in danger of being submerged, but Europe itself is in danger. Even if we can slow down the advance of the United States, Europe must be strong enough, and powerful enough, to compete successfully with China and India as they continue to emerge over the next decades."

He gestured expansively. "Are we going to focus our attention on building inefficient wind-powered electrical generators in every backyard, and granting constitutional rights to animals, and all the other illusions which pass for political priorities these days, or are we going to, as the Americans say so eloquently, *kick butt?* I accept your invitation, and offer myself to you, Jean Luc, as the group's Machiavelli."

It occurred to the others that Jean Luc had stage-managed these endorsements in advance, and that they were being set up. Pierre Truffaud considered the possibility—he had done similar things himself. There is nothing like a couple of quick 'yes' votes to get the crowd moving in your direction.

He glanced around the table. Unlike the others, he had not risen to power and influence through the ranks of management and high society, and his considerable wealth had been obtained illegally and was well-hidden. He was a diplomat. He was probably the most powerful man in the room beside Jean Luc, and in some ways he was even more powerful, for he could take explicit political action and his government's potential veto could be wielded like a club against his opponents. In addition, he had many friends across the diplomatic class of Europe and beyond, and his influence therefore extended far beyond the borders of France.

He was a little older than some of the others, and he could just remember the GIs who liberated his village from the SS, and handed out chocolates to the kids and cigarettes to the adults. He remembered the American doctor who had saved his father's life; the cheerful, purposeful engineers who had fixed the bridge across the river and repaired the electrical generating plant; and the handsome young man who had carried his older sister off to a life of happiness and plenty in California.

"Fuck'em," he said. "I'm in."

They were all in: the banker, the retired general, the communications entrepreneur, the senior trade union representative, the hedge fund manager, and the shipping magnate. An elderly servant refreshed their coffee and replenished the decanter.

"How will you...we...proceed, Jean Luc?" Truffaud asked. He was wondering how Jean Luc planned to take advantage of his position as a senior diplomat in the Foreign Ministry. This was going to be *fun!*

"We will simply present the United States with a series of challenges," Jean Luc replied, smiling to acknowledge their support. "These challenges will have two characteristics: first, regardless of what the US does, it will be isolated from world opinion; and second, the challenges will have no military solution. Whatever position the President takes will create a firestorm of criticism, domestically as well as internationally.

"In those circumstances, international public opinion will turn even more against the administration and the President will be forced to compromise. The more challenges we present, the weaker he will appear, and since appearance is everything, the weaker he will be. Indeed, the process is beginning quite literally as we speak."

"You will create events which damage him?"

"I will place the balls of the American President in a nutcracker, and then I will squeeze."

CHAPTER 2

Perception is far more important than reality.

—Jean Luc Lafarge

Maria Menendez flew into Paris the following morning. Her taxi inched its way into the center of the city where she checked into the Intercontinental Hotel. She made several phone calls and indulged in a luxurious bath before dressing for the evening. She dressed conservatively—a black, loosely cut silk evening gown with a demurely high neckline, long sleeves and a hemline at her ankles. Yet somehow the dress seemed to convey the fact that she wore nothing beneath it.

Her escort arrived promptly and took her to a gallery where a charity auction was being held, arranged and underwritten by the generosity of Jean Luc Lafarge. The vast rooms were crowded and the sound of several hundred people talking at the tops of their voices was overwhelming. The event has attracted the ministerial and diplomatic crowd as well as the pretentiously wealthy and the self-appointed intellectual elite.

"You are interested in this work, mademoiselle?"

Lafarge had spotted Maria's striking profile from across the room and had worked his way over until he stood at her shoulder as she examined one of the exhibits. She glanced at him briefly: the classically handsome profile, the perfectly groomed silver hair, the elegantly cut suit, the friendly but appraising eyes.

"No, not really, monsieur, to tell you the truth, I'm here simply out of politeness. As far as I'm concerned most modern art is a complete hoax."

She gestured to a pile of old newspapers tied with string and carefully encased in Lucite, with the inscription 'Futility, 2002'.

"Why is that art?" She examined the catalog. "And why is it worth fifty thousand euros?"

"Be careful, my dear, or you'll be thrown out of the gallery," he replied, chuckling. "It's a highly significant work of social comment."

"It's a piece of shit," she responded succinctly, turning away.

Lafarge smiled broadly. "Permit me to present myself. My name is Jean Luc Lafarge. Do I detect an Italian accent?"

"No, I'm Spanish. And, just to save you valuable time and effort, Monsieur Lafarge, let me tell you I'm here with someone. It's been very pleasant to make your acquaintance, but now I must rejoin him."

Jean Luc smiled and bowed, accepting the rebuff with equanimity. "Then I will wish you a pleasant evening, Señorita."

She nodded politely and moved away through the crowd. His eyes followed her until she reached a man with ash blond hair with whom she linked arms. He whispered something in her ear and they both laughed.

Lafarge retreated to a distant corner of the room and took out his phone. "There is someone at the gallery I wish you to follow. I will find my own way home."

He provided a brief description and disconnected.

Lafarge's driver had positioned his large black Mercedes directly outside the gallery, and it was easy to spot the attractive dark-haired woman and her blond companion when they emerged half an hour later. They took a taxi to an upscale restaurant on the left bank. Two hours later the couple took another taxi to the Intercontinental. Lafarge's driver drew up behind them and left his car.

"Five minutes," he said to the doorman, handing him twenty euros, and followed them into the hotel, where he spotted them heading into the dim recesses of the ornate lobby bar.

An hour later he left the hotel and gave the doorman another twenty euros, with an apology and a complaint about customers who order cars and then change their minds. The doorman pocketed the money and shrugged. The driver phoned his employer.

"Her name is Maria Menendez and her address is in Barcelona. She's staying at the Intercontinental Hotel and she's booked in for three more nights."

He had waited until she charged the drinks to her room number and then bribed a reception clerk to tell him the name of the guest staying in that room.

"The blond man did not go to her room and I'm following him now."

Over the next twenty-four hours it developed from Lafarge's extensive sources of information that Maria Menendez was the marketing director for a real estate company building condominium complexes along the Spanish coastline. The company maintained small sales offices in Paris and Berlin. Her company credit card accounts revealed that she traveled to both cities frequently. Jean Luc's Spanish associates reported she had a wide circle of friends but no permanent relationship. Her principal leisure activity was sports cars; she belonged to an amateur racing club and owned a Porsche 911 Targa.

Her blond escort at the gallery was a married mid-level Dutch diplomat who had purchased a condominium the previous summer. He was evidently pursuing her but, so far as could be discovered, without success.

On the last night of her stay in Paris she dined with the blond man at an elegant restaurant. Lafarge arrived shortly afterward. The couple was still at the tiny bar sipping aperitifs as they waited for their table.

"Well, it seems we meet again," said Lafarge, coming up to her as if the encounter was entirely accidental. He noted she was again dressed demurely but somehow, at the same time, provocatively.

"I'm sorry, monsieur?" she responded vaguely.

"We met at an art show three days ago. You did not admire the exhibits." He turned to the diplomat and nodded. "Jean Luc Lafarge, monsieur. I hope you will forgive this interruption?"

The diplomat was not pleased at the intrusion, but his manners compelled him to be gracious. Jean Luc engaged him in a conversion with regard to the state of Dutch football, to the point the diplomat was charmed, and Maria was virtually ignored.

Eventually Lafarge turned back to her. "Forgive me for indulging my passion for the sport, mademoiselle. I must admit, I still do not know your name."

"Maria Menendez," she responded, making it clear she was providing this information solely out of courtesy and with reluctance even then.

Lafarge chatted amusingly for another minute or so, and then, with fresh apologies for his intrusion, withdrew to join another elegant silver-haired gentleman already seated at their table.

"Who is that gorgeous creature?" Michel Leclerc asked. "Another of your conquests, Jean Luc?"

"Not yet, Michel, but it is merely a question of time. I met her by chance on Monday."

"How long will it take to work the legendary Lafarge magic? A week? A month?"

"Come, Michel, it's rude to pry. She visits Paris only occasionally, so I understand. Besides, she shows no signs of being interested."

"I'll wager she resists you for more than a month, Jean Luc. She has that hard-to-get look about her."

"How much?"

"Oh, I don't know...enough to make the bet worthwhile without being outrageous. Shall we say a quarter of a million?"

"You're on, Michel!" They shook hands across the table.

"Excellent. I have the feeling there's more to her than meets the eye. I must start planning how to spend your money. Now I understand why you changed restaurants on me at the last moment."

"Ah, Michel, you know me too well! You have discovered one of my little secrets!"

A waiter appeared and they ordered, balancing the delights of the menu against its calorific consequences. Then they turned to business.

"Speaking of secrets, when I agreed to join your most recent enterprise, Jean Luc, I made it clear that I want to be more than a passive investor. When will you begin?"

"Our first activity is already underway. It started quite literally as we were speaking a few days ago. It fits the general target market we discussed last week. The staff is in place and the equipment has been delivered. We have already produced a sample batch of the product and I expect full production will begin in another week."

Lafarge was unconcerned with being overheard. He might well simply have been describing one of his numerous industrial ventures.

"The first sample surprised the market, I think, and the effect will be cumulative as production continues. I have every confidence in the on-site manager and I have given him complete discretion in terms of timing and output volume. If he's successful, we may want to start a second production unit as well."

"I would like to offer a suggestion or two, if I may?"

"Of course, Michel."

"One thought is that there are certain market conditions we can anticipate. We can, perhaps, turn these to our advantage; the proposed African venture that you mentioned, for example, there's absolutely no reason why this venture should not be self-funding."

"That's brilliant, Michel! So brilliant, in fact, I should have thought of it myself!"

Lafarge glanced over Leclerc's shoulder, and observed that the diplomat had left Maria for a moment.

"Excuse me, Michel, for one minute, if you would be so kind. I have to start earning your money."

He rose and walked over to her table.

"Ah, mademoiselle, or I should say Señorita, are you enjoying your dinner? I always find the lamb exceptional in this restaurant."

"I am, thank you, Monsieur Lafarge," she replied coolly. She regarded him calmly, waiting for his next gambit.

"Are you often in Paris?"

"Often enough."

"Perhaps you will permit me to take you to dinner next time you are here. If this cuisine is to your liking, I know another little place you might enjoy. Would that be convenient?"

"Perhaps."

"Then, let me give you my card. You can telephone me if you wish to take up my offer." He bowed politely, and returned to his table.

"Did you make progress, Jean Luc? Should I be reaching for my check-book?"

"Not yet, my friend; however, in these cases the difficulty of the pursuit merely increases the satisfaction of the reward."

They talked of other matters until dinner was over.

"Coming back to our new venture, you say you will be in full production within the week, Jean Luc? Will you be packaging this as an individual brand, or simply as a generic?"

"Oh, we're branding it, Michel. I have always thought a distinctive brand image is most important. It heightens consumer awareness and creates the perception of scale. In this particular business, I believe, perception is far more important than reality."

Moshe Aaron studied the simple typewritten notes in their protective plastic covers. The first had been received a week ago, and read, 'The Sons of Hebron will strike in Jerusalem on Sunday, April 4th.' It had been sent by mail, addressed to the prime minister and mailed in Jerusalem, one of the hundreds of threatening letters that the government received each week, indistinguishable from the rest; its specificity had been unusual, but with no further information and no collateral intelligence, it had not been actionable.

The grenade attacks had not been followed by a credible claim of responsibility from any known terrorist organizations, but the official who had read the note recalled it and brought it to the Mossad's attention. Of course, there was nothing in the note to suggest it was referring to the grenade attack, but on the other hand, it was the only significant event that had taken place that day.

The second note had been mailed yesterday and received this morning, and read, 'The Sons of Hebron will strike in Tel Aviv on Sunday April 11th.' The official who had opened the first note recognized the style, and sent it over to the Mossad immediately.

Unfortunately there was little Moshe could recommend to his superiors beyond increasing security patrols in Tel Aviv. Intelligence was already working overtime to discover the perpetrators of the grenade attack, and it was known that the major Palestinian terror organizations were doing the same: the conclusion had to be that this was the work of a new group or individual who had emerged from the churning hatreds of the West Bank. Yasir Arafat was believed to be annoyed; he did not like terrorist attacks to occur without his foreknowledge and approval.

The modus operandi was novel. The perpetrator was not explicitly suicidal and the target area had not been particularly busy: the attacker had not waited for a bus to enter the intersection, for example. The launch of a second attack against the rescue crews was unique. It was possible that the first attack was designed as bait to lure the security forces into the target area.

That suggested a level of sophistication in planning and tactics which potentially made this new group very dangerous. On the other hand, the actual mechanics were decidedly low tech—grenades lobbed almost at random.

The consensus was that one man, acting alone, had hurled the grenades down from a rooftop overlooking the intersection. He had crouched beneath the parapet and lobbed them blindly into the square, which accounted for the fact that he had hurled one in the wrong direction so it landed on the roof of the adjacent apartment building.

The second attack had probably been perpetrated from one of the apartments in that building. Presumably the man had come down from the roof and crossed to the apartments unnoticed in the melee following the explosions. The military had been very slow in conducting its search after the first grenades, and there would have been time for someone to lob the second set through the windows of a vacant apartment and leave the building undetected, probably by a rear fire escape. Inconclusive forensic evidence suggested the grenades were of Russian origin, but that was rather like saying that tea comes from India.

Who might be responsible? Hezbollah had been fairly quiet, and it didn't seem much like Hamas or the Al Fattah Martyrs Brigade, or any of the usual groups even though the name 'Sons of Hebron' would suggest it. The scale was far too modest for Al Qaeda and, in any case, Al Qaeda didn't attack Israel directly. Even though the attack was modest in the scheme of things, its randomness was worrying, and the pre-announcements implied a great deal of confidence. The whole thing lacked emotion. Moshe formed the opinion that the Sons of Hebron might be more interested in drawing attention to themselves than in inflicting damage. But to what end?

Kamal finished testing his two automatic grenade dispensers. They each had a rack down which the grenades would roll, and a powerful spring-loaded throwing arm at the bottom of the rack. The arm had a cleverly designed lever which detached the safety as the grenade was launched. The whole thing was a bit like a baseball pitching machine, or a tennis ball server.

He installed each dispenser in a rusting metal cabinet which made it look like an elderly electrical junction box, complete with a sun-bleached warning of high voltage. The door would open immediately before the attack and close immediately after. It was possible the dispensers would not be noticed in a quick search.

On Thursday night he positioned one dispenser on the flat rooftop of a grocery store, and the second in the eaves of a synagogue. This was undoubtedly the most dangerous part of the entire enterprise, for there was no easy explanation for why he should be climbing on buildings with an electrical junction box strapped to his back in the middle of the night. He had chosen buildings with fire escapes above dark alleys in commercial areas which would be deserted at night: even so, any passerby might see him and raise the alarm. Although he was not detected, he was sweating from nervousness as well as exertion.

Including the slingshot in the back of his van he would be able to launch three attacks. He chose consecutive intersections along a main road in Tel Aviv as his targets. He would use the van to launch the first assault on the central intersection, and then the automatic dispensers would fire on the adjacent intersections ten minutes later. He decided not to use delayed follow-up attacks. He was interested to see whether the security and rescue teams would behave differently after his strike in Jerusalem.

On Saturday night he positioned his van with extreme care two blocks from the central intersection and adjusted the slingshot aiming mechanism. A police car and a military truck came slowly down the dreary street as he was waiting, but they were not checking parked vehicles. He assumed there were heightened levels of patrolling all over the city.

At eleven he opened the roof and started the attack. Six grenades disappeared into the night sky at five second intervals. Thirty seconds later he closed the roof and climbed back into the driving seat. The sound of distant sirens started almost immediately, and a police car raced past him.

He drove slowly away, threading his way through the dark backstreets until joining the main highway back to Jerusalem. Naturally there was a roadblock and a massive traffic jam. Kamal's papers were inspected and his van was searched, but his ID was impeccable and the slingshot was simply part of the supports for his worktable, and a bag of onions disguised any scent of explosives the dogs might have been able to detect. The young soldiers waved him on.

Twelve vehicles behind Kamal's van was a scruffy Toyota driven by a youth trying to come to terms with the fact he was almost certainly about to die. A stranger had approached him a few days before and offered him a hundred dollars US if he would transport a cardboard box containing twelve grenades from Tel Aviv to Jerusalem on Saturday night. There would be another hundred waiting for him on delivery. Quite apart from the cash, it was a way of impressing his friends by being part of the intifada without having to commit suicide, and the chances of getting caught were very low.

Now, however, he was ensnared in a roadblock. He could surrender and face a long and harsh incarceration; he could try to make a run for it although there was an excellent chance he would get shot; or he could use the grenades. He always thought of himself as a tough guy, but in this moment of real danger he discovered his bowels were discharging themselves.

He had achieved little in his life. He had never had a girl. His only real moment of distinction was when he had been paid twenty dollars by a Belgian

TV crew to crouch by the corner of a building and fire an AK-47. The crew had cut the image into footage of Israeli tanks in an urban area to create the impression that he had been firing at them rather than into open desert. The reporter had intoned a piece about brutal military repression driving desperate Palestinian youths to fight back for their legitimate fatherland. She had ended the segment with "Typically, the Israeli Defense Forces deny the incident ever took place."

But now there were real soldiers and no TV crew to shape events. The box of grenades was beneath the passenger seat. The line of cars and trucks ahead of him inched forward. He formed a desperate plan. He would throw one of the grenades at the soldiers by the roadblock, killing as many as possible, and make his escape into the olive trees beside the highway. The grove of trees was only a few yards away and it would be pitch black in there. He forgot, or didn't know, about night vision glasses.

He opened the passenger door, climbed out of the car, and reached beneath the seat for one of the grenades. He turned it over and over in his hands as he figured out how to release the safety pin, and finally extracted it. The driver of the truck immediately behind him saw what he was doing and pounded on his powerful Klaxon horn. The youth jumped in fright and the grenade slipped from his sweaty fingers and rolled into the gutter. He willed himself to run, but his legs seemed to have turned to jelly. All he could do was stare at the grenade.

Kamal saw the explosion in his rearview mirror as he drove away from the roadblock. He pulled over and ran back, along with several others. In spite of all the years and all the incidents, the basic public response to mayhem was still to run toward danger, to do whatever could be done for the injured. The Toyota and the car in front of it were in flames. Two soldiers were dragging the youth's body away from the fires at considerable risk to themselves, while another was pulling the limp and bleeding truck driver from his cab. The remaining soldiers were trying to push the growing crowd back to a safe distance. The heat reached the point at which the Toyota's gas tank exploded, and that, in turn, detonated the remaining grenades.

Kamal backed off with the rest of the crowd and returned to his van. He had been feeling pleased with the success of his attack, but now he was annoyed and, perhaps as a consequence, his neck was aching more than ever. He called his girlfriend.

"Are you asleep?"

"No, I'm watching the news," she replied. "There's just been another bombing."

"Yes, it's on the radio. Do you want to stop by in half an hour?"
"Okay, I need someone to cheer me up."

CHAPTER 3

The objective of terrorism is not to kill or damage, but to create terror.

—Jean Luc Lafarge

Maria telephoned Jean Luc to say she would be in Paris on the following day and would accept his invitation to dinner, if it was still open. Her tone was pleasant although she also managed to convey the impression that his response was a matter of indifference to her. Jean Luc assumed there were numerous men she could have called; she was giving him the opportunity to become of interest to her. He smiled. Nothing gave him more pleasure than the seduction of reluctant women, and all too often women threw themselves at him, hoping for one of the expensive gifts for which he was notorious, or even a weekend on his yacht in the Mediterranean: such women robbed him of the gratification of conquest.

Dinner in the dark restaurant he had chosen, where the candles lit the faces of the diners if they were conspirators, reminded him a little of a fencing match. He was urbane and witty, and she was coyly aware of his advances yet unwilling to yield much ground. She was perfectly prepared to talk, but not of personal matters. She described her company's latest real estate project, and he asked a number of the financial details, not only to get her to talk, but also because he was always looking for tax-advantaged investments.

"They're looking at a property in Fort Lauderdale. The market is primarily Canadian snowbirds, of course, but they're hoping for European interest as well."

"Does that mean you'll be spending time in Florida, my dear?"

"No, not at all. I won't be working on the project."

"You're too busy with your current properties?"

Maria shrugged. "No, it's just that I refuse to have anything to do with Americans, and I'm sufficiently well-established at work that they don't hold it against me."

"Really, don't you think the popular anti-Americanism is a little overblown?"

She shook her head impatiently. "I'm not motivated by that media nonsense. I've never liked bullies, that's all."

"My dear, you intrigue me. Are you referring to current American foreign policy, or something else?"

"I have no interest in politics." She hesitated and Jean Luc sensed for the first time, she was speaking of something that mattered to her.

"There was a boy at school, who was an American and a bully. His father was something in the American air force, in NATO. The boy's name was 'Chuck'—such an ugly syllable. He tried to take advantage of me when I was twelve. Since then I've loathed all things American. I must admit I was delighted to hear he was a passenger on one of the September 11th planes."

She shook her head in dismissal. "The whole thing was very unattractive. Let's talk of other things, if you don't mind. What do you do when you're not working, or attempting to seduce women?"

Lafarge raised an eyebrow and chuckled. "And I thought I was being subtle!"

He touched his hair, and she took it as a gesture of vanity. This was important, because vain men are insecure, and insecure men can be manipulated.

"To answer your question, I dabble at this or that, but I don't have a consuming hobby. I suppose I just don't have enough patience or energy left over after business affairs. So, it's whatever takes my fancy. For example, I've recently found myself involved in racing."

"You own racehorses?"

"Well, I do, but this involves racing cars. I've found myself in possession of a small racing venture as a result of a bankruptcy, and I've become quite interested."

"Really? How intriguing! Racing is my favorite thing!"

Her enthusiasm was obvious and genuine. She leaned forward, and suddenly she looked younger and more alive as she dropped her mask of indifference. Jean Luc felt a prickle of desire and allowed himself a silent grunt of satisfaction: at last he had found an avenue of attack.

"Yes, it could be a good promotion opportunity. I also have an interest in the Sassal brewing business, and since I own the cars anyway, I might as well put our logo on them at Le Mans: 'Team Sassal' or something. The PR people think it will give the beer a high-tech masculine image. The target market segment for the beer is affluent thirty and forty-year-olds."

"What sort of cars are they?"

"You know, my dear, I really have no idea. I must have read it somewhere…they may be Renaults or perhaps they're Jaguars. It doesn't matter. I wish I had more confidence in what the PR people are telling me. You're in marketing, what do you think?"

"Well, racing does project an image of high-tech masculinity, as you say, and it also projects affluence and calculated risk. That could be extremely appealing to upwardly-mobile thirty-something's—a fantasy play."

She was now fully engaged in the conversation, speaking quickly, and Jean Luc saw a tiny wrinkle of concentration appear on her delightful forehead.

"You'd need to tie the cars and the advertising in with a promotional campaign, like Team Sassal apparel or something like that, with one of the designer labels perhaps, something mid-market, like a Nike Sassal Grand Prix line. Not Nike, of course, but someone…incidentally, they're far more likely to be Audis or Porsches—if they were Bentleys you'd know."

She was clearly excited.

He frowned. "Despite my reputation, I'm really very risk adverse. The real question I have is whether it helps our branding if the cars do poorly. Would you expect the market to respond favorably if the cars blow up on the first lap, or will we get a lift just by being there? The question is whether it's more cost-effective to run the cars, or to buy conventional TV advertising—models in bikinis, the usual stuff."

"I might consider combining the two, sexy girls driving the cars, that sort of thing. The man can't get the girl until he offers her a Sassal."

Lafarge had gained control of the racing organization through a debt workout process in which the assets of the spendthrift scion of a wealthy family had been seized. It was such a pity. The old man had worked forty years to build a decent plastics business before dying of a heart attack, and then his son had managed to squander the entire thing in less than three years through personal extravagances and catastrophic business decisions.

Lafarge would normally not have given the racing organization a second thought, selling off the assets to the highest bidder, but it occurred to him to dangle it before Maria's eyes. It played to her reported passion for sports cars and her professional interest in marketing, and she seemed to be instantly entranced.

"Perhaps you're right, but it's all incredibly expensive. You know, on reflection I'm fairly sure I'll shut the whole racing organization down and use a more predictable advertising medium for the beer."

"Oh, don't do that!" Maria exclaimed, as if horrified. "At least, not before you've taken a second look. Racing enthusiasts have wonderful consumer purchasing demographics."

Lafarge appeared unconvinced and casually suggested she might like to do him an enormous favor and look over the organization and the marketing play, and give him a recommendation. She accepted with alacrity.

"I'll gladly pay your fees, of course."

"Nonsense, it will be fun! I'll enjoy it, and I'm sure my bosses won't object."

"My dear, I can't let you do it for nothing. Name your price."

"You can take me out to dinner again."

The group was gathered in Jean Luc's Paris residence. He took his place at the head of the table and the others settled down. Only coffee was served, this was a working session.

"Gentlemen, I wish to give you an accounting of our enterprise. First, as far as finances are concerned, we have all made our initial contributions, with the exception, by common agreement, of Francois, whose contribution is intellectual."

There was a sense of satisfaction in the room, for these men knew that promises and commitments meant nothing until they were backed up by cash and their contributions had turned a theoretical discussion group into a practical criminal conspiracy, all of which created a certain camaraderie.

"In terms of action, our first project is well underway. You have doubtless seen reports of a new form of terrorist activity in Israel, and I assure you the pace will continue."

"That's us?" asked the general in surprise.

"That's us," Jean Luc responded, smilingly. "It will take, I estimate, two to three more attacks to goad the Israelis into retaliation: less if we're lucky."

There was complete silence around the table.

"Let me explain what we are doing in some detail," Jean Luc continued. "First, we have established the notion of random attacks, but at regular intervals. What has not been reported in the press is that we are *pre-announcing* these assaults to the Israeli authorities. We send them a message, so they know when and in what city the attack will come, but not *exactly* where.

"That gives our operation a distinct image; a brand identity, if you will. They know we exist, but they don't know who we are."

He made a gesture of satisfaction. "It must be quite irritating, and irritation leads to impatience and poor judgment, and the compulsion to act without a rational plan."

Pierre Truffaud listened carefully. Initially he had joined the group in order to get closer to Jean Luc. In the maturity of time there were several business ventures in which he hoped Jean Luc might take an interest. Naturally his government position prevented him from direct ownership, but his brother-in-law was his secret partner and Truffaud was an expert in manipulating EU regulations. In the meantime, he realized, he was getting an education in how Jean Luc operated—an inside track on his legendary skills at managing situations to his advantage.

"In addition," Jean Luc continued, "We're varying the operational details each time so we don't become too predictable. This makes it harder for them to catch us, and to clean up after us. Our objective, of course, is to get them to retaliate, but in order to do so they must think they know where the attacks are coming from.

"That leads to the second part of our operation. We are providing them with disinformation that will, hopefully, lead them to conclude that this is state sponsored terrorism, and that the sponsor is Syria."

"Excuse me, Jean Luc, but isn't this all a bit indirect?" Truffaud asked. "I thought our target was America?"

"Yes, indeed it is, my friend. Let me explain. In searching for the source of the attacks, Israel will be directed by a disinformation campaign toward Syria. With sufficient provocation, they will strike. A raid against a sitting member of the Security Council will undoubtedly produce universal condemnation, and set in motion a diplomatic chain reaction which will be very damaging to the United States. Perhaps you'll permit me to give you more details as events unfold."

Truffaud wondered for the twentieth time why Jean Luc had formed this group, rather than doing it all himself. The only explanation he could think of is that Jean Luc wanted to share the financial burden. The total contributions were twenty five million euros, and that was significant money, even to Jean Luc. Or, perhaps, he needed this secret cabal simply so he could parade his cleverness and trumpet his successes.

Kamal would still have been annoyed if he had permitted himself any normal emotions. He had given that kid several clues to suggest he came from Damascus, and then the kid had been stupid enough to blow himself to smithereens at the roadblock before being caught and coughing up it all up during interrogation. Now Kamal would have to go to a second form of misdirection, and it would be far more risky.

But first things first. He had to complete his preparations for the next attack. He loaded his next set of automatic dispensers. The two he had used in Tel Aviv had worked like a charm and had still not been noticed, as far as he could tell, and he saw no reason to change his approach just for the sake of change. He dismissed the notion of going back to retrieve them. There was no point in taking unnecessary risks.

The next attack would be in the port city of Haifa, and the dispensers would be installed in dummy transformer boxes set high on utility poles. He loaded the dispensers alternately from two boxes of grenades. The first set was completely conventional. The second set was not. He was wearing a full protection suit with its own air supply as he worked.

He drove up the coast to Haifa and stole a small truck with a 'cherry picker' elevator and transferred the dispensers to it. There were twelve identical trucks parked in the utility maintenance depot and he doubted anyone would count them in the next few hours. As dusk was falling he set out orange cones in the roadway by the poles he intended to use and lit arc lights. Utility repairmen do not work in darkness or in secrecy. The highway ran beside the sea and there was a sharp tang of salt in the air. He manipulated the cherry picker mechanism and the platform lifted him into the air.

He was strapping the first dummy transformer to the pole as a police patrol passed by without a second glance. When the installation was complete, he set the timer that would trigger the attack. Then he moved half a mile and repeated the operation.

He returned the stolen vehicle unnoticed and drove the plumber's van to Safad, close to the border with Lebanon and the disputed territory of the Golan Heights, and left it in a lockup garage he had rented. He stole an elderly pickup truck, redolent with pig manure, and drove back to Jerusalem.

It was two in the morning when he returned to his apartment but there was still much to do. He washed the black dye out of his hair and shaved off his mustache. He grimaced as he ripped off the artificial hair he had glued between his eyebrows, taking several layers of skin with it.

He surveyed the other elements of his disguise. The work boots he had been wearing ever since arriving in Israel were one size of small, which had given his gait a short, springy sort of action as his feet had automatically rebelled against bearing his weight. He had been sleeping with his head propped up on a rock-hard pillow, which gave him a permanent ache in his neck, so that the movements of his head were slow and tentative, and his shoulders were thrown back to relieve the pain.

Tinted contact lenses had darkened his gray-green eyes. The first and second fingers of his right hand had been bandaged together as if he had been suffering from a bad sprain: the effect had been to encourage him to use his left hand. In all, he had moved awkwardly and with a certain clumsiness, and his bushy artificial eyebrows had, somehow, robbed his face of much of its intelligence.

He looked at himself in the mirror. From his untidy sandy hair and rimless glasses, to his faded tee shirt with 'Who gives a shit?' emblazoned on the front and 'Assholes' on the back, to his worn khaki cargo pants and comfortably shabby sneakers, he was once again a post-graduate international student, one of those cheerfully self-absorbed souls who apply for scholarship after scholarship in order to avoid actually having to work for a living.

He ran his eyes around the room one last time, searching for some surface he had forgotten to wash that might still hold his fingerprints, some area of carpeting that might hide a strand of hair. But he knew the room was cleaner than an operating theater in a hospital. He had gone to the length of cleansing the U-bends in the bathroom. His cleaning woman would come in tomorrow, and she was a thorough woman. If the room was ever examined, there would be traces of her handiwork, and her fingerprints would be scattered at random.

He took a taxi to Ben Gurion airport, arriving not much after four, and submitted himself to the security processes which make El Al the safest airline in the world. He spoke French and adequate English and a smattering of Yiddish and Arabic.

His backpack contained his thesis on 'comparative socialism' comparing social benefits in various countries and their effect on society, all contrasted with the dire straits of the downtrodden working poor in the United States; notebooks filled with scrawled notations and references; and loose printed copies of e-mails to and from his supervising professor who, in real life, he had never met. Two over-ripe bananas, thrown into his bag and evidently forgotten, were fast reducing the entire collection to a complete mess.

"Yesterday's fucking lunch," he groaned to the baggage inspector, trying to wipe goo off his thesis. "I never had time." She lent him a wad of Kleenex.

His passport, visa, ID and ticket were genuine. He had no criminal record. He had arrived in Israel to study six months ago and the contents of his backpack were ample evidence of how he had spent his time. His big floppy carryall contained nothing to raise any alarms.

The flight left at seven right on time, and soared into the morning above the sparkling Mediterranean, bound for Orly Airport in Paris. 'Henri', for that was his new name—at least for the present—took off his sneakers and wriggled his toes luxuriously, and then craned back in his seat to see the coastline of Israel receding behind the Airbus until it was no more than a long smudge in which no details could be distinguished, and certainly not three timers ticking quietly away.

Henri arrived in Paris and passed through customs and immigration without incident. He stopped for a double espresso, perching on an uncomfortable aluminum stool at a small round table which he shared with a businessman who left his newspaper behind. Henri glanced at the sports pages casually and then headed to the toilets. Folded into the newspaper were a new set of documents, as genuine as those he had used in Israel. 'Charles' flushed his old documents into the sewage system and boarded a plane to London.

❦ ❦ ❦

'The Sons of Hebron will strike in two places on Monday at 8 pm. You have not met our demands and you will pay the price.'

Moshe read the latest missive with a cold feeling in his stomach. There were several reasons for alarm. First, the terror campaign was being escalated to two simultaneous attacks. No one, certainly not Moshe, doubted that whoever had written the note would strike again. Second, the target cities were not identified. This made detection or prevention almost impossible.

After the last attack in Tel Aviv several of the prime minister's advisors had been recommending that the public should be warned in advance of any future attacks. Then people would stay off the streets, and there were be tens of thousands of eyes searching for signs of the attackers. The prime minister had been wavering in that direction, but this latest note made that strategy impossible: you could not watch the whole country.

But the third and most troublesome point was the suggestion that the perpetrators had made demands to which Israel had not responded. It was as if there had been a missing letter. Every single piece of correspondence the government had received was searched for the missing information, every e-mail, and every phone log. But how could anyone tell the difference between the thousands of crank calls and threatening letters the government received and the demands—whatever they were—of the Sons of Hebron?

"He's pissed at us, whoever he is," Moshe grunted. "He's asked for something and we haven't responded. We're missing something."

"Let's review everything we know, from the beginning," responded the man at the head of the battered conference table, who represented the prime minister directly.

This was a meeting of hard men, toughened by dozens of attacks on their country over the years. They were embittered men, for they had failed in their most basic duty, to protect innocent citizens; and they were frustrated men, for nothing, *nothing*, had succeeded: not olive branches and concessions, not retaliations and assassinations, not crackdowns and incursions. Whatever they did, the world condemned them, for the world had managed to convince itself against all the evidence that their enemies would settle for less than the complete destruction of the State of Israel.

And, worst of all ironies, Yasir Arafat, surely the least competent of all terrorists, isolated in his compound in Ramallah, with nothing for company except his Nobel Peace Prize and his fat Swiss bank accounts, still controlled the fate of Israel.

"We received a message saying there would be an attack in Jerusalem on a particular day," said the prime minister's representative. "There was an attack and it was unusual. It was as if the 'Sons of Hebron' were announcing their arrival.

"We received a second message. The second attack was similar to the first: a relatively mild initial attack followed up by secondary attacks on the security and rescue teams. It was probably the work of three men, although Moshe has suggested it could be one man using some kind of a throwing device. We're testing the feasibility of that theory now.

"Shortly after the second attack, a Palestinian kid from Hebron was caught in a roadblock and blew himself up. Obviously he wasn't the originator of these notes, they're far too sophisticated. So he was some kind of a legman, or a crazy kid planning a copy cat attack, or maybe one of the actual attackers but not the brains behind them. In other words, we have no fucking idea who he was, although Moshe has a theory. Moshe?"

"He may have been a decoy. It may be that he was *meant* to be caught, and he had been given some sort of disinformation."

The man at the head of the table grunted neutrally. "Now we have this third note, and we're facing another attack. I, for one, believe the attack *will* be carried out. In the meantime, all the intel is negative. The other side doesn't know who's doing this. The raid we conducted two days ago into Hebron turned up nothing of any use, and the prime minister is taking a lot of heat for it, from the opposition as well as internationally. And we seem to be missing whatever demands were made.

"I am reaching the conclusion that this entire thing is unlike any other we've experienced. The attacks are not suicidal, and they're not designed to create maximum damage."

"These attacks are designed to achieve what they *have* achieved," Moshe said. "They're designed to get us to focus on the Sons of Hebron and to get us worried."

"Fuck!" said the prime minister's representative, and there was no disagreement with his assessment.

CHAPTER 4

Power is like money: It must be put to use in order to amass more power.

—Jean Luc Lafarge

Jean Luc pursued his conquest of Maria at a steady pace, so that he would not seem to be hurrying her, although his progress was always forward toward his ultimate objective. He was not impatient as long as he judged he was gaining ground, and his bet with Michel gave him a good framework by which to gauge his advances. He had complete confidence in his eventual victory. The Le Mans racing project was a perfect situation for them both: they could spend hours together on the project and, in that context, develop the casual intimacies of friendly colleagues with a shared enthusiasm.

He was greatly impressed by the professionalism with which she approached the task: she combed through the marketing information provided by Sassal, and compared it to the demographics of other racing sponsors. She took the approach that a Sassal Le Mans marketing campaign would be an investment to be recouped by improvements in future sales. Jean Luc admired the way she balanced her flare for innovative PR techniques to enhance the image of the beer in the marketplace with a coldly objective approach to cost effectiveness. He was becoming as interested by her work as he was entranced by her tightly cut jeans.

Maria had spent her adult life observing the strategies of the numerous men who tried to seduce her, and she was impressed—very impressed—by his campaign. She had the more difficult task of maintaining her persona of independence while seeming to fall gradually under his spell, as if her enthusiasm for the project was steadily becoming balanced by an enthusiasm for Jean Luc.

The inevitable took place on a rainy Thursday evening. They had attended a cocktail party and gone on to dinner with the chairman of the Sassal brewing company and Jean Luc's chief financial officer, and their wives.

The women assumed the elegant señorita was Jean Luc's latest mistress, although they were wrong by a few hours, and wondered, as they often did, about their own husbands' arrangements. Biology is particularly cruel to the wives of wealthy and successful men, for once they turn forty, just as they begin to obtain all the things they always wanted, with the resources and leisure to pursue them, their husbands begin to look elsewhere. Even the most strenuous of health spas or the most skillful of plastic surgeons cannot turn back the clock, and familiarity is all too often the enemy of passion.

Maria laid out her conclusions for the Sassal marketing campaign and her performance dazzled everyone. The staid 'Sassal Lager' was to be renamed 'Sassal-France' and the ornately cumbersome label featuring muscular brewery workers was to be replaced by a stark 'S-F' with 'Grand Prix' beneath it in smaller script, and the lettering was offset to create the impression of speed.

The motto was to be 'Premium Lager: For Winners' and the advertising campaign, built around sleek images of the Le Mans cars, would feature successful men—men who were winners. Each thirty-second vignette of success—in business, in an academic setting, in sports—would finish with a similar shot of a successful man seated on a balcony or patio with an S-F bottle on the table and an S-F Le Mans car in the middle distance, from which one or more scantily-dressed nubile women would emerge, attracted by his magnetism.

The chairman of the brewing company shook his head sadly. Although her idea was wonderful, he could not possibly create a new premium lager in less than a year. The basic processes of brewing are simple, but it takes time and money to change the production facilities. She explained the beer should remain exactly as it always was: only the labels were to be changed. The difference between a lager and a premium lager is the label, and 'premium' has no legal definition.

"It's simply commercial speech," she explained. "You can advertise that you have the 'best tasting tomatoes in the world' without having to prove it. You can say 'premium' or 'superior' without having to justify it."

She gave him a lengthy legal opinion written by a law firm with EU regulation expertise to support her claim. The financial executive began to ask about costs, but she produced a thick analysis for him, full of graphs and tables with such titles as 'Relative Price Point Sensitivity' and told him the unit price should be raised ten percent to reflect the beer's new premium status, and at that price the profit margin would rise by thirty-four point three percent. The CFO adjusted his steel-rimmed glasses, riffled through the pages, and fell silent.

She excused herself and went to the crowded, noisy bar, where she ordered a Sassal and drank it straight from the bottle. Most people hold their drinks in front of them, for fear of spilling, but she held her bottle at arm's length by her right thigh. Somehow the gesture seemed both relaxed and provocative. Naturally she was surrounded by men within a minute, and Jean Luc's party, watching from the table, saw that soon they also ordered Sassal. Jean Luc was amused to see the men begin to hold their bottles as she was doing. He decided on the spot to adopt her entire plan, regardless of what the others might say, but they were already as captivated as he was.

Maria disengaged herself and returned to the table. "So, what do you think?"

"As my namesake would say in the movies, 'Make it so'!" he said gaily, invoking the Star Trek character Jean Luc Picard, and they all laughed.

"Goodness, Jean Luc," one of the women said coquettishly, to her husband's intense annoyance, "It must be wonderful to be able to say that, and everyone scurries to obey."

She detected her husband's unspoken vibrations, and hurried on. "I can't even get the au pair to do what I want."

But Jean Luc was not offended in the least, indeed he was beaming. "Power is like money. It must be put to use constantly in order to amass more power."

In the car Jean Luc asked Maria whether she would like to come in for a nightcap.

She did not pretend to misunderstand his meaning. She turned and looked at him fully.

"Thank you, Jean Luc. That would be very pleasant."

He led her directly to his bedroom where they embraced gently.

"Permit me to assist you," she said, and Jean Luc smiled as she began to undress him.

He offered a silent prayer of gratitude to the biochemists of the appropriate drug company as she completed disrobing him, for he had reached an age in which reinforcements were helpful, if only as insurance. Michel would soon be a quarter of a million euros poorer. It was only twenty-one days since the bet had been made.

She stood back and removed her pantyhose and skirt. She was wearing nothing underneath. Jean Luc's eyes were riveted and then, to his complete amazement, he completely lost his self control. In a few seconds it was over.

He was shocked and furious at himself. This was not the masterful yet considerate conquest he had planned, the leisurely exploration that would wipe away the remains of her casual indifference and reduce her to genuine submission. His body had reacted as crudely as if he were an impetuous and totally inexperienced adolescent. Worse yet, he would not be able to try again for several hours—the biochemists could only achieve so much. And worst of all, she was wryly amused.

His dignity was shattered. He began to splutter an apology, some crass offer to pay for dry cleaning her blouse, but she interrupted him.

"Don't be silly, Jean Luc. It's a compliment I haven't been paid in quite some years," she told him smilingly, and touched his lips to silence him.

"Please don't apologize. I think it's very touching." She reached up and kissed him. "I'd adore a long hot bath—will you join me?"

The promised attacks came exactly when the Sons of Hebron had warned. The first attack was in Haifa, and in mathematical terms of the number of dead and injured, it was no more damaging than the others. The first volley killed three civilians and injured eight more. The follow-up volley, in an alarming variation from previous attacks, fell not on the target intersection, but into the forecourt of the nearest hospital, just as the ambulances bearing victims were being uploaded.

Moshe, like all the men at the conference table, felt a wave of fury and frustration. The meeting had been called in anticipation of the attacks, in order to coordinate intelligence and plan an immediate response. But *what* response? The prime minister's representative was reduced to pounding his fists and muttering filth. The senior military officer thought of the retaliatory strikes into the West Bank which had been provisionally scheduled, but knew with grim certainty they would do nothing to deter or disrupt the Sons of Hebron.

Each attack—all the attacks, in and of themselves—were less damaging than the havoc caused by one deluded teenager strapping on explosives and detonating them in a crowded bus or cafe. But there was something utterly inhuman about the 'Sons of Hebron': the sense of a cold mastermind toying with them.

A bank of TVs stood along one grimy wall, and the men watched as each station interrupted its usual programming and switched to live news coverage. A reporter from the BENS, the British European News Service, stood in front of a hospital emergency room (a completely different hospital, in a different city, but that didn't seem to matter).

"This latest incident in the Palestinians' desperate fight for freedom..." she was saying.

Moshe and all the men at the table braced themselves for news of the promised attack in a second city, but there were no reports. Perhaps the note was wrong, or perhaps the Sons of Hebron had encountered an operational problem which had prevented the attack. As the minutes dragged by a wisp of optimism crept into the room, but then CNN abruptly interrupted its own interruption. News of a second attack came in and the optimism abruptly vanished.

The actual attack was exactly like all the others; simply two groups of grenades tossed seemingly at random into a crowded city intersection, but with one huge difference: It was in London. Six grenades fell into the intersection of Knightsbridge and Sloan Street at eight in the evening London time, killing eight pedestrians and wounding twenty one from shrapnel and shattered plate glass. The second wave, thirty minutes later, killed six more and injured nineteen.

The London attack dominated the global news. Within a day most of the pundits came to the conclusion that the attack could be laid at the doors of Israel, the American President, and the British Prime Minister.

If Israel was not so intransigent in obstructing progress toward 'peace', there would be no need for terrorism, or 'legitimate armed resistance to illegal occupation' as it was generally described. If the United States was not so supportive of Israel it would be completely isolated and therefore more willing to compromise; and if Britain were less supportive of the American administration, the United States would be less contrarian and unilateral. Thus, it could be seen clearly that the British government had, by its ill-advised trans-Atlantic policies, called down this attack upon its citizens.

The attack also had the effect of changing an Israeli problem (which, after all, was their own stupid fault) into an international problem, with all the consequences that could be predicted. The Security Council took up a resolution condemning Israel for repeated human rights violations, and 'fostering global insecurity through its repressive policies' toward those who had suffered for so long under its heel. Naturally the resolution never saw the light of day, because the United States was sure to veto it.

But the General Assembly has no veto system and set up a UN study group to analyze the 'root causes' of the attacks. Neither the US nor Israel were asked to participate on the panel, but they were required, under the terms of the commission, to provide 'any and all intelligence that the commission might request'. The fact that they both refused was simply evidence of their antagonism to the 'collective will of the global community'.

Almost unnoticed in all the commotion was an explosion in Safad, in which a van blew up in a rented garage. No one was injured. Analysis of the wreckage revealed grenade shrapnel. This was the second time in eight days that a vehicle containing grenades had blown up, and the site was cordoned off and the Mossad took over the case. The working hypothesis was that this was a Sons of Hebron van.

❦ ❦ ❦

Twenty-four hours after the attacks, several of the Haifa rescue workers and victims fell ill with severe flu-like symptoms. For almost another day the doctors missed the significance. After all, if one is treating an acute trauma victim one does not look for some independent cause of a high temperature and low blood pressure. Then several of the rescue workers and people who lived at the scene of the attack were brought into emergency rooms with high fevers and respiratory distress. Then within hours two Safad policemen were transferred in with similar symptoms.

It was the triage nurse in the emergency room at Haifa's largest hospital who spotted the pattern and sounded the alarm. All the patients were abruptly transported in sealed ambulances to a military isolation hospital, where the cause of their illness was identified.

"What the hell is ricin, anyway?" the prime minister's representative demanded. He had been chosen for his calm and patience, and his ability to manufacture compromises between bitterly opposed political factions, but since the 'Sons of Hebron' campaign had started, his calm and patience seemed to be receding into distant memories.

"Ricin is a naturally occurring cytotoxin which causes red blood cells to agglutinate and burst by hemolysis," the Mossad doctor responded. "It's a heterodimeric Type 2 RIP which...."

"What the *fuck* are you talking about?"

The doctor was offended. "A RIP is a ribosome inactivating protein, typically an N-glycolated 30 kDA monomer that...."

Moshe cut him off before the next explosion. "Ricin is a deadly poison found in castor beans. You eat it and it enters your bloodstream and destroys the red cells. Or you can inhale the ground-up dust with the same results."

"By irreversibly inactivating the eukaryotic ribosomes," added the doctor in a misplaced attempt to clarify the situation.

"Thank you, doctor, that's extremely helpful," said the prime minister's representative with some semblance of his old self. "What are the symptoms?"

Moshe jumped in before the doctor could speak. "If you eat it: acute stomach pain, fever, vomiting, diarrhea, and then dehydration and loss of blood pressure. If you breathe it in: fever, coughing, nausea, laryngitis, and then respiratory failure. It's easy to confuse with a severe attack of flu or a bad stomach virus. Death usually occurs in two to five days."

"And what's the antidote?"

"There is none," said the doctor. "As I said, the damage is irreversible. Once the RIPs have bound to the surface galactosides and entered the cytosols to reach the ribosomes...."

His voice trailed away so that for once he did not need to be interrupted. Everyone in the room had a vivid vision of brutal trench warfare at the cellular level, with endless advancing columns of merciless RIPS and the battlefields littered with the burst and bloated corpses of helpless cytosols in their billions.

The prime minister's representative pulled himself back from the vision. "How do you get poisoned?"

"Normally you chew castor beans by accident," said Moshe. "However, the process can be weaponized by grinding up the chemicals and releasing them into the air as a fine dust. If it gets into your mouth and you swallow it, it'll get into your digestive system. If you inhale it, it gets into your lungs and into your bloodstream that way. If you ingest enough, you'll die."

"How hard is it to make?"

"You can't cook it up in your garage, but any small commercial pharmaceutical lab could do it. The equipment isn't particularly unusual. The principal challenge is to keep the manufacturing process absolutely safe."

"How much is enough?"

"One milligram."

"Where does it come from?"

"Ricin is like a dirty bomb. It's a poor man's weapon of mass destruction. A dirty bomb, just packing radioactive material around an explosive, is relatively easy to make but it has limited effects. Ricin is the same. It's easy to make but, unlike a biological weapon, it doesn't reproduce itself and the victims can't spread the effects to others."

"Known sources or uses?"

"Ansar al-Islam, the terrorist group which was based in Northern Iraq and has ties to Al Qaeda, and our old friend Abu Musad Zarqawi, who, as you know, is the Jordanian who was the link between Osama and Saddam."

"The guy with one leg?"

"Exactly. As far as uses are concerned, there have been more threats than successful attacks, although it's probably been used more than once in Chechnya. Ansar al-Islam has been active up there, and they probably produced a substantial stockpile before they were thrown out of Iraq. Oh, and there was a bizarre case in London in the '70s when the KGB scratched someone's leg with an umbrella with ricin on it. The Soviets made tons of it."

"What happened to the Ansar al-Islam stockpile?"

"The Americans bombed the camps, but we assume some of it went to Syria along with Saddam's other WMD goodies."

'Jules' saw the news of the attacks when he landed in Johannesburg. There was no reference to ricin and he wondered if that part of the attack had failed. The explosion in Safad was too small an event to mention on the international news, and so he had no way of knowing if his third and last timer had worked.

He was completely exhausted. He had been in London less than forty-eight hours, and he had almost slipped off a rain-slicked roof and fallen into Sloan Street the night he installed the grenade dispensers. He had just managed to grab an old corroded TV antenna and haul himself back to safety before it snapped off its mounting. Then he had thrown up. At least the grenade launchers had worked.

After setting them up he had changed identities again and gone straight to Heathrow airport for the grueling flight to South Africa. He would be here less than three hours before heading north.

The balance had shifted between Jean Luc and Maria. His moment of weakness, so unexpected to them both, had transformed him in an instant from a masterful, urbane sophisticate into an awkward moonstruck schoolboy. He had begged her to stay with him whenever she was in Paris, and she had willingly agreed, but he found himself in an agonizing dilemma. Without chemical assistance he was unable to achieve his objective, despite her skillful efforts, and with chemical assistance he was unable to restrain himself for long enough. She was maddeningly sympathetic and patient, and kept assuring him that she was perfectly happy to wait until his importunity worked itself out.

He struggled briefly with his conscience before accepting Michel's payment on their bet, and donated the entire amount to a clinic which researched sexual dysfunctions.

The more understanding and considerate she was, the more desperate he became to justify himself in her eyes. At night she would snuggle close to him and assure him she liked him just the way he was, while his self-loathing rose like bile deep within him. She conducted herself as if she eagerly expected each night would be the night on which the problem was resolved, but it never was.

Unable to perform that most basic function, he began to do all the things he had always despised in other men. He began to boast of his achievements and his power and his influence. He made extravagant displays of his wealth. He pressed ludicrously expensive gifts upon her. He began to tell her the little secrets and peccadilloes of the rich and famous, and to brag of his connections. He held a small dinner party and, cashing in some political IOUs, arranged for the President of France to attend. Maria was appropriately dazzled and that night she told him she wanted to move in with him on a permanent basis.

Jean Luc had arranged for Maria's Barcelona apartment to be bugged and her mail to be intercepted. Three teams of his men working eight hour shifts kept her under constant surveillance. Her e-mail account was hacked. Her cell phone had been 'lost' in a restaurant for half an hour, during which the circuit board had been replaced with another that provided the additional feature of relaying all her conversations to a recording device.

Jean Luc built a comprehensive understanding of Maria's life from these intercepts, and particularly from her cell phone conversations. Jean Luc learned a great deal about the condominium business, including details of two plots of land her company was considering acquiring. He thought of jumping in and buying them and then turning a quick profit by reselling them to Maria's firm.

He discovered her boss was urging her to take over the new and fast expanding business venture in Florida, and had offered her a hefty pay increase and a fifty thousand dollar bonus, but Maria flatly refused.

"Please don't ask me again, I'm not changing my mind."

"Is this about your new French friend?"

"That's none of your damn business! The point is, as you very well know, I hate everything American, and I'm not going over to live in the land of Mickey Mouse and B-52s."

Hans, the diplomat, called frequently. He was a genuinely funny guy, almost good enough to be a standup comic, and Maria was clearly fond of him, but there was an underlying strain in their relationship.

"Hans, we've done this before. You're married. Can't we just be friends? You know I love seeing you."

"But why not? That billionaire is married too."

"He's different."

"Please, just once? I'm going out of my mind! Am I repugnant, or something?"

"Of course you're not. It would just spoil our friendship, and that's very important to me."

"No it wouldn't! Just once? Will you at least think about it?"

"Well, okay, I promise to think about it, but I don't want to get your hopes up."

"Nobody ever called it that before."

She talked to her best friend Be-Be almost every day; long, voluble conversations which covered every topic under the sun, from feminine hygiene to current events, from diets to decisions to be made, from gossip about friends to problems at work, all poured out with startling intimacy and detail.

"So what's with your latest? Are you really interested in him?"

"He's fine. He's a nice guy, Be-Be, I like him."

"What's not to like about a billionaire?"

"I don't care about money, you know that."

"Is he good in the sack?"

"He's fine."

"Fine? Is that all you can say? Does the earth move?"

"We have a good relationship."

"That's it?"

"No, really, Jean Luc's great in bed. He's amazing!"

"Bullshit, Maria. I know you too well. Are you getting serious? What about Bernardo?"

"Bernardo? He's fantastic, really fantastic, but it's just physical, nothing else. What's with you guys? Why aren't you pregnant yet? Did he go to the doctor to get his sperm count checked?"

"He's too embarrassed. He won't jerk off into a bottle in a doctor's office."

Jean Luc played this conversation several times. It was acutely painful to hear her defending his physical prowess to her friend. That act of secret loyalty was probably the nicest thing anyone had ever done for him, and he wondered if his wave of affection for her was based in gratitude or the first stirrings of true love.

There was nothing, nothing in the tapes to suggest she was anything other than what she appeared to be, or her interest in him was anything but genuine. Still, just to be on the safe side, he would have his surveillance extended to Be-Be and Hans. You could never be quite certain who knew what—just like that Jeannette Bois woman, the bank clerk, who had known what she shouldn't have known.

For very different reasons, he would institute a search for Bernardo, whoever he might be, and for whom he felt an overwhelming hatred.

CHAPTER 5

In real life one has to be realistic.

—*Jean Luc Lafarge*

"As you doubtless know," said the Israeli, "Several of our citizens are suffering from ricin poisoning. The ricin was packed into hand grenades and released into the air when they exploded. There have been a number of civilian and military casualties."

"I have no idea what you're talking about!" the Syrian responded. "If someone's attacked you, it certainly wasn't us!"

They were strolling along the once-glamorous seafront in Beirut. In the fifties and sixties Beirut had been bursting with life, a rare example of a country in the Middle East which was not dominated by the politics of hatred. Then the bad times had come, and Beirut had been transformed from the 'Paris of the Mediterranean' into a battleground. The buildings which lined the promenade still bore the scars of conflict. Today the Mediterranean was a sullen steel gray, reflecting the bitter enmity between the two countries that the men represented.

Sometimes even enemies must talk face to face without go-betweens, in order to ensure complete clarity of communication. Thus it was in the old days of the cold war, when the President of the USA could talk directly to his counterpart in the Kremlin over the 'hotline', and thus it is today between Israel and its opponents.

"Yes, it's unfortunate," the Israeli continued. "Things are difficult enough as it is, without some idiot using chemical agents. In fact, it's completely unacceptable."

"I can only repeat myself. We know nothing of this."

"The ricin has been traced to a vehicle which originated in Damascus."

The van's VIN number had been legible after the explosion and it had indeed been imported to Syria.

"That's a monstrous suggestion! We have absolutely *no* knowledge of this attack. It is clearly in our best interests to prevent such a thing from occurring." His indignation seemed genuine.

The Israeli paused. "Do you need to call to verify that? Or are you sure?"

"I'm certain. I've received a complete briefing, and there's nothing remotely like that. And you mention hand grenades—we don't know anything about this new group. It's not us, it's not Hezbollah, and I'm fairly certain it's not the Palestinians, although they're so disorganized it's impossible to be sure. You may or may not know that the Iranians are just as puzzled."

Both men stared at each other. The Israeli was a former prime minister, and there could be absolutely no question that he carried complete authority as his government's representative. Similarly, there could be no doubt the Syrian spoke for his President. Both men could make a binding deal on the spot.

"I'm not interested in whether your government is behind the attack. With due respect to your President, he may not know what is going on. He's not the man his father was, and the *mukhabarat* are not exactly a single group under his complete control."

"I can speak for the entire government," responded the Syrian, obliquely acknowledging the younger Hassad's weak authority.

"Let me simply explain our policy, exactly as it was explained to me. There are eight possible groups we have identified which may be behind these attacks, and four of these have a presence in Damascus. Of course, it may be someone else, but, nonetheless, we will destroy them unless you destroy them first."

"What are you demanding?"

"That you immediately arrest these groups and every other group you know of, *anyone* who could *conceivably* be involved, and tell us—accurately—of all their known active or sleeper agents operating in Israel. We will participate in the interrogations.

"In addition, we require immediate access to certain storage facilities which house...let me say 'materials' that were imported from Iraq when the Americans invaded. We haven't touched them because we thought—we hoped—they wouldn't be used. On that basis we will not take military action, at least until we have exhausted every other possibility."

"What you are asking is impossible—you know it's impossible," the Syrian replied calmly. Obviously he did not take the threat at face value. "If we take action against these groups—alleged groups—we would not survive. All hell would break loose. You can't even prove these attacks are of Syrian origin. You have no justification for randomly attacking whoever you think might be involved."

The Israeli had spent his adult life alternatively fighting with, and negotiating with, his country's enemies. He began to walk again, and the Syrian followed.

"You know, it's all such a waste. All these ruined countries, all these wasted lives. Your side, because you need an enemy to justify your repression, and us, because we have nowhere else to go. I wanted to be a historian, a teacher, perhaps I could have written a book or two, and perhaps students might have still been reading them a hundred years from now—who knows?

"Instead I've been forced to be a soldier, and then a politician. As a kid I remember asking my father before he died in the '56 war, 'Why won't they leave us alone? What do we have to do to get them to leave us alone?' It was a good question then and it still is. It's the question that has defined my entire life."

"Perhaps things could have been different, but they are not," the Syrian responded. "I have two brothers and a cousin buried on the Golan. And now you expect us to do your bidding or suffer the consequences?"

The Syrian felt the deep anger of the old blood feud boiling up inside him. He turned and spoke directly to the Israeli.

"We *always* suffer the consequences. We always have consequences which involve suffering! I could have asked my father the same question as you asked yours. Listen to me carefully. We have *nothing* to do with these attacks, directly or indirectly. Those materials you mention are secure and untouched. Any steps you take will be upon your own heads."

"Let's just call it our 'Hamah strategy,'" replied the Israeli. "In 1982 you destroyed your own town of Hamah in order to kill the PLO inside. Twenty thousand people died. Most of the victims were innocent Syrians, but that didn't stop you, and you drove Arafat out successfully and into Lebanon. Using the same logic we're going to destroy as much of Damascus as it takes to destroy whoever is behind these attacks."

The Syrian realized the Israeli was in deadly earnest. The grenade attacks had spooked the government sufficiently that it was prepared to lash out, even at shadows.

"Such an action is completely unacceptable, even for Israel," he growled.

"Then get rid of whoever is using ricin against us."

"That's not Syria's problem!"

"It is now! You have seventy-two hours."

"But...."

"Oh, and don't worry," the Israeli added, turning to leave. "We'll be very careful to miss the French embassy."

The Syrian's face took on an expression which mixed incredulity with anger and fear, but the Israeli was already walking away.

Maria was staring at the television with a frown on her face, gripping the remote control as if it were a weapon. She and Jean Luc had been lounging in his comfortable sitting room, sipping chardonnay and relaxing before dressing for the evening, but now she was tense and grimaced as she pointed at the screen.

"I see the Americans are refusing to support the famine relief effort in Central Africa. The news says that up to a quarter of a million people are at risk this coming summer. And that's not counting deaths from AIDS. Don't they have consciences?"

"In fairness, my dear, I believe they *are* offering to supply food. They're just saying that they'll send their own grain and distribute directly, rather than pay for the UN to buy non-US grain in the market."

"They're trying to force the poor Africans to accept their genetically altered Franken-foods. Can't they do anything without some kind of an ulterior motive?"

"Don't you think the starving Africans would rather have grain of any sort than die of malnutrition?"

"They're just trying to undercut the UN again. It's all politics. I just wish there was something more that could be done. Why doesn't everyone get together and put the bullies in their place?"

Jean Luc smiled. "That's easier said than done," he explained patiently. "There are many reasons to stay on America's good side and far fewer to oppose it. People talk about David and Goliath, and the Lilliputians combining to defeat Gulliver, but these are just stories. In real life one has to be realistic."

"I don't accept that," she said with some heat. "We can't live in a world in which there is one superpower that picks and chooses which treaties to obey and which to ignore. Fundamental human rights demand that one country can't boss around the other two hundred, and threaten everyone who doesn't fall into line with B-52's."

"Why this sudden interest in politics, my dear?" He found her naivety quite touching, like a child asking why people have to die.

"It's not really a new interest. I told you I can't abide Americans. It's not political, it's personal. Anyway, I met a woman in the Green Party. She's incredibly persuasive. She says we can't just sit around and do nothing. Some of her policies are ridiculous, I admit, but the main thrust of her argument, that the US must be stopped, is absolutely correct. She says she has connections. It's all a bit vague, but she suggested I could make a donation. She said the money would be put to good use against the Americans."

Jean Luc frowned. "Such people can be very dangerous. Many are completely genuine, but others are not. If you contribute to a group that has certain kinds of known or suspected connections you'll get on all sorts of lists."

"What connections?"

"Money that you devote to some worthy cause, like famine relief, can wind up at a very different destination, and you, my dear, could wind up in jail for the rest of your life. I urge you to break off all dealings with this woman."

"Are you suggesting she's associated with terrorists?"

"My dear, I have no idea, but such things happen, particularly in groups with highly anti-American agendas."

"Well, perhaps you're right, she is a bit weird, but I don't think I can do *nothing*. It's time for people to stop talking and start acting. If it means taking a risk, so be it!" She jumped up and began pacing in frustration.

"Please, I beg you. I don't want to lose you!" He also jumped up, genuinely alarmed. "There are other ways of attacking the problem without throwing in your lot with a bunch of left wing loonies."

"They may be left wing loonies, as you put it, but at least they've got the guts to try to do something about it, something more than simply moaning and groaning. As the saying goes: 'My enemy's enemy is my friend'."

"My dear, I respect your convictions, but, as I said, there may be other ways of achieving the same objective without exposing yourself to personal danger." He seemed to be speaking obliquely.

"Like what?" she shot back. "What do *you* do, Jean Luc? Go to Davos every year with a bunch of other super-rich people and complain politely? Jesus, you've got more money than God—you could make a real difference if you bothered."

"Really, my dear, what's got into you? I'm just trying to look after your best interests. I…."

For the first time in their relationship she seemed truly annoyed with him.

"This isn't a question of personal comfort or even personal safety. This is about starving children and the environment being poisoned, while people like you drive around in chauffeur-driven Mercedes doing sweet fuck all."

He was shocked by her venom. "That's extremely unfair, and you know it!" Jean Luc bristled. "Can we please return to a rational level of conversation and get dressed for the reception tonight?"

"Why? So we can eat canapés we don't need while half the world is malnourished?" She stalked off in high dudgeon.

That night she did not snuggle with him and he felt painfully rejected.

"Have I done something to offend you, my angel?" he asked nervously into the darkness.

"No, Jean Luc, you have done nothing, as far as I know, nothing at all." Her voice had a dead quality. "That's precisely the issue. I might as well tell you I've decided I'm going to see that woman again. I take your point about funding terrorists, but I have to have a higher purpose in life than simply selling expensive condominiums to upwardly mobile overweight Germans, or convincing gullible men to drink more Sassal by appealing to their testosterone."

"I…I was hoping that perhaps, well…." His voice fell silent in uncertainty, and there was an empty feeling in the pit of his stomach.

"You were hoping for what?"

"That *we* might be becoming a higher cause…." It sounded so pathetic in his ears.

There was a long pause as she digested his confession. He found he was holding his breath as he waited for her response. Finally she moved over and entwined herself around him.

"Jean Luc, you're the nicest man I've ever met, you know that, and you know it's got nothing to do with your money. I want nothing but your company."

Jean Luc felt a surge of relief, even as she continued. "But it still bothers me that, in spite of all your power, and all your success, you've never done anything really important; something for the good of mankind. Don't be offended, but to me it's as if you're wasting your life, just as I'm wasting mine. You could make such a difference! It doesn't change what I feel for you, it just makes me sad, that's all."

She kissed his chest and took a huge leap into the unknown.

"I…I think I may be falling in love with you," she murmured. "I'd like our children to think of their father as a great man, as well as a wonderful man."

It was completely unexpected.

"Oh, Maria," he gasped before he knew what he was saying, and she felt tears on his cheeks. "I love you so much," he whispered and realized it was true.

They kissed, and he discovered to his unadulterated delight that, at long, long last, his newly discovered passion had conquered all his problems.

'Jerome' felt at home. He liked the sights and sounds of Africa, the heat and the smells, the slow rhythms of life. He loved waking up at daybreak to a cacophony of noises—dawn was so damned *noisy,* with every single animal and bird intent on announcing its existence, and the clattering of pots and pans in the kitchen as the staff prepared breakfast.

He loved sitting slumped on the veranda of the ramshackle building which passed as the best hotel in town, awash with sweat as the noon sun beat down and reduced life to a crawl, watching the women swaying slowly by with bundles on their heads, as if they were posing for *National Geographic,* as if Africa was timeless, and as if, statistically, they wouldn't be dead from AIDS in five years.

He loved dusk, bringing relief from the heat at long last, and another burst of noise as the animal and bird kingdoms arranged themselves for nightfall, and it was time to gather with the few other guests to open their carefully sealed bottles of alcohol.

He had spent two years as a mercenary in the Ivory Coast, supporting this faction or that, defending his employers' piece of the conflict diamond pipeline. His group had changed sides several times as the fickle fortunes of war tilted one way or another, but the objective was always the same, and smuggling is strictly a cash business. Occasionally they'd intimidate some wretched village by killing a few men at random, and carrying away a selection of the women, but there was little actual fighting, and by unspoken agreement the mercenary groups were always careful to avoid each other.

He had left with half a million US dollars in a bank account in Zurich and a sock-full of uncut diamonds. The diamonds had disappeared into the back-streets of Amsterdam at a ridiculous discount, but his bank account had still doubled.

Now he was back, and even though the Ivory Coast was more than a thousand miles away, this was still Africa, still the same magnificent and mysterious continent bent upon destroying itself. A baldheaded man plopped himself down in the cane chair next to Jean's and fanned himself with a sweaty straw hat. An ancient clerical collar, worn despite the heat, identified him as a Catholic missionary from the crumbling and overflowing orphanage up the street. His words coincided with Jerome's thoughts.

"This was once a thriving town, when I first got here, over thirty years ago. We had schools, churches, clinics, even a hospital. There was plenty of work in the plantations, and plenty of food. Now the town's dying, like this entire country. In five years there won't be anybody left here at all."

"I thought the UN was supposed to be taking over?"

"I rest my case."

Jean let the old man ramble on while he considered his plans. His task was infinitely easier for this part of the mission. There were no grenade launchers to build, no slippery roofs to cross in darkness, no roadblocks to pass through. All he had to do was break into a dilapidated warehouse stuffed with bags of grain. There were guards, but they were inept and untrained. Thankfully the Americans were not directly guarding their famine relief convoys.

And he felt much more comfortable handling ricin in liquid form, rather than near-invisible dust; that had been *scary*, even though the grenades had been hermetically sealed in plastic coatings, and in spite of his protective suit.

His cover for this part of the operation was as a freelance journalist on contract with a respectable periodical, and therefore he asked the old man a couple of questions and for permission to quote him. Two German aid workers joined them and he made a show of writing down their comments and checking the correct spelling of their names. When an American with the US relief project drifted over, they received him frostily.

"We should be getting another ton of food tomorrow," the American announced. "It's rice this time—they've promised four light trucks. Can you use any in the eastern villages?"

"I don't know how you have the gall to show your face around here," began one of the German doctors, and there was real malice in her voice. "How can you force these poor people to eat unsafe food?"

"Has the danger been proven scientifically?" the old priest interjected mildly.

The German turned on him.

"Fuck off, child abuser. I don't talk to Catholic priests, or any other organized perverts for that matter," she spat back.

That evening it took less than ten minutes for Jerome to break into the warehouse, contaminate half a dozen sacks of grain, and leave quietly. The worst part of the whole thing was that he now faced a journey of two thousand miles all the way back to South Africa, then all the way back to Europe, and then all the way to Canada. At least his neck had finally stopped aching.

CHAPTER 6

Few things worth doing are done in public.

—Jean Luc Lafarge

Rachel, Moshe's wife, hung up the phone. "Sorry to interrupt dinner," she said. "But that was my friend Belle. Her boyfriend is still missing and she keeps wondering if he was killed in one of the terrorist attacks and they haven't identified his remains."

Moshe and Rachel were entertaining Moshe's brother Josh and his wife Sarah to a relaxed family dinner.

"Kamal, the Algerian with the biggest what's-it in Israel?" asked Josh. "The guy she brought to dinner?"

"Really, Josh, I really shouldn't have said what she told me in confidence."

"Mr. Foot-Long is missing?"

"He's actually an Israeli citizen, and he's a perfectly respectable plumber, and it's less than a foot. Why are all men so obsessed by size?"

"It's a plot to get our sympathies," said Sarah. "They claim to feel inadequate, so we will feel sorry for them and give them a blow job to make them feel better."

"Does Josh do that too? Moshe's always trying that one on me. It must run in the family."

"If Kamal's missing and she's worried," Josh said, "Maybe Moshe's people can find him. His guys know where everybody is."

They all looked at Moshe, but he had pushed aside his dinner plate half-eaten and was staring blindly into middle space. He kept going over it and over it. Something was wrong. It just didn't add up.

"Moshe?"

"What?" he asked vaguely. "Sorry, I wasn't listening."

"We were saying Belle's plumber Kamal is missing. Could you find him?"

"Mr. Huge is AWOL?"

"Could you get your guys to track him down as a favor? She's worried out of her mind."

"Well, we could, but from a professional perspective we'd probably approach it by searching for his you-know-what. It's big enough to be obvious. It would, if you don't mind me saying it, stand out like a sore thumb. And the rest of him would be attached to it."

"There we go again," said Rachel. "Penis envy."

"It runs in the family," said Sarah, but Moshe was still half distracted.

"What's up, Moose?" asked his brother Josh.

Josh was the physical one, compact and powerful, dark and handsome, a captain in the IAF, while Moshe had the brains. Family legend maintained their father had both the brains and the brawn, before he was killed in Lebanon in '82, and bequeathed one set of attributes to each son. Moshe was as thin as a rail, with a weak chin and a nose far too big for the rest of his features; he was the one that had won all the scholarships, while Josh was the natural athlete and later the dashing fighter jet jockey.

"There's a note and an attack," said Moshe quietly. "There's a second note and a second attack. There's a third note saying we haven't done something and a third set of attacks, which are much more serious: one is in London, and they use ricin here. Okay, so we have a pattern of note and attack, note and attack, note with reference to demands and attack. Observe a change, like a gear shift, between the second and third note and attack sets. Let's call that 'part one.'"

The cheerful family kitchen with its bright red and white checked tablecloth suddenly seemed colder. Josh, Rachel, and Sarah were hearing all this for the first time, for these were closely held security secrets. Moshe almost never talked about his work, just as Josh seldom mentioned his. Security resides, above all, in keeping your mouth *shut*, even at home.

"Are you sure you should be telling us this?" Josh asked uneasily, but curiosity drove him on. "Notes? What notes?"

"*Ricin?* You mean that chemical weapon?" Rachel demanded.

"Is this about the grenade bombers?" Sarah added.

In the paradoxical way of their family, cerebral Moshe had married a pretty and vivacious wife, while handsome Josh had fallen helplessly and happily for a quiet plain girl.

"There's a group called the Sons of Hebron. They send us a note before each of these grenade attacks, announcing where they're going to hit us."

"The Sons of Hebron? I've never heard of them."

"Nobody has. We haven't, the Palestinians haven't, the Syrians haven't, the Iranians haven't, even the Afghans, as far as we can tell. They've appeared out of thin air."

"Is that why we went back into Hebron the other day and blew all those buildings up?" Josh's wife asked.

"Yep," said Moshe. Josh shifted in his seat, and they all guessed he had been part of the raid. The Palestinians were claiming they'd hit a kindergarten, and the civilized world had been appropriately shocked without bothering to find out if it was true.

Moshe had returned to his soliloquy.

"Okay, part two is a Palestinian kid blowing himself up at a roadblock following the second attacks in Tel Aviv and a van blowing up all by itself following the third attack in Haifa. Both vehicles have grenades and the second one has ricin."

"Listen, honey," Rachel interrupted him. "Are you quite sure you should tell us all this? I mean, obviously you can trust us, but you never talk about your work."

It was as if Moshe had not heard her.

"Now, what do we do? Let's call it part three. After the first attack we basically do nothing, because we don't know anything and we don't see there's going to be a pattern. After the second attack we search Hebron and find nothing, and we blow up a few suspect buildings. It wasn't a kindergarten, incidentally, Josh, it was a whorehouse."

Josh wondered if there was *anything* the Mossad didn't know, and Moshe continued his soliloquy.

"After the third attack we threaten Syria. In other words, our responses are escalating as we perceive the threat to be increasing, but we still have no knowledge of the enemy or his ultimate intentions. We're striking out at random."

He was silent for a moment and then continued.

"Then there's part four, international reaction. After the first attack there's nothing—just the usual 'it's all your own fault' bullshit from the Arab League.

After the raid on Hebron, there's lots of serious international noise from the usual European sources and the human rights groups, but still nothing out of the ordinary. After the attack in London: *Bang!* Huge international reaction, with all the trimmings. The Arabs press the buttons at the UN; our prime minister gets yelled at by the White House—I mean *really* yelled at—I heard the tapes."

"We've been through all this a dozen times in the past, Moshe," said Josh. "A wave of killings and then Arafat turns them off again when it suits him or the Europeans send him more cash. What's so different about this time?"

"I honestly don't know. It's just that I believe we're being played—suckered into something, and not by the usual suspects. Someone is using us as a pawn in some other game. Someone is pushing us to escalate our responses. It's too…symmetrical."

"You still didn't explain the part about ricin," Josh's wife broke in.

"A few hours after the Haifa attacks, the rescue and security people started getting sick. They were all isolated and they'd been poisoned with powdered ricin. We hushed the whole thing up to prevent panic."

"Dear God! We think the ricin came from Syria, so we're threatening them?" Josh asked.

Moshe nodded. "Yes. It's the logical thing to do, except none of this makes any sense at all."

"Why are you telling us all this?"

"Because I'm scared shitless."

⁂

"Good morning, my little one." Michel Leclerc stood before her in the morning sunshine, impeccably dressed and with a superb topcoat draped elegantly over his shoulders.

"Michel, what a surprise, how are you?"

"All the better for seeing you, I assure you. Can I persuade you to join me for an aperitif before lunch?"

Without waiting for a reply he took Maria's elbow and steered her to a sidewalk café, where they sat down in the sunshine. He had all of Jean Luc's charm and self assurance, Maria thought, but somehow he was a little softer, as if he lacked Jean Luc's most predatory instincts. While Jean Luc saw life as a competition he was driven to win, Michel seemed to see life as something to be savored.

"So, you have fallen under my old friend's spell? If you ever grow tired of him, or he of you, I insist that you choose *my* shoulder to cry on!" He grinned at her roguishly.

"Michel!" Maria exclaimed as if scandalized. "How can you say such a thing?"

"If I do not say it, it might not occur to you, and so I have nothing to lose and everything to gain. Besides, I am two years younger than him, and therefore a much more suitable match."

He clutched his heart in pantomime, and smiled coyly. "I admit I am smitten."

His eyes undressed her, and then he sat back and laughed, robbing the situation of any offense and somehow creating a charming conspiracy between them.

"How kind," she said vaguely, not quite certain where this conversation was going.

He continued. "However, I must admit, I have never seen Jean Luc conduct himself in this fashion. He is completely infatuated. I wouldn't be surprised if he speaks to Louise."

A waiter appeared.

"I don't think it's too early for champagne, do you?" Michel asked her, and ordered without waiting for her to reply.

"To Louise, his wife, you were saying? About me? Why would he do that? Or do you know something I don't?"

"Does he speak to you of her?"

She frowned, torn between curiosity and discretion.

"I know you're a close friend of his, but I'm not sure we should be speaking of such matters, Michel."

"Ah, let me explain. As you know, Jean Luc and I have been friends since our school days, close friends, and you should think of me as part of the family. Indeed, Louise is my cousin and it was I who introduced them."

"I didn't know that."

"Louise is a remarkable woman," he said, settling back more comfortably and adopting a tone of casual intimacy. "Her family is one of the most prominent in France, and, of course, she's extremely wealthy in her own right. Old money, as they say. When Jean Luc left university and was casting about for an appropriate wife, it occurred to me that she would be perfect for him—her social standing could open many doors for him, her capital could enhance his chances of building his business—and I was right.

"They made an ideal couple, and in many ways they still do. She lives down on the estate, of course, and is becoming more and more reclusive as the years roll by, but that suits Jean Luc very well: a successful marriage of convenience."

"Why do they live apart, if they're so well suited?"

He took a sip of champagne.

"My dear, she's like a china doll. Perfect, exquisite, and, alas, completely frigid, if I may use that term!"

Michel clearly drew a great deal of pleasure from divulging such intimate details.

"It's such a pity! Jean Luc, as of course you know well, likes his women hot-blooded, if I may say so without offense, as indeed I do! But now, my instincts tell me Jean Luc wants to be free of her, after all these years. You've made an amazing impression on him, my dear!"

"I…I don't know what to say, Michel. We're very happy—but divorce? That's a huge step for him. He scarcely knows me, and it's only been a few weeks."

"True, but the best few weeks of his life."

"Why do you say that?"

"Because he told me. As I said, he and I are extremely close."

His tone was conspiratorial.

"To be frank, he's asked me to speak to Louise on his behalf. I tell you this because his well being is important to me, as if we were brothers."

"I'm speechless!"

He ordered more champagne before continuing.

"My little one, be gentle with him. In spite of all his strength, he's very vulnerable, and you can cause him as much pain as pleasure."

"What do you mean?"

"He's extremely sensitive where you're concerned. I've never seen him like this before. You've been goading him to take more of a direct position in politics, to use his power and influence, and he feels inadequate. Perhaps you haven't been goading, but he still feels pressured to justify himself in your eyes."

"I admit I've been a bit vocal about America, but…."

"He's desperate to impress you, but he is bound by an oath of secrecy."

He paused and leant across the table, taking her hands in his.

"Listen to me. If you knew what I know, you would not question his involvement in these matters. I promise you, Jean Luc is indeed shaping world events, in ways you cannot possibly imagine. You can trust me absolutely on this! You can feel proud of him!"

"I…."

"Be patient with him, my little one. I promise you, in a few weeks you will be delighted, and we will all have Jean Luc to thank."

Moshe stared at the latest note. There was the usual bleak announcement of impending death and destruction, but there was also something else. 'The old man is still in Ramallah. The Sons of Hebron will strike twice on a day of our choosing.'

"What the hell is this supposed to mean?" Moshe asked the room at large.

The prime minister's representative lit a cigarette and inhaled deeply. It had taken him months of struggle to beat the habit, and now he had succumbed again under this new pressure.

"God knows. The old man is presumably Arafat, but what are we supposed to do? Release him? Remove him from power? Deport him? What do these sons of bitches *want*?"

Moshe frowned. It just didn't make sense.

"We assume that the missing note told us what to do?"

"Right," said the man from the Defense Ministry. "But what do we do? Go on TV and say we're sorry, your demands got lost in the mail, please fax us a duplicate as soon as possible? You notice they increased the ante to 'two strikes' and no date?"

"The Prime Minister is worried, needless to say," said his representative. "He has to make his mind up about Syria. In fact, he's decided to go ahead unless we come up with a powerful reason not to. Besides, we've made the threat and we have to deliver on it. The Syrians have done nothing except keep denying everything."

The room was silent. Everyone understood the implications and consequences of assaulting Syria, but everyone also understood the consequences of doing nothing.

"The next attack will be worse, and it will undoubtedly involve at least one foreign city. If they use ricin overseas, it will be catastrophic. Syria is the most probable source. Therefore we *must* attack Syria."

"Why Arafat?" asked Moshe. "Why do the Syrians care about Arafat? They hate him!"

"I don't know. But I have to report to the Prime Minister. Does anyone have anything to add?"

One by one the men around the table voted for striking Syria. Finally the prime minister's representative motioned to Moshe.

"Okay, bear with me for one minute. I think we're being fooled. I don't think there was another note—we've just assumed there had to be one and we lost it before we realized what it was. Now we're assuming that we have to do something with Arafat. But look at the note, it doesn't say 'therefore.'"

"What the hell do you mean?"

"It doesn't say Arafat is still in Ramallah, *therefore* we'll attack again, it just says we'll attack again. It could equally well say, 'It's a sunny day, period, we'll attack again.'"

"So what are you suggesting?"

"I'm suggesting we stay out of Syria—we're being led into a trap."

There was a long silence. "I'll present your view to the Prime Minister, Moshe, but I don't think he'll buy it. There's not one shred of evidence to support your view."

"With due respect, sir, there's not one shred to support yours either."

❧ ❧ ❧

"My angel," Jean Luc said to Maria. "I have a meeting here this evening. It's just a group of friends. We pool donations to charities and agree how to allocate the proceeds and so on."

"It sounds very noble."

"Well, perhaps, but we don't talk about it. Few things worth doing are done in public. But in fact it's pretty damned boring—financial reports and so on. Michel's in it and a couple of others. Anyway, at the risk of offending you, would you be gracious enough to remain upstairs? It should be over by nine and then we can go out for a bite to eat."

"The same group that was here last week? With Michel and the professor who sounds like he should be Henry Kissinger's twin brother? Of course, but eating is the last thing I should be doing. I'm putting on weight and it's all going to my ass. Look at it!"

She gave him a clear perspective.

"You need exercise," he responded roguishly. "Something to get your heart pumping. I'll see what I can think of."

"I'll look forward to it."

He smiled and turned away before matters went too far. He had always tired of his women quickly, but in Maria's case the reverse was happening. It was as if some seismic shift was taking place within him. Even the intense excitement of bringing the American hegemon to its knees was beginning to be eclipsed by this woman, so icy cool on the public surface and so fiery beneath.

He wished she could join the group downstairs, and realize the true breadth of his power and the soaring height of his ambition, rather than being hidden away like some cheap call girl he was keeping on the side. But trust is given far more reluctantly than love, and he was still sufficiently in control of his emotions to know that revealing this ultimate secret carried more risk than reward.

It was almost as if she had read his mind—or at least one part of it.

"Don't feel badly about leaving me out of your meeting, Jean Luc," she said. "I still have a ton of work to do on the Sassal campaign for the board meeting next week, and there's a presentation to the bankers on financing the new condominiums to get ready for. I've been seriously remiss about earning my salary."

He decided, on the spot, to buy the condominium real estate company lock stock and barrel—it was actually a pretty reasonable investment on an after tax basis, although the debt structure would need to be revamped—and she would become the managing director. He'd relocate the company's headquarters to Paris and he'd be spared the painful nights he spent alone when she was traveling. Perhaps she might even take over marketing for all Groupe Lafarge consumer products—the Sassal-France GT campaign was nothing short of brilliant. 'Sassal for winners' he thought as he hurried downstairs, 'ultra-cool with an attitude problem'; it was so *right* for the market, just as she was so *right* for him. Poor Louise, he thought disjointedly, ice on the surface and ice beneath. She has to go.

CHAPTER 7

Vanity is the most powerful emotion of all.

—Jean Luc Lafarge

The two squadrons of IAF F16-I aircraft that took off from Ramat David Air Base were perhaps the most advanced fighter aircraft in the world, with capabilities which exceeded even those of the F16s flown by the USAF. There was quite literally no way the Syrians could possibly stop them but, even so, the Israelis suppressed several SAM sites and were ready to deal with any Syrian Air Force Mig 29 Fulcrums or Tu 27 Flankers which happened to be airworthy and piloted by men stupid enough to take off. The only conceivable threat was an extremely lucky hit by a shoulder-borne triple-A missile.

The attack was completely unopposed and sixteen targets were hit; five in Lebanon, three in remote areas of Syria, and the remainder in and around Damascus. All the aircraft returned to base within ninety minutes of taking off. Moshe's brother Josh was among the pilots sent to the Damascus area.

The world let out a collective primal scream.

Street demonstrations took place in twenty seven countries, culminating in a synchronized Global March for Peace which consisted of protest marches from cold, wintry Christchurch in New Zealand in the middle of the night to Fairbanks, Alaska in the mid afternoon. At exactly the same moment, all around the world, effigies of the Israeli prime minister (and for good measure the American President) were set afire. In many locations the demonstrations extended to attacks on Israeli embassies and El Al offices and, particularly in Europe, on synagogues.

The American administration was furious. They had seen the attack developing from AWACS surveillance aircraft high over the Persian Gulf. In the first few minutes of the raid, they had to face the issue of what to do if the IAF crossed into Iraqi airspace en route to Iran; a contingency for which they had no plan, and the thought of IAF F16s and USAF F16s engaged in combat was something US Central Command simply could not contemplate, and there was real concern about which side might gain the upper hand.

The US Secretary of State was so angry he literally did not listen to the explanation offered by the Israeli foreign minister. He lost his usual self control, screamed into the phone, and hung up. A meeting of the US National Security Council bickered for half an hour over the wording of the administration's statement condemning the Israeli raid, with the Secretary of State insisting on 'extremely unhelpful' to the peace process and the National Security Advisor holding out for 'very unhelpful'. In the end they compromised at 'very unhelpful indeed'.

The United Nations had no such linguistic difficulties. A resolution was prepared within hours which squarely condemned the attack as an unjustifiable act of aggression and a crime against humanity and, with intended irony, threatened 'serious consequences' if any such attack ever took place again. The detailed wording was designed to trigger the International Criminal Court, which, within a day, announced it would consider indictments and called for briefs from the peace loving nations of the world.

* * *

'Robert' liked Montreal. It is small and cosmopolitan, and combines the sophistication of its French origins with the edginess of an American city. Upon arrival, he spent the better part of the day sleeping off the effects of jet lag, and then set out to find the bars and cafés frequented by the student population. Montreal is home to the University of Montreal and McGill University. He found a bar just off Sherburne, and in it he found a young lady wearing a tee shirt which read 'Harvard is the McGill of America'. All around him twanged the unique accent of Québécoise, riddled with harsh vowels: 'Kay–Beck–Kours', and so loaded with Americanisms and butchered grammar, as pungent and energetic as the city itself, that he could scarcely understand it.

"Je suis comme 'whatever', et elle est comme 'fuck you'," said the girl to a young man as he approached them, recounting an argument.

"Quelle bitch," he replied.

Robert ordered a beer—Sassal GT—and the girl broke off her conversation in a minute or two and came and stood beside him.

"*Sassal aussi*," she said to the bartender. "You are Robert?" she asked him in English.

"Yes. George says 'hello'."

"That bastard owes me a hundred dollars."

"He owes more a lot more."

"Okay. I'm told you need contacts with political activists. I'll introduce you around. The kid I was talking to is as good a place to start as any. There's a party at my place later on, with the right kind of people."

✦ ✦ ✦

The first few deaths were put down to dysentery, or, indeed, almost any of the acute gastro-tract problems which preyed upon the people. People weakened by months—years—of malnutrition and outright starvation can and do die of almost anything. Does the specific cause really matter, when twenty five percent of the population has AIDS, and the other seventy five percent is waiting to contract it?

It was a doctor from 'Doctors without Borders' who noticed the unusual pattern, and a review of cases over the previous ten days confirmed his suspicions: people were dying at an unusual rate in the villages supplied with American-donated food. He was an Indian who did not share his colleagues' universal distaste for America, and he knew that the anti-genetic food campaign was simply protectionism to defend inefficient European farmers from their more productive counterparts in the US, without any scientific basis whatsoever.

Still, the comparative death rate statistics were unquestionable and he could not ignore the facts. The most likely explanation was the milky-green liquid from the local village wells which passed for potable fresh water, but he couldn't be sure.

Africa's self-inflicted wounds were bad enough without more misery being imported. The huge eyes of starving children with grotesquely inflated bellies haunted his dreams. Now he had a new nightmare, a nightmare of children wracked by abdominal pain, too weak to whimper; and their eyes, dulled with excruciating pain, staring up into his in silent condemnation, 'Doctor, I suffer. Why do you not heal me?'

He raised his concerns that night during dinner at the crumbling hotel, asking the other relief workers if they had seen anything untoward among their own patients. Had there been an uptick in digestive illnesses? How recently had the well water in the outlying villages been analyzed? Were the historical death-rate statistics reliable, so that before and after comparisons could be made?

The conversation followed professional lines until one of the German doctors turned to the American sitting beside her.

"You bastards!" she said. "You *fucking, murdering, BASTARDS!*"

She slapped him as hard as she could. Shocked by her assault he fell backward from his chair, and she leapt on him, raking his cheeks with her fingernails and punching him with all the force she could muster. She was considerably stronger than him, and he squirmed weakly. Eventually the others pulled her off. His nose was clearly broken, and his face was streaming blood.

As luck would have it, a TV crew from the British European News Service—BENS—was visiting the area, and the next day the whole world knew.

"Doctor Shah," asked the reporter, "I know you said that the most likely cause is some form of contamination of the local well water, but you can't rule out the possibility that these genetically-altered foods have poisoned people, can you?"

"Until we can complete our analysis of the well water, and conduct autopsies to establish the real cause of death, we simply don't know."

"But in good conscience, Doctor, can you unreservedly recommend that these people continue to ingest artificially engineered substances? Would it not be safer to switch to a more reliable source of wholesome nutrition without these unknown and deadly side effects?"

"Well, we must always be cautious, of course," and his remaining, "But I see no evidence so far that this has anything to do with the food" was edited out. In her closing remarks, the reporter said, "And so here, in this remote corner of the world, desperate and helpless men and women are paying the ultimate price of American policies, as they are in so many other corners of this planet. Tracy Williams, BENS World News"—she paused to wipe away a tear—"Central Africa."

Back in the studio, the anchor shook her head in silent horror, and was forced to clear her throat before continuing with the next segment of the show, an update from a hospital in Damascus filled with the civilian victims of the recent Israeli air raids. Given the statistical distribution of the human race by gender and age, it is remarkable that the victims of Israeli bombs are almost exclusively children and pregnant women.

Moshe broke into Kamal's apartment. It took him less than two minutes to conclude that Kamal had gone from Belle's life forever. There were no personal belongings. He certainly had not gone out one evening and had the misfortune to be turned into red goo spread on the inside of a bus by a suicide bomber. When he had left he had taken everything.

Moshe looked around more closely, and frowned as a suspicion began to form. It was not just that he had taken everything; he had taken *everything*, every single trace of his existence. Even the tidiest person leaves something behind, some scrap of soap dropped in the bathroom, some paper napkins in a kitchen drawer, some half empty bottle of washing up liquid beneath the sink, a bent wire clothes hanger in a closet. But Kamal had left nothing: the place was hygienically clean.

Moshe unscrewed the telephone mouthpiece. It was one of the older models, at least ten-years-old, with little holes which let the sound of the speaker's voice reach the microphone inside. Over years of constant use, tiny particles of humanity—saliva, flakes of dead skin, grease—gradually build up inside the holes. The holes were clean. Moshe did not have a microscope, but he was prepared to bet that the entire telephone had been scrubbed and sterilized. There was only one conclusion: Whoever he was, Belle's Mr. Huge was a bad guy.

He used his cell phone to call in a forensic team. They would find nothing, he bet, but that would confirm his suspicion. He locked the door and ran downstairs. On the front steps he stopped in mid stride.

"Oh shit," he said softly to himself. The lab analysis of the remnants of the blown up vehicle in Safad had speculated that the vehicle might have been used by a plumber, based on fragments of piping and tools. A huge pipe wrench had been found impaled in the remains of one of the walls by the force of the explosion. Kamal had been a plumber.

Over the next twenty-four hours the pattern became clear. Mossad agents combed the neighborhood and found some of his customers, and they all reported he was the cleanest, tidiest plumber they had ever heard of. Not only did he clean up after himself, but he wore rubber gloves to avoid leaving greasy fingerprints all over his customers' kitchens and bathrooms—so thoughtful.

No one was quite sure of his last name, not even Belle, and there were no records of his existence. He had sublet his apartment from a friend and had signed no documents. The friend knew him only as a guy who frequented the same coffee shop as himself. The forensic team confirmed the complete sterility of the apartment. The only human traces belonged to the cleaning lady and Moshe himself.

There were no photographs. Belle said he was camera shy and complained that his eyebrows always made him look like a Neanderthal. With great embarrassment she admitted he had permitted her one snapshot, but this served only to confirm that his reputation in the family was based on fact.

Between them they constructed a remarkably detailed composite of his face, for Moshe recalled him quite clearly from the two times he had shared their dinner table. Unfortunately, there were no good matches in any government data bases, and no one of that appearance had entered or left Israel.

"So why did we think he was Algerian, Belle, or from Algeria originally?"

She screwed up her eyes in concentration.

"He wouldn't talk about his background, he said it was too boring to mention. I thought he was Algerian because he cut himself one time and swore in French: That's all. And he seemed to know *about* things, but not the things themselves...I can't explain it exactly. He knew how to find his way around Jerusalem—more than I do, and I've lived here all my life—but it was like he had learned it from a map, and he didn't recognize the actual streets. I don't know. It was just a feeling."

"What did you talk about?"

"To tell you the truth, not much. It was mostly physical, if you know what I mean."

"We'll have to go over your apartment with a fine toothcomb."

"He never went in it. We always met at his place."

"Shit."

The Mossad and the CIA are close, even intimate allies, even closer than the CIA and the British MI6, and 9/11 had brought the two organizations closer than ever. Almost all the CIA's reliable human intelligence on the Middle East and terrorism comes from the Mossad, and much of the Mossad's electronic intelligence comes from US surveillance assets. Even so, the two organizations do not trust each other completely, and the CIA and the Mossad devote considerable resources to spying on each other. Besides, the Department of State can be counted on to minimize the reliability of Mossad information.

Therefore, Moshe did not send Kamal's likeness to the CIA directly, but to one of the Mossad's operatives inside the CIA. The search results were negative. In addition, Algeria knew nothing; Interpol knew nothing. Kamal had never existed.

"Did he ever say anything that surprised you, Belle?"

Moshe had grown hopeless. His colleagues and bosses agreed that Kamal was probably one of the Sons of Hebron, but without any intelligence they could not progress.

"Did he ever mention the names of Egyptian soccer players, or make a comment about the weather in Chechnya, or a coffeehouse in Damascus, or anything out of the ordinary? Anything at all, like the one time he swore in French?"

"He knew about diamonds."

"Diamonds? What happened?"

"Oh, we went past a jeweler's once, and I stopped to look at the rings in the window, and there was one big expensive one, on a sort of magnifying display thing, and I looked at it and said I liked it, and he peered at it for a long time and said it was flawed. It was just a casual comment, but it struck me at the time he knew what he was talking about."

"*Bingo!*" Moshe exclaimed.

"You know where he is?"

"No, but I know how to find him."

Moshe presented his conclusions and his proposal to his boss.

"That's *very* tenuous, to say the least, Moshe."

"That's true, but tenuous is all we've got. Can I go for it?"

His boss stared at Moshe, his big nose and weak chin, his gawky limbs and his eyes shining with excitement. Moshe was over thirty-years-old, and he'd never grown out of his teens. He was always coming up with a unexpected view or an implausible connection, but his logic was always impeccable, even if a bit far out, and his operational scorecard was outstanding. He had a flair for the unusual, the knack of getting inside the enemy's head.

"Okay, go for it. We've got nothing else. Just don't eff it up, Moshe."

It was impossible to tell where the idea originated, because success has many fathers, but the best claims are probably those of McGill University in Montreal, and it is a verifiable fact that their 9/11 committee held meetings even before the University of New South Wales in Sydney.

The idea was simple and compelling. On September 11th students all around the world would gather in silent vigil and burn models of the Twin Towers.

The motto of the movement was *'c'est possible'*—'it is possible'—which meant it is possible for a few ordinary, powerless people to rise up and strike a blow for peace and freedom against the ruthless and all-powerful United States. The idea caught on like wildfire, spreading across the globe through the ubiquitous Internet, and soon the world coordinating site at McGill was reporting its thousandth participating institution. It was particularly significant when the Chinese government gave approval for a 9/11 parade and demonstration in Tiananmen Square.

There were numerous attempts by established groups to hijack the movement for their own particular purposes—environmentalists, anti-corporates, human rights groups, and so on—but the students managed to stay ahead of the pack, bundling all such isms into its single message 'c'est possible'. The genius of the idea lay in its lack of specificity. It avoided long laundry lists of demands, and it avoided all debate about what to do about any particular subject, and therefore everyone could interpret it in any manner they chose, with the one, easily acceptable proviso that the principal impediment to world harmony, prosperity and justice was the United States.

The movement caused particular anguish in the US. When Berkeley announced it was joining 'c'est possible', the Justice Department filed suit against the students on the grounds, when you cut through the legal mumbo-jumbo, that the entire concept was seditious. The ACLU leapt to the students' defense, arguing that their first amendment rights of free speech permitted them to burn a model of the Twin Towers, just as it permitted them to burn the American flag. The court ruled in favor of the students and the appellate process soon brought the case to the Ninth Circuit Court of Appeals, which not only supported the protest, but went further. It found that 'nothing in the constitution permits the United States to act in defiance of the freely expressed will of the global community'.

Nowhere was the anguish more acute than in New York City, where the local supporters of 'c'est possible' applied to the police department to march through the streets of Lower Manhattan to Ground Zero itself for their ritual burning. The city ducked the issue and refused a permit, citing public safety, but a judge swiftly intervened and issued an order compelling the city to permit the demonstration to go ahead.

Public debate was intense and sometimes violent, and included a barrage of editorials back and forth between the city's two leading newspapers. "As painful as this might be to the families who lost their loved ones," wrote the *World Journal*, "It will serve the public good by reminding us all that the policies of this administration are a grave danger to this country as well as to the global community." The other fired back a brief editorial: "New York to the *WJ*: Go screw yourselves."

Maria swam lazily across the pool and climbed out. Jean Luc offered a wolf whistle at her nakedness and she rewarded him with a few disco dance steps. Then she swayed with an exaggerated undulation across the patio and leaned over to kiss the top of his head. The Mediterranean sun beat down upon them as she arranged herself on a chaise and giggled as he slowly applied sun lotion to her glistening torso. This was one of Jean Luc's 'little hideaways'—a spectacular rambling villa on the shores of Sicily near Aci Costello with magnificent views of Mount Etna behind them and the deep blue sea spread out before them. The tiles around the pool were a genuine Roman tessellated floor which had been perfectly preserved beneath the black volcanic ashes of Mount Etna for almost two thousand years.

"Can we stay here forever, Jean Luc? Can we live here all the time and make babies in the sunshine?"

For once he did not yield immediately, but sat down beside her.

"We need to talk. That's why I brought you down here, where we could relax."

"Oh God, is this going to be something awful?" she asked, in sudden alarm.

"No, no, my angel, it's more a question of making plans, I promise you."

He took her hand gently.

"I've started the process of a separation from my wife, from Louise. I think that can be achieved in a civilized manner, provided her dignity is kept intact. As you know, she keeps to a small circle of friends, and seldom leaves the estate. In the scheme of things, she's being remarkably reasonable: The chateau and the wine business, the stable and the stud farm, the big yacht, the Monaco apartment, the money in the Caymans—that kind of thing. Her most curious request is to meet you."

"Why would she ever want to do that?"

"It's a question of self-esteem. She doesn't want the press to formulate the idea that she's being thrown over for a showgirl or something like that. She wants this all done with decorum. She wants an annulment on the grounds that she prefers not to have children, and doesn't want to stand in my way.

"In fact, believe it or not, she's proposing to attend the wedding. That might sound strange, but it's the way she thinks. Everything must be civilized. I sometimes think that vanity is the most powerful emotion of all. Everything must be done with grace; everyone's face must be saved."

"But...."

"But, of course, I realize I am presuming a great deal."

He knelt beside her and took a leather box from his robe.

"My dearest Maria, would you do me the infinite honor of becoming my wife?"

He opened the box and revealed a diamond ring. The gem, cut in a square, was as wide as her finger.

"Oh, Jean Luc," she whispered.

He slipped the ring onto her finger.

"I have two conditions for saying 'yes', Jean Luc."

"What are they?"

"First, we must have no secrets. None. Whatever happens, we must be completely honest and open and work things out together. Whatever we do, we do as a team."

"Of course, I promise. And the second condition?"

"You must promise to make love to me at least once every day, beginning right now."

"I promise," he smiled.

"I love you, Jean Luc," she said in a broken voice, holding out her arms to him, and her eyes filled with tears; although not tears of joy as he presumed, but tears in memory of her long lost self-respect.

CHAPTER 8

Uncertainty is the mother of failure.

—Jean Luc Lafarge

Jean Luc took his place at the head of the table. He always radiated self-confidence, but this evening Michel thought he seemed particularly pleased with himself. Perhaps it was the remarkable success of the new Sassal campaign, which was generating genuine public enthusiasm as the day of the Le Mans race approached. Perhaps it was due to his remarkable new Spanish mistress, for whom, so rumor had it, he had great plans. There could be no question that there was a youthful spring in his step these days. Or perhaps it was the surge in anti-American sentiment around the world.

"Now, gentlemen, I believe our trap has been set. Let me take a moment to review what we have accomplished during the past few weeks."

He looked around the table and such were his high spirits that he laughed infectiously before continuing, and they all laughed with him.

"First, we have created a chain of events which resulted in Israel's attack on Syria. The world is united in condemnation. The British government was successfully marginalized by the attack in London. The United States is in, shall we say, an acutely difficult position. It cannot condone Israel's action, but, on the other hand, it cannot condemn Israel's act of pre-emption without condemning its own policies.

"The UN and the International Criminal Court, and the International Red Cross and all the rest, are like a cloud of mosquitoes about the White House, and cannot be swatted away. In sum, the Americans are in a lose-lose position, as they say. The Middle East has been further destabilized. That mission has been accomplished, and we plan only one or two further attacks to maintain momentum, which, coincidently, lowers our risk profile."

He paused for a sip of coffee.

"Second, we have created another chain of events, this time bringing into question the safety of American humanitarian relief. In this case also we can let the global community carry the ball, and as a result we will have also effectively isolated the United States from the world's commodity markets. We can safely rely on the WTO and the WHO to regulate US genetic foods out of the markets for at least five years, until European research and development have caught up, and we will declare our own European strains safe after all. We were planning another outbreak of mad cow disease in America, but that may no longer be necessary. Again, mission accomplished!

"As an aside, I'd like to offer you all the opportunity to buy into Genetaire, the biochemical company, on the ground floor. The name combines genetics with 'sanitaire'—'safe'. At the very least your return on capital will repay your investment in our secret endeavor. I have to give Michel the credit for the whole idea. After all, what's wrong with making a little money at America's expense?"

There was a buzz of appreciation around the table.

"Third and last, we have created the 'c'est possible' campaign. I am frankly astonished by the way it has spread. In a way our other initiatives have been, shall we say, technical, weakening the US diplomatically and economically, but 'c'est possible' is nothing less than a universal popular revolt. Once again, mission accomplished!

"All of this is generating a deep sense of uncertainty in the American population, the same sense of national shame that the liberal movements of the '70s created so successfully over civil rights and Vietnam and all the rest. Uncertainty is the mother of failure. America is a house divided, and a house divided will fall."

Jean Luc gestured dramatically to illustrate the fall of the United States, and the table burst into applause. He bowed modestly before continuing.

"Now, gentlemen, we progress to the next stage of our campaign. We have hooked the fish, shall we say, and now we must reel it in. Our good friend Francois Diderot, our own in-house Machiavelli, will step to center stage!"

❦ ❦ ❦

"I assume you're joking, Moshe." Daniel stared at his old friend and shook his head. "No, knowing you, you're dead serious."

They had been to college together and had followed generally similar career paths, although the differences in the profile of security threats to Israel and France had led Moshe into deeper and more dangerous waters.

Daniel had become an international crimes expert, focusing on the drug and arms trades, fighting these shadowy organizations from behind his desk by tracking suspicious movements of large sums of money. He had achieved a spectacular and career-enhancing coup in closing down a large conflict diamond operation run out of Amsterdam by way of Morocco.

He had sunk his teeth deeply into the ex-Soviet arms smuggling business, tracing payments through various European and gulf state banks, but just as he was tying the nexus of arms payments and embezzled UN relief funds transfers, that investigation had been peremptorily cancelled for reasons he had never really understood. Now he was pursuing the flow of heroin from Afghanistan into Europe by way of God-alone-knew-where.

His sedentary occupation and the endless hours at his computer screen were compromising both his waistline and his eyesight. He felt himself turning inexorably into a bureaucrat. The noble cause of fighting secret battles in defense of his country's security seemed increasingly remote.

Moshe, on the other hand, dealt in terrorism, terrorism, and terrorism. Find the bad guy, kill the bad guy.

"Can you give me anything else without compromising your operation?" Daniel asked Moshe.

"You have the composite of his face," responded Moshe. "He was almost certainly disguised, so the other composite shows his facial features without his hair and eyebrows. You'll have to get a match on his face from his bone structure and the shape of his eyes and ears. Judging by the description of his body hair, he may have lighter hair—mid-brown rather than very dark brown to black. We have a good, accurate picture of his body, including the feature that I mentioned."

"His Mount Vesuvius?"

"Exactly. He speaks Arabic and Yiddish, but he swears in French. It's not unusual for people to swear in their mother tongue if they're startled, so conceivably he's Algerian or even French.

"Let's see, what else? He's a competent plumber. He knows something about diamonds, more than the average guy on the street. He's between twenty eight and thirty two. Now for the guesswork: If he's the guy I'm looking for, he has some military training, possibly including urban guerilla warfare."

"I don't know if I like where this is going, Moshe."

"Let's connect the dots. If he's Algerian or French, with military counter-insurgency training, he could be Troupes de Marine or Legion Etrangere. I'll guess the latter, because they teach plumbing, among other things. If he knows diamonds you'd have to think Cote d'Ivore or Sierra Leone, possibly through Executive Outcomes or Sandline, or one of the other mercenary outfits.

"Last but not least, he absolutely does not want to be found. He went to extraordinary lengths not to leave his fingerprints behind, which means that his fingerprints are on file somewhere."

"But you don't have prints?"

"Nope."

"Shit, Moshe, you know the size of his dick to the nearest millimeter, but you don't have his prints—is there something about the Mossad I should know about?"

"Don't be a prick."

"Is this the grenade bomber?"

"I can't tell you that. It's a possibility. But he's definitely a very bad guy."

"Did you ask the Brits? They must want him almost as much as you do."

"Not directly."

"Jesus Christ, Moshe," Daniel said in exasperation. "Is there one *single* intelligence or security service *anywhere* that the Mossad had not penetrated?"

"Well, naturally we haven't penetrated yours."

"Naturally. So...you want me to try to find him?"

"If you can, Daniel. And I bring you some intel in return."

"I'm not sure if I want it."

"Why not?"

"The last time you gave me a suspected terrorist cell operating on French soil we put them under surveillance and then—poof!—they get blown away, and I'll bet you guys did it."

"Those were very bad guys and your guys were pissing around doing squat! The intel was good. You should've grabbed them."

"Listen, Moshe, we're friends, and God knows I've broken a lot of French laws for you over the years. But I'm not going to tolerate Israeli hit squads operating in France. If it happens again, I'll arrest you for murder, and I'll make it stick. I mean it, so help me God!"

"I know you mean it. I'd do the same thing to you in Israel. Do you want the intel or not?"

"I'll take it, but I mean what I say," Daniel said tersely.

"Point taken."

"Point agreed?"

"Point taken."

"Shit, Moshe, you guys are impossible! Who do you think you are? God's chosen people?"

"And my guy? Will you look?"

"Why should I?"

"I'll offer you refugee status and a nice new identity. There's a really great kibbutz I know that grows olives and watermelons. You could wear a yarmulke and learn some songs from 'Fiddler on the Roof' and you'd fit right in."

"Fuck off!"

Robert flew back to France. At long last he would be able to relax. Jean Luc was a generous boss and he was fairly certain he'd be sent somewhere to unwind with a high quality call girl to keep him company, all expenses paid. He smiled in anticipation. Women were always so surprised the first time, with the same silly expression on their faces and the same long drawn out exclamation of '*Oh...my...God!*' from the soft and stupid, like Belle in Jerusalem; to the bitchy and superior, like that doctor in Africa; to the frankly weird, like the student in Montreal.

Safely back in Paris he placed a phone call to an answering machine and waited for a return call. In the meantime, he went to the gym—travel had wrecked his regular workout schedule and he had a lot of catching up to do—ate alone in his favorite local bistro, and planned to spend the rest of the day catching up on sleep. Flying across the Atlantic from west to east was always more difficult than the other way around, for some unknown reason. His phone rang before he had finished his main course, and he listened for some time before hanging up. Shit! Now, instead of getting a good night's sleep he had to go out and steal a car.

At least he did not have to keep remembering his name, or trying not to respond if someone mentioned the name Paul. He drank a silent toast to all his aliases—Kamal, Robert, Jerome, Jules, oh, and Henri and Charles, he was already forgetting.

"Guys," he said to himself, "You did good work. Meet Paul Rennard: super hero and all-around tough guy!" He tossed back his drink and called for another.

There are two kinds of police forces in France, as there are in many countries. There are the guys who direct traffic and hand out speeding tickets and investigate crimes and arrest burglars. They are hemmed in by dozens of civil liberties constraints, oversight boards, judicial reviews, transparency rules, and regulations covering every aspect of their work. They are hated or beloved depending on whether an individual citizen has or does not have felonious or criminal intentions.

But then there is also the notion of 'public order'. The idea that a society, however free and open, still needs a group of enforcers when things get out of hand, and the state, however benign, must also be coercive to protect the public welfare; a group for whom the rights of the many sometimes outweigh the rights of the individual. In France this second notion is embodied in the Gendarmerie Nationale, a national civilian police force—within the Ministry of Defense.

Daniel ran Moshe's request as a missing person case, checking the extensive sources of information available to him as a senior member of the GN.

The facts provided by Moshe produced a list of one hundred and nine possible candidates, which Daniel reduced to a possible twelve based on the composite likeness of Vesuvius. All had served in various branches of French Special Forces, all had received at least some formal vocational training in the building trades, and all were known or suspected mercenaries. Eight were French and four had served as foreigners in the Legion Etrangere. A little further checking revealed that two were in jail serving long-term sentences and two others were dead, leaving eight live suspects. It was as far as he could go. If Moshe had a fingerprint, Daniel would be able to pinpoint Vesuvius, but Moshe did not.

* * *

Michel flew into Beijing. It was not at all his kind of city. The endless miles of featureless slab-like buildings created an oppressive atmosphere, and the frenetic scuttling of Beijing's people seem to emphasize their antlike status within the People's Republic, rather than their prodigious energy and industry. Michel, and the man he had come to meet, sat side-by-side in ugly armchairs with a side table bearing a vase of dusty artificial flowers between them. Michel had often been in China and wondered if there was a government regulation dictating that all meetings must be held in the same depressing ambience.

The man named a price for the service Michel wished to buy. It was ludicrously high.

"That's far too steep, I'm afraid. We simply don't want to make that kind of a cash investment."

"Then perhaps we can consider part cash, part goods—payment in kind."

They dickered for two days. Michel's contact clearly had severely limited authority and had to check with his superiors frequently. Michel, on the other hand, had Jean Luc's agreement to use his own judgment within the overall parameters of the deal. In the end there was only ten million dollars between the price the man wanted and the value of the goods and cash Michel was prepared to pay.

"Very well," said Michel finally. "I'll agree to the extra ten million provided it's part of the cash on delivery. I'm already giving you fifty million in cash and fifty million in industrial equipment up front."

The man from North Korea agreed—reluctantly—but he agreed. Michel flew to Hong Kong and decided to stay a day or two to celebrate his success: another piece of the puzzle was fitting into place.

* * *

Television is a remarkable medium. Two people sit in a cheap little stage set, alone in a cavernous room, observed only by the unemotional lenses of bulky cameras and a few ill-kempt technicians. The room is cold except under the ruthless lights which seem to create a separate and antiseptic environment on the stage. The technicians observe the participants as if they are specimens under a microscope, making minute adjustments to their equipment. The director and his assistants sit in the control room selecting images of the participants from a bank of choices before them. The images are curiously detached from the real people on the stage.

A huge digital clock in the control room is the god before whom they worship, for the seemingly natural flow of conversation must fit within a schedule timed to the exact second. The director speaks softly and the interviewer hears his voice in a tiny earphone: "Five minutes to commercials. Speed him up a little if you can." All is sterile.

And yet, at the other end of the heavy cables and the satellite uplinks and downlinks and coaxial connections and all the rest of the bewildering technology, the barren scene in the studio is transmuted into an intimate conversation taking place in the audience's very living room, as if the viewer were also sitting at the coffee table with a glass of water before him, also in an ugly leather chair with stainless steel arms, glancing back and forth between the interviewer and the interviewee.

"History is full of examples of freedom fighters facing enormous odds and yet changing the course of nations," said Professor Diderot with his customary gravity. "Their names are evocative of the unconquerable human spirit and the struggle for human dignity and freedom: Mahatma Gandhi, Yasir Arafat, Nelson Mandela, Osama Bin Laden, Martin Luther King. I think that the new 'c'est possible' campaign is a recognition, indeed a celebration, of their spirit."

The interviewer spoon-fed him his next line.

"Does that mean that opposition to the United States has the same moral authority as, for example, opposition to apartheid?"

"Let us not be too harsh on our American friends," responded the professor, obliquely accepting the comparison without having to say so. "Let us not fall into the trap of so-called 'moral clarity'."

He smiled sadly. "I prefer to think of the old story of the prodigal son, who erred from the ways of righteousness, but was welcomed back into the fold when he saw the error of his ways. I think—I hope—we have a similar situation now."

"Surely you do not support American unilateralism, and all that it implies, and the pain and suffering it causes?"

"No, but I would urge us all not to be too judgmental. All of us, as individuals, have made mistakes. Nations have made mistakes. We must be fair."

All over France viewers felt themselves nodding, accepting the nobility of spirit he offered.

"We must draw a distinction between people and their governments. It's not easy to live under a corrupt regime. After all, it's not so long ago that our good German friends elected Hitler to office, and perhaps America is going through a similar phase. As I said, let us not be too judgmental."

The interviewer had an acute ear for nuance. It was clever to tie in Hitler, as if the American electorate had made a similarly innocent, but disastrous mistake in electing their President, but it was also potentially highly controversial. It was best to give the professor the widest possible range for his next comments.

"It took a world war to remove Hitler."

"That, I think, is too narrow a definition of history. It took a world *movement*, a universal global sense of *revulsion*, as perhaps we are seeing now. Unfortunately we are all being forced to think in crude military terms these days. World War II was a struggle of *ideas* far more than it was a struggle of *armies*.

"My point is simply that the actions of governments do not necessarily reflect the wills and aspirations of peoples and turn them into what we could call 'good guys' or 'bad guys'. Ordinary Americans are just like you and me—even those in Texas," he added with a smile.

"You sound hopeful, Professor," said the interviewer.

"I am. Fundamentally I'm an optimist. We all get impatient, but it takes a long time for outmoded ideas to die away. But I like to think we are finally seeing the death-throws of the old idea of national sovereignty, the last convulsions, if you will, before we can all move forward together."

The interviewer prepared to begin his wrap-up, but Diderot held up his hand imperiously.

"Let me be clear. We cannot find a solution by simply blaming everything on America. For example, America is by far the world's biggest polluter, but it is not the world's *only* polluter. As another example, a B-52 in pursuit of a preemptive national policy is an instrument of terror, but a B-52 dispatched by the combined will of the UN Security Council can be an instrument for good, as it was in Serbia.

"Rather than simply trashing all things American, we should be reaching out with a hand of friendship, a willingness to forgive, offering them a chance to redeem themselves, a way back into the international community. That's our policy toward Libya, and it's working. That same policy applies equally well to North Korea, the United States, Iran, and any other nation which endangers its neighbors and the world community."

"Including Israel?"

"Ah," said the professor with a rueful smile, as if the interviewer was trying to catch him out. "For that answer you'll have to invite me back again."

This interview received wide acclaim, and was the first airing of what was instantly dubbed the 'Diderot Doctrine'.

PART II

CRACK

CHAPTER 9

Of course America loves Europe—that's why they screw us so often.

—Jean Luc Lafarge

"Shit," said the President of the United States. Most administrations start off with a bang and then gradually get bogged down. The first couple of years had gone pretty well, but then the steady acidic drip, drip, drip of partisan politics, the remorseless hostility of the media, and the sheer exhaustion of the White House staff, had shifted the balance. Now it looked like this could be another one-term presidency.

"Sir, you *must* sit down with the Europeans. Sixty percent of likely voters think our foreign policy is headed in the wrong direction. Almost *seventy percent* think you don't care enough about world opinion."

The President came from a gritty northeast rust belt town, and his appeal to the electorate was his 'honest Joe' plain speaking and his belief that policies should be based on common sense. He had run against the Washington intelligentsia, and had struck a chord with the electorate. He came into office with a three-plank platform: radical surgery to the tax code, which he described as 'eighty thousand pages of gobbledygook that even the accountants don't understand'; support for small business—'getting America out of the hands of Wall Street and into the hands of Main Street'; and a moderate foreign policy—'we can't solve every problem in the world and we shouldn't try to'.

There had been something appealing about his blunt slaps at special interest groups, his habit of wearing a quaintly formal vested suit with construction boots—'this country was built by guys wearing boots, not fancy lawyers and politicians wearing shiny black loafers', and his cheerfully arbitrary judgments: 'environmentalists can't see the forest for the trees'.

His signature issue had been successfully brokering the ANWAR/CAFÉ deal through the Congress, in which he had traded steeply increased fuel economy standards for automobiles, which the environmentalists loved and businesses interests hated, for oil drilling access in the northern wilds of Alaska, which the environmentalists hated and big business loved. As he said, 'If it upsets everybody, it *has* to be a good idea'.

It had all worked very well for two years, but then the press of world events had opened up the door for adjectives like 'isolationist', 'disengaged', 'uncaring', 'unilateral' and 'dangerously simplistic'; and a couple of domestic miscues had diverted attention away from the healthy economic recovery.

During his third year in office, the President had shifted strategies, cutting deals with his opponents in Congress to try to take the sting out of the raging partisanship, but that had led to a burst in pork-barrel spending and messy compromises, and the growing sense that 'honest Joe' had lost his way and turned into just another slippery Washington politician.

"Sir, I know you always say you won't be driven by opinion polls, but the voters really *do* believe we're encouraging Israeli aggression. They really *do* believe we should put troops into the West Bank and force the Israelis back to the '67 Green Line. Christ, almost a *third* of the country would support a *war* against Israel. This country invaded Afghanistan and Iraq to crush dictatorships with gross human rights violations and secret weapons programs. They just don't see how we can let the Israelis get away with the same stuff."

The White House Chief of Staff was frustrated and didn't pull his punches.

"And, Mr. President, maybe most people don't care deep down if some starving Africans die, but they care if they died because we poisoned them, and they care very much if our own food supply is dangerous. Organic food is the fastest growing industry in this country. People are scared, Mr. President, and they don't care that there's no scientific basis.

"In fact, they think you're hiding something. Over half the country responded 'yes' to the question 'do you think the government is being dishonest about food safety?'"

The President's likely opponent had proposed a massive subsidy for organic food production, paid for by a federal sales tax on most other foodstuffs, and the idea was proving extremely popular.

"And now there's this 'c'est possible' campaign. In their gut, most people hate it, and they expect you to stop it, and you haven't. Junior judges have stopped you in your tracks. It makes you look weak."

The President did not respond. He knew his chief of staff was right, and he knew his grip on his office was slipping.

"Sir, you can't change everything, so you must change what you can. I urge you, sir, sit down with the Secretary General and the Europeans at the G8 summit. Make a deal. One deal if they agree to back off and put their pressure on their media to take an easier line. More than one deal shows too much weakness. I don't care what you choose: just pick one thing to change the conversation. It could be Kyoto or the Anti Ballistic Missile Treaty, the ABM. It could be a NATO takeover of the West Bank and Gaza, by force if necessary.

"In return, get commitments from them to propose a UN resolution condemning this 'c'est possible' garbage. That will take the wind out of the students. If they go ahead, they'll be protesting against the UN. I don't know, Mr. President, but we can't simply keep eating crap forever."

He was pacing the office in his agitation.

"Maybe the key is the ABM treaty. Maybe North Korea will give up the nukes if we give up on the ABM and give them lots of money. That will please China because it makes Taiwan vulnerable. Crap on Russia over Chechnya and put it back on the front pages. Then, a couple of months before the election, we'll use the private dirt we've got on your opponent and you'll win next November—not by a lot, but you'll win."

"I agree completely," said the Secretary of State. "That will shut them all up internationally and give you a chance to deal with your domestic issues. I get to sit in the UN and get the crap beaten out of me for a couple of days, so what's new?"

"We can't reverse fundamental policies with our oldest allies just…" began the National Security Advisor, but she was cut off.

"This is a political issue, not a security issue," said the Secretary of State. "If you want to be sitting here after the elections, we're going to have to make some adjustments."

"I agree," said the Chief of Staff. "I don't give a rat's ass about the West Bank, or whatever you pick, but I care a great deal about California's fifty-four votes in the electoral college. We *must* keep California."

The President liked his closest advisors to give him frank advice and criticism, with no holds barred. He welcomed disagreements: it helped him to think things through. The beauty of this bunch was that, once he made a decision, they all locked step and supported him, even if they'd lost the argument. The National Security Advisor was already imagining a Sunday morning talk show. "No, we haven't changed our policy toward Taiwan at all, Kevin, we've simply clarified it."

"What's the strategic impact of reversing course on missile defense and rejoining the ABM treaty?" the President asked the Secretary of Defense.

"Zero," he replied. "We cancel the project in public and keep right on going under a covert status. In fact, we'll be able to juggle the funding and speed it up if nobody knows about it."

"Any input on all this anti-Americanism from the intelligence community?"

"There's input from the CIA..." began the National Security Advisor.

"*Puh-leeeze*," interrupted the Chief of Staff. "The same guys that said Iraq was littered with WMDs?"

It seemed a consensus was forming, with the NSA in a minority of one. It wasn't so much that the President wanted another four years in office—he was coming to think of the oval office as a prison cell—it was just that he could not tolerate the thought of losing the election, particularly to *that* slime ball. He looked at the Vice President and raised his eyebrows.

"I have a different view, Mr. President." He glanced around his colleagues. "This President was elected because he struck a chord with the American people. We're in trouble because we've compromised. They used to say, 'Let Reagan be Reagan' and it worked. I say, let's all get out of the way and let the President follow his own instincts."

"The world community..." began the Secretary of State.

"Fuck the world community," the Vice President interrupted. "The last time I looked, the world community doesn't vote in the elections. Jesus Christ, do you want this President to go down in history as another Jimmy Carter?"

They all looked at the President. He pushed back his chair and put his feet on the desk, and they all stared at his construction boots.

"We'll do it my way," he said.

The oval office could be a prison cell or the most powerful place in the world: it just depended on your perspective.

"Lafarge has some sort of a secret group," Maria said to Hans. Their voices were lost in the babble of conversation all around them. She and the blond diplomat stood in the center of the throng, facing each other but slightly to one side, so that each could scan the crowd behind the other's back. Maria was making gestures with her hands, as if she were telling a joke involving drinking from shot glasses.

"There's his industrialist friend Michel Leclerc, Pierre Truffaud, General Giamente, Francois Diderot, the intellectual, and a couple of others."

She pretended to toss back a drink.

"They meet regularly at his townhouse. Lafarge says it's a low profile private charitable organization, and he mentioned a couple of beneficiaries you can check out—one has something to do with AIDS relief in Africa, I think. However, it struck me that the firepower he's assembled is completely disproportionate to the objective. At first I thought it was illegal arms trafficking, as the intel suggested, but the inclusion of Diderot makes it political. I think it's dirty."

She gestured as if tossing back another drink and Hans laughed easily.

"That's pretty thin. Why do you think it's significant?"

"Because it's the only thing he hasn't told me about, or, at least, he's resisted telling me about."

"Jesus, Maria, we pissed around for four weeks waiting for him to notice you, and now that you're on the inside, you've still got squat."

He laughed again, and said, "Well, okay, I'll see what Langley has to suggest, but they're getting pretty antsy."

"I don't want Langley told, at least not yet. It may be nothing and I'd look like an idiot. I'm hoping you can run this through Dutch channels."

"It seems to me that you've got him eating out of your hand. Can't you get more out of him?"

"I'm trying to, but I can't push too hard."

She began to gesture again, as if starting another joke.

"I've started playing my anti-American card and hoping for a reaction. In hindsight, we chose the wrong target. If anything is going on, Lafarge is undoubtedly the leader, but Michel Leclerc is less discrete. I could probably have gotten far more out of him. He's made some vague hints, but he definitely wants the usual quid pro quo."

"Could you switch from Lafarge to him?" he asked, laughing again.

"No, not without spoiling everything. Jean Luc is being extremely possessive. He even wants to marry me, for God's sake! If I have an affair with Leclerc it would kill my relationship with Lafarge."

"What about evidence? What about Lafarge's safe?"

"This is not a James Bond movie, and I don't have X-ray eyes. I haven't even been able to locate it yet. There's one in the bedroom for jewelry and things, and he's even given me the combination. I think it was some sort of trust test, to tell you the truth. But there are no secret papers in it; just jewelry and stuff. I assume he has another safe in his study."

"Well, you can't hang around without results forever. Maybe you should go ahead and seduce Leclerc anyway. Perhaps the intel on Lafarge was wrong. Who knows?"

A waiter approached with a tray of champagne glasses. He handed one to Maria, together with her cell phone discreetly wrapped in a napkin. The waiter nodded subserviently and moved on.

"So he's tapped your phone as we thought he might," Hans said. "He's definitely up to no good. Anyway, I have to tell you Langley has identified a German they're interested in. If you don't get anything definitive out of Lafarge or Leclerc in the next couple of weeks, we'll have to give up on him and you can try this German woman. In the meantime, we'll check out this charity group."

He made a gesture signifying copulation.

"So, the Irish nun says to the priest, 'and all this time I thought there *were* no snakes in Ireland!'"

"Hans, that's awful," Maria groaned. "That's not even funny."

"What isn't funny?" Lafarge asked from behind her.

"It's a well-known fact that jokes involving three nuns are never funny," she said, turning and smiling at him warmly. "Do you remember my friend Hans?"

"Of course," said Jean Luc, shaking hands amiably, as if delighted to renew the acquaintance. "I was just speaking to the Dutch trade minister."

Maria had been studying Jean Luc for weeks by now, and was beginning to read the signs. She knew he was annoyed to find her with Hans although his face exhibited nothing but bland geniality. His poker face was legendary in business circles. Only the slight, almost undetectable flexing of his fingers betrayed his emotions.

Others drifted into the conversation. It seemed there were trade delegations in Paris from all over Europe, all pleased to meet one of Europe's premier business leaders, all accepting his flattery at face value, all wondering what it must be like to be a real, genuine, billionaire.

Maria and Jean Luc were officially an unofficial couple. Everyone knew they were together, but everyone pretended they weren't. Such was his influence that Jean Luc was even able to suppress any reference to them in the scandal sheets and buyers of paparazzi services. There were ugly rumors about a photojournalist who had taken some compromising pictures of Jean Luc on the Riviera some years ago. No one was prepared to take that risk again.

"Do you think the Americans will make a deal on agricultural subsidies, Monsieur Lafarge?" someone was asking.

"Oh, I'm sure they will, in spite of all the issues."

"Why, because they love us?" the delegate asked sarcastically.

"Of course America loves Europe—that's why they screw us so often."

❧ ❧ ❧

Jean Luc stared at the newspaper incredulously. He put it down on the breakfast table and picked it up again, as if he could not believe what he was reading.

"*Oh my God!* I can't believe it! I'm so sorry, my dear, but your friend Hans was killed last night!"

Maria jumped as if she had been scalded.

"*What?*"

"I'm so sorry, my dear," he repeated, and read out loud the article as she listened as if she were carved out of ice. 'Dutch embassy official Hans Blucher was struck and killed instantly by a hit-and-run driver on the Quai D'Orsay last night at eleven. Witnesses said Blucher was crossing the street when a speeding black sedan hit him and crushed him beneath its wheels. Blucher was returning to his car after a diplomatic reception and witnesses described him as sober. The black sedan continued at high speed and has not been located. The police have asked the public for help in identifying the vehicle and driver. "This is a tragedy," said the Dutch ambassador, who was a witness.' The rest seems to be about Hans...let's see, the police basically have no clues...."

He stood and came around to Maria's side of the breakfast table, enfolding her in his arms.

"What a shock for you, my poor darling. It must have been right after the reception when we talked to him. My God, and he only had minutes to live!"

Jean Luc fussed over Maria, insisting she lie down for a while, telephoning his doctor to come *immediately* to ensure that the shock had not been too great for her, calling a senior police official to find out if there was any unpublished information, and insisting that he would cancel his planned business trip to be with her.

"I'm all right, Jean Luc," she kept saying, and finally convinced him that it was a bit of a shock, but Hans had not been that close. She would not hear of him delaying his trip.

He left reluctantly.

"I'll be back tonight, my dear, and we'll drive down to Le Mans tomorrow. A change will do you good. Call me at any time. Don't worry about interrupting a meeting."

He hovered as he tried to think of something to cheer her up. "Try to be brave, my angel. Death is harder on the living than the dead. I'm sure he didn't suffer."

"I think we should carry the offensive to them, sir," the NSA told the President at her daily meeting with him in the Oval Office. "I think we could start by taking on that slimy bastard Professor Diderot."

"Is Henry Kissinger available? Can we afford his fees?"

"Very droll, Mr. President. I'd like to go to Europe and take him on myself."

"I'd like to take him on *my*self...."

"The UN Secretary General has put Diderot on one of his 'global architecture for peace' committees."

"Really?"

He raised his eyes to the ceiling at the endless obstructionism which emanated from the UN Headquarters.

"I'll call the Secretary of State to make sure we don't sit on the committee and we won't fund it."

"He already did, sir. He's also come up with a complete nonentity as ambassador to France and he's scaling back the size of the embassy."

"Good. I'll say one thing for the Secretary," grunted the President approvingly, "He may not agree with a decision, but by God he supports it in public."

"Diderot is floating a plan for regional votes in the Security Council, sir, basically that each continent has input, so that major decisions are more balanced and more democratic. It sounds good, but of course the real objective is to give Mexico and Canada and even Cuba a veto over our foreign policy."

"Fuck'em all."

The NSA was fiercely loyal to her boss, and believed deeply in his political abilities: like Houdini, he could wiggle his way out of almost any box, but the constant hostility pouring in upon them from every corner of the globe was grinding him down. Perhaps he was too fundamentally decent to be the leader of the free world.

"Sir, with respect, we can't just go isolationist, not in a world economy, and we won't beat the Europeans just by saying 'no'. Disengagement is not an option. We're in the Middle East for keeps: energy, Israel, and the consequences of Iraq and terrorism. We're in Asia because our economy is fundamentally linked to theirs. We're in the Americas because this is where we live. We're in NAFTA and NATO and WTO and all the rest because we need them."

He changed the subject.

"Did we get autopsies on those poor wretched Africans who died from food poisoning?"

"No, all the victims were cremated as a health precaution."

"What?"

"In case scavengers ate their bodies and the genetically modified stuff somehow got into the local ecology. So there's no scientific data, pro or con. It's against their culture, but some local aid doctor advised them to do it."

"And we're left to prove a negative. *Shit.*"

The President struggled to his feet. One day, everyone secretly agreed, his habit of sprawling with his boots on the desk would lead to disaster. His chair would slip backward and he would land on the floor in an undignified heap—but not today.

"Okay, let's put aside all the crap. Let me ask you a stupid question. What's our foreign policy?"

"What's yours, sir? As the Vice President said, 'We're letting you be you.'"

"I actually get to steer the ship of state? Wow!"

The President began to pace. One of his habits was to reduce policy to its most simple, fourth grade elements. He called this process his 'checking his moral compass' and it was the root of the two fundamentally opposed views of his presidency, His opponents argued that he was simply too dumb to be President, and his supporters argued that only clear and simple core principles could generate a consistent policy in the vast complexities of domestic and foreign affairs.

"Okay, we always try diplomacy first, but we don't let people lie to us forever, and we won't be suckered twice. 'Fool me once, shame on you, fool me twice, shame on me.'"

"Agreed. Like the kid's game 'truth or consequences.'"

"'Truth or consequences'? I like that. I can use that in a speech. Okay, there is and never will be forgiveness for terrorists."

"Good."

"There may be lots of shades of gray, but when push comes to shove, we will always choose a democracy over a dictatorship, and a free market over a closed one."

"What about Kyoto? The International Criminal Court? The Anti Ballistic Missile Treaty? Land mines?"

"We sign and work within good treaties, but we don't and won't sign bad treaties."

"Sir, that's good, but with respect it's not enough. It sounds defensive. And, in any case, how can we continue to support Israel if it attacks Syria without provocation? How can we justify sending dangerous foods to Africa instead of the safe foods provided by the UN? How can we ignore the universal support for 'c'est possible'?

"That's what Diderot and all the rest are saying. That's what your probable opponent is saying, and the polls say he's got real traction. We may think we have good intentions, but we produce bad results. Let's 'fess up and admit we've been wrong all along."

"We haven't been wrong!"

"Tell that to the mothers of the kids we killed in Africa!"

"They can't prove we did."

"We can't prove we didn't, and in this climate that's all that matters."

"*Shit!*"

"Exactly, sir. We're balls deep in shit without an exit sign."

CHAPTER 10

Love is more easily given than trust.

—Jean Luc Lafarge

Maria went to the visitors entrance of the US Embassy, eased her way through the waiting lines of visa applicants, passed through a metal detector, submitted to a search by polite Marine guards, and eventually reached a reception desk marked General Enquiries.

Her route to the embassy had been tortuous. First she had left the house and wandered aimlessly. Then she had taken a metro and done some window shopping. Jean Luc's driver had followed her all the way. Then she had gone down into the metro again, traveled a couple of stops, and jumped out of the train at the last moment. She was fairly sure she'd lost the driver, but it was possible that Jean Luc had a second tail on her. She had lingered in the long shopping arcade at the Ritz, but she couldn't detect anyone loitering behind her. Finally she had taken her chances and gone to the embassy: she had no choice.

"Yes, m'selle?"

"I need to speak to someone in security, please."

"Your passport, please."

Maria handed over her passport for the third time. The receptionist thumbed through it without apparent reaction.

"What is it about?"

"I'm afraid I can't tell you."

"If you write out your inquiry it will get to the right person," said the receptionist politely, but firmly. "There are forms over there. Alternatively, you can e-mail us if you prefer."

"No, thank you. I have to speak with someone in person; it's a matter of some urgency."

The receptionist had to decide whether Maria really had genuine business with the embassy, or she was simply some screwball off the street, as so many are. His job was like that of a triage nurse, assessing the urgency of medical emergencies at a hospital. Maria passed whatever tests his experience had taught him.

"Very well, please take a seat over there. I'll keep your passport for just a moment, if I may, and return it when you leave."

Maria waited forty-five minutes. If Jean Luc was having her followed it would be difficult to explain what she was doing, but she had no alternative. Her only local contact with the CIA was Hans, but now that he was dead, she had only one other way of getting in touch with the Agency: a computer ID and password, but they only worked on a secure US government network. If she couldn't get through here, if the bureaucrats judged she was a nutcase or a proto-terrorist, and she was thrown out, she'd literally have to go to Langley, Virginia, and present herself to the guards at the gate.

She had no idea who Hans reported to, and she knew no one else in the Agency in Europe. Perhaps she was too junior, or perhaps it was 'need to know'. If she was somehow captured and interrogated she would have no secrets to betray. Perhaps she should sit tight and wait for someone to contact her, but that might take forever, and she sensed that whatever Jean Luc might be doing, it was coming to a head.

"Miss Menendez?" A tall Marine captain stood before her like a Greek god, rescuing her from her stream of thought.

"Yes," she said, standing up.

"I'm Captain Sandler. How can I help you?"

"Can we speak in private please, Captain?"

He looked doubtful, and then led her to a quiet corner of the cavernous room.

"This is the best I can do, I'm afraid." He clearly had no intention of taking her into the interior of the embassy.

"I need to speak to an intelligence officer."

He did not look surprised, and she guessed he guessed she was a screwball after all.

"I'm afraid that isn't possible," he said politely. "What can we do for you? If you tell me I'll relay the message."

"Just ask an intelligence officer to search on the secure system for the word 'rosebud': r-o-s-e-b-u-d. Then he'll see me."

"Rosebud? Like the movie? What was it, Citizen Kane?"

He smiled. A little spark crossed the space between them, and she thought, 'Wow, in other circumstances…', but she said, "Listen, I don't make these stupid words up. Please ask someone to do it right away."

"Do you have any other ID, Miss Menendez?"

"Just a driver's license, but it won't tell you any more than my passport."

She handed it over.

"You are a Spanish citizen?"

"That's what it says, doesn't it? Please speak to an IO with authorization for the secure system, will you?"

He reached a decision. "Please wait."

He was gone less than five minutes, and his manner was considerably warmer when he returned.

"Please come with me, Miss Menendez."

He led her past additional security barriers and she was searched more thoroughly by a female Marine before being escorted through a maze of corridors to a tiny drab office.

"Good morning," said the non-descript man behind the desk. "What is 'rosebud'?"

"It's just an ID, sir. Please put in the password 'shoemaker9', just like it sounds, all one word, lowercase. Then you'll be in a messaging system. Tell them anything you want."

He sat down at his keyboard and was busy for some time. Maria stood before the desk, unable to see the dialog on the screen, and the attractive Captain Sandler stood behind her, discretely guarding the door.

"They say 'please wait'," the intelligence officer reported eventually.

Ten minutes passed and the electronic dialog started again.

"He wants to talk to you," said the officer, standing up and making way for her. She sat down at his desk and saw the last few lines of dialog on the computer screen.

Shoemaker says:	Paris embassy
Rosebud says:	just a minute
Rosebud says:	who is with you?

Shoemaker says:	A Spanish national name Mendendez, Maria
Rosebud says:	repeat name
Shoemaker says:	Sorry, Menendez
Rosebud says:	describe her.
Shoemaker says:	Brunette, 120 pounds, 5 foot 6, late twenties, brown eyes, suntan complexion
Rosebud says:	gorgeous looking?
Shoemaker says:	Very
Rosebud says:	put her on the system

She smiled and said "Thank you" to the intelligence officer. Then she typed:

Shoemaker says:	Who is this?

The screen came back and the dialog began:

Rosebud says:	frank, what am i?
Shoemaker says:	TDH
Rosebud says:	really?!?
Shoemaker says:	VTDH
Rosebud says:	who is cindy?
Shoemaker says:	Sgt Wilson's little girl. Who is Gina?
Rosebud says:	the waitress in the diner what happened to hans?
Shoemaker says:	Don't know, maybe my mark
Rosebud says:	cover blown?
Shoemaker says:	Don't know could be jealousy or genuine accident Need everything on Diderot, Francois, professor, Leclerc, Michel, industrialist, ref illegal arms transshipments

There was a short pause.

Rosebud says:	ok, in the works do you need out???
Shoemaker says:	No, need local contact, legwork

Rosebud says: ok, wait

This time the pause lasted five minutes.

Rosebud says: ok? anything else?

Shoemaker says: Nope Seeya

Rosebud says: seeya

The door of the office opened to reveal a man like a granite boulder.

"Miss Menendez? My name is Jake Stone." He reached out and briefly wrapped her hand in his vast paw. "I just got off the phone with your boss. It's okay, Captain, you can stay. How much time do you have, Miss Menendez?"

"I've been here too long already. My mark is traveling, but I may be followed."

At that moment her cell phone rang. She smiled an apology and checked the number before answering it.

"Jean Luc?.... No, I'm fine, truly.... I went out for a walk.... No, on the metro.... I'm near the Place Vendome, I thought I'd have some coffee at the Ritz.... No, truly, please don't worry, I'm pretty much over it.... Me too. I'll see you tonight."

She hung up. "I'd better get to the Ritz PDQ. It's a good thing I can disable GPS on this phone."

"Okay," said Stone. "Then I'll be brief. Your boss is sending someone else to take over, but in the meantime I'll assign these two gentlemen to assist you. It's the best we can do immediately."

"I appreciate that, but they'll need a credible cover and I'll need face-to-face contact in public. I need a personal bug with this model of dictation machine." She held it up and the gorgeous captain wrote down the model number. "I'm going down to Le Mans tomorrow for the car race. Do either of you know anything about racing?"

"I drive a little, and I know something about Le Mans," said the handsome Captain Sandler. "I have a friend on one of the teams."

"Good," said Stone. "We'll get you down there and fit you in somehow. I assume you have no objection to temporary Marine Corps involvement, Major?" He smiled and continued. "Now, let's get you out of here the discreet way, and into the Ritz."

When she had left, Sandler asked Stone, "What was the 'Major' reference, sir?"

Stone chuckled. "I understand she holds the rank of Major in the USMC. Just remember to salute and stand to attention when you speak to her, Captain—she outranks you!"

Moshe could not possibly persuade his boss to give him the resources and money necessary to track down all of Daniel's possible suspects. Hell, they weren't even suspects, to tell the truth; just a collection of profiles which might or might not match his guesses about Kamal's background.

"Why did we find no fingerprints in the van that blew up in Safad?" Moshe asked.

The Mossad scientist stared at Moshe as if he were a rebellious teenager demanding 'why can't I stay out after eleven?' in one of those endlessly repetitive arguments in which the parent is ultimately reduced to 'because I say so' or simply 'because'.

"Because fingerprints are deposits of human grease and oils excreted from the skin, which coagulate on the surface with dust and other microscopic material to form a lasting residue. An explosion creates heat, which melts the grease."

"What was the Safad explosion site like?"

"It was a charnel house," replied the scientist. "The explosives guys estimate there were at least two cases of grenades, and detonators as well. They did a chemical analysis of the residue. It's all in the report. Unfortunately, it did not occur to us to look for ricin until it was too late."

He had lost his brother-in-law in that disaster; his sister was having terrible nightmares and the kids were afraid to eat.

"And of course there was gasoline in the tank and we found the remains of a couple of spare four gallon tanks as well. Most of the walls were knocked down. They were pretty flimsy, just cinder blocks with no structural ability to withstand a lateral blast. The roof disintegrated. One end of the garage was still standing. It was much older and built of stone. There was debris all over the place."

"Can I see it?" Moshe asked.

"It's still cordoned off because of the ricin scare."

"What sorts of debris?"

"Bits of the van, bits of copper piping, a few tools scattered around, stuff like that."

The scientist was becoming impatient. Moshe was living up to his reputation of stubbornly refusing to accept the obvious.

"What happened to the tools?"

The scientist sighed. "We collected everything and bagged it after we realized that ricin was involved. It was part of the routine environmental survey for toxic substances."

"Did you dust the tools for fingerprints?"

"I don't think so. We didn't have a reason to. As I explained, fingerprints don't survive heat. Really, Moshe...."

"Could we check them now?"

"I suppose so, but it's a waste of time. You won't get anything."

But Moshe did.

A heavy wrench had been blown out of the back of the van and impaled itself in one of the remaining walls like an arrow. The initial shockwave of the explosion consisted of normal air forced outward from the point of ignition by the expanding gasses of the explosive materials. The wrench was lying on top of the makeshift workbench and was accelerated from rest to a speed of twelve hundred miles per hour in two linear feet. It passed through the thin metal of the rear door panels before these had time to disintegrate, traveled horizontally handle-first across the garage and struck a seam of soft mortar between two large stones in the rear wall, in which it was decelerated to rest in twelve inches.

The large wrench jaws remained exposed to the following blast of heated gasses, which contained significant levels of finely powdered ricin, but the massive old stones remained in place and sufficiently cool that the wooden surface of the handle, although severely abraded by being forced through the grit-like mortar, did not experience a significant rise in temperature.

The wrench was subsequently jerked out of the wall by the salvage crew and tossed into a plastic bag, more as a curious example of the unpredictable ballistic events which occur during an explosion than as a potential piece of forensic evidence.

And there, in a shallow indentation on the greasy old handle, like a coy girl waiting to be discovered, was one big beautifully preserved thumbprint.

The town of Le Mans lies in the bucolic heartlands of France, and is home to the world's oldest and most famous automobile race, *Les 24 Heures du Mans*—The 24 hours of Le Mans. Eighty sports cars race continuously for a day—from noon on Saturday to noon on Sunday—on a thirteen kilometer track. Each car has a team of three drivers. The race tests the endurance of both the cars and the drivers, and is a fascinating balance between speed and reliability. There is no point in having the fastest car if it breaks down.

Another enduring attraction of the race is that the cars are not all the same. There are ultra-engineered cars entered directly by the manufacturers, and there are also many cars entered by private teams. Thus the race is many races, and has many winners: the fastest privately entered Porsche, the fastest production car, and so on. Indeed, any car that survives the twenty-four hours of mechanical torture is considered a real winner.

The first race was organized by the Auto Club d'Ouest, the ACO, in 1928, and was won by a Chenard and Walker Sport which averaged sixty two miles per hour. In 2003, the race was won by a Bentley averaging one hundred forty two miles per hour. The rules and the track have been modified innumerable times, often for reasons of safety, and the art and science of building automobiles have gone through many revolutions, but the modern race still manages to preserve the traditions of the past and its perennial attraction to racing enthusiasts throughout the world. There is still the exhilaration of highly-tuned cars screaming down the Mulsanne straight, and the fascination of drivers testing the limits of their skills in the serpentine corners of the Maison Blanche chicane.

Maria and Jean Luc drove down a week before the race. In the spirit of the occasion, Jean Luc insisted on driving himself, taking his vintage 427 AC Cobra. AC is one of those famous old specialized British firms which build much beloved high performance cars while perpetually hovering on the brink of bankruptcy. The AC legend is based on combining the raw power of huge American engines with the delicacy of a lightweight European body and suspension. The cars are absurdly overpowered for all but expert drivers.

Maria had always realized her profession could bring instant death, but she had never imagined it coming in the form of a five hundred horsepower, open sports car driven by an inexpert driver. Even before they reached the outskirts of Paris, she was begging him to let her take over and after another ten kilometers he agreed, as self-preservation finally triumphed over machismo. He excused himself on the grounds that she was still edgy over Hans' death, and needed to take her mind off things, although part of his mind acknowledged that he had been really *stupid* to try to overtake that bus.

Jean Luc settled into the passenger seat, buckled his belt tightly, and let his mind drift. Maria had kicked off her shoes and hitched up her skirt to drive.

Her seatbelt crossed her chest at an angle which left little to his imagination. She drove with smooth competence and an obvious, sensual pleasure. She glanced over and grinned at him and his heart performed a summersault.

Jean Luc never did anything without a plan. He never let his emotions overcome logic. He was famous for it. Yet in the matter of this girl, with her long silky thighs displayed so casually, he was throwing discretion to the winds.

Well, to be fair, almost to the winds. If he wasn't able to come to a reasonable agreement with Louise, which wouldn't compromise his social standing or most of his wealth, he would not go through with the divorce. He was fairly sure Hans had not been Maria's lover, yet he had arranged his death anyway, as a precautionary measure. He knew there would always be men around Maria like bees round a honey pot, and he couldn't kill every man she smiled at. In fact, it was an immense boost to his ego to see them slathering over what only he could possess. Still, he simply could not tolerate the thought of those thighs wrapped around another man.

Power was something to be used, he always said. He had exerted his power to build his commercial empire until it had no weak links. Each business was profitable in its own right, and he only retained businesses with real growth potential. He would probably have sold off Sassal—nothing wrong with it except the limited demographic expansion of its market segment—if it hadn't been for Maria's new marketing campaign. If the cars did well, and if sales took off, he'd keep it. If not, he'd sell it to the German consortium who kept offering to buy it. He was known as a turn-around artist, buying troubled or exhausted companies on the cheap and redirecting and re-energizing them, but a huge part of that was knowing when to sell strategic losers.

His empire was well-diversified and pumping cash; his after tax return on capital was excellent and well hedged. He had a small, but very promising stable of young businesses like Genitaire, any of which might mature to replace an existing company in his stable which happened to lose its edge.

It wasn't clear that he needed to keep building and expanding indefinitely. His portfolio was just right, the product of thirty five years of hard work and sound judgment. Besides, once your personal net worth exceeds five billion euros, it isn't clear that you need a lot more money, and he wasn't a playboy like Dick Branson or a wiz kid like Bill Gates. He wasn't going to cling to power forever like Hank Greenberg or Sandy Weill, and he wasn't going to turn into a high profile amateur politician like George Soros.

The power he had always nurtured and used in business could be turned toward other goals. The challenge of rebuilding France's position in the world was like a classic case of turning around a once-powerful company which had lost its edge and direction. The strategy in this case was to weaken the market leader by tarnishing its brand image, and then structure a joint venture which could offer an attractive alternative product mix within a conglomerate. The words might be different—'America' instead of 'market leader', 'foreign policy' for 'brand image', 'international alliance' for 'joint venture', 'UN' for 'conglomerate'—but the strategy and logic were just the same.

It was an infinitely more interesting project than simply buying yet another company or doing yet another under-the-counter energy deal with the Russians. And, he reflected, for an amateur in political manipulation he was doing pretty damned well!

Maria shifted downward and the car burbled and then roared, jerking Jean Luc back to the road stretching before them, to the wind in his hair and the sun on his face. He vaguely recalled something called 'double clutching'. She had turned off the autoroute and was exercising the car on country roads. She glanced over and laughed in delight. The car leapt around an elderly truck piled high with bales of straw.

They bought wine and cheese and bread in a tiny village and drove up a cart track to picnic. Maria was bubbling with high spirits. They had a corkscrew but no knife and no glasses, so they tore the food apart with their hands and passed the bottle back and forth. When lunch was over she pushed him down on the grass and pulled off her panties.

"Someone might see!" Jean Luc protested.

"Who cares?" she asked gaily, as she knelt over him and hitched her skirt up to her waist.

Back in the car Jean Luc fell into a comfortable torpor, lulled by the wine and the fresh air, and the sunshine flashing through the branches of the trees which lined the roads. The engine of the open roadster rumbled and roared as she led it through its paces. She had not put on her panties again and they fluttered from the gear shift like a totem.

She seemed to have shrugged off Hans' death completely. Perhaps he had been wrong to imagine there was something between them. She had been upset at the first shock, naturally, but she'd gone out and walked it off. His idiot driver had lost her on the metro, but she had been at the Ritz, just as she had told him, when the driver finally got there.

He had no grounds for suspicion. It was just that love is more easily given than trust.

Maria had become his other great project, totally unexpected and delightfully welcome. Originally, she had been simply another routine seduction, with the challenge of overcoming her casual aloofness, leading to the disaster of their first night together. But she had shown tact and gentleness, and gradually an emerging passion. In retrospect, he could even laugh about it. She had been so *sweet.*

This was an arena in which his power had no meaning. He had come to realize that in all his fifty-five years and in all his relationships and affairs, he had never felt love, and now that it had finally come to him, he was overwhelmed by its intensity. When Le Mans was over, he would tell her his one remaining secret, and she would see him as he really was and their love would be complete.

There were a thousand reasons not to tell her, of course, but he *wanted* to. Besides, even if he was powerless in his love for her, he was not completely powerless, as Hans had discovered and as would any other man who so much as looked at her twice. He had put a price tag of a quarter of a million on Bernardo's head.

CHAPTER 11

Over the long run, violence can be very cost effective.

—Jean Luc Lafarge

Moshe carried an impression of the precious fingerprint to Daniel, and waited while he traced it. Daniel's beat was financial fraud and illegal funds movements—he had a bloodhound's nose for financial impropriety—but his investigations certainly permitted him to conduct searches for individuals, and the fingerprint guys saw nothing unusual in Daniel's request for a high priority search. A day later, Daniel called Moshe to meet him in a downtrodden bistro in a part of Paris that tourists seldom visit.

"Vesuvius is Rennard, Paul Rennard. French national, Legion Etrangere, mercenary in Sierra Leone, the whole bit.... Okay, so I admit it, you were right! He didn't work for the big mercenary firms, he was a subcontractor for a couple of South Africans. He has an interesting background. His parents were French Algerians who were killed in a traffic accident and he was brought up by Jewish foster parents until he ran away and joined the Legion."

"Halleluiah! Vesuvius has a name. Where is he now?"

"He's an upright citizen, no arrests, no convictions. Works as a security manager for a company called Genitaire, perfectly respectable, address in Paris."

"Who or what owns Genitaire?"

"It's part of the Groupe Lafarge. It's a scientific research firm, genetics and that sort of stuff."

"Lafarge? The billionaire?"

Daniel had heard the implications in Moshe's tone.

"Listen to me carefully, Moshe. Remember, this is France and you are decidedly *not* the law here. I can more or less overlook it if your guys knock off a couple of foreign Arabs, but I absolutely cannot permit you to go after French citizens, and Lafarge is one of the most powerful men in Europe.

"He's completely respectable, ultra-well connected, and way, way out of your league. His company's revenues are larger than your government's tax receipts. He's far, far out of my league, too. And there is nothing which implicates Lafarge. Rennard was probably moonlighting for his old connections. Am I being clear?"

He stared at Moshe and Moshe stared back calmly.

"I understand."

"I mean it. Listen, in this climate the Mossad is as unpopular around here as the CIA, and that's saying a lot. I'm absolutely *not* going to help you on this."

"Daniel, I really do understand, believe me. Is Rennard in France now?"

"Yes, although he travels quite a bit. There was a reference to him being in South Africa recently, but that's not confirmed. What are you going to do? I have a right to know, Moshe."

"I'm going to defend my country."

"You're turning into a prick, Moshe."

"Yeah, but not as big a prick as Rennard, by all accounts."

Jean Luc's driver for the past eight years was an admirable man, but he was getting a little long in the tooth, and had managed to lose track of Maria for several hours in Paris. Jean Luc felt he had to make a change. Still, the driver was very loyal and an excellent intel guy; he'd seen the implications of Jeannette Bois' banking discoveries immediately. As a former member of the Soviet forces (he had deserted in Afghanistan) he still had useful connections. Jean Luc re-assigned him to a desk job, and Paul Rennard now sat behind the wheel.

"I've asked a lot of you recently, Paul," Jean Luc told him. "And you've been outstanding. You're entitled to a break You can drive me and provide personal security, and I want you with Maria every time she leaves the house."

Paul liked his new assignment, and he liked the way Jean Luc had fattened his Swiss bank account. He did not feel his new status was inferior to his old one at Geniture—even assassins must think about their careers—and his business card read, 'Group Security Coordinator.' He had worked for Lafarge for several years, but had spent little time with him. Their arms-length relationship had consisted mostly of instructions given over the telephone and subsequent cash payments.

His work was dangerous, but the pay was excellent. His strongest impressions of Jean Luc up to now were that he was very businesslike and efficient, and Jean Luc evidently found and admired the same qualities in Paul. There was also a mutual dependency. Paul knew enough about Jean Luc to have him put away forever, while Jean Luc could undoubtedly snuff out Paul's existence at any time.

Their relationship had begun when Paul gave up his mercenary career—too much risk and hardship—in favor of a conventional job as a security guard at Genitaire Laboratories. The company had expanded rapidly and Paul's job had expanded with it, until he was head of security with eight men under him.

He had first met Jean Luc during an ugly episode when a group of animal rights activists were attempting to close down Genitaire's extensive testing site. The leader of the rights group was a particularly pugnacious woman. On a visit to the labs, Jean Luc had suggested in jest that someone should break her legs.

Paul had not done precisely that, but he had done so to her closest supporter and explained to the pugnacious woman that the same thing would happen to her if there were any further protests. In addition, he had given her a thousand euros from the company's petty cash account and suggested there would be more to come if the woman transferred her campaign to the facilities of Genitaire's closest competitors.

Jean Luc believed business is a brutal battle and had succeeded in large part through ruthlessness, but he had never thought of physical violence as a corporate strategic option. Paul's actions at Genitaire opened Jean Luc's eyes to the possibilities and thereafter, from time to time, he called on Paul's talents, but only when there was no possibility of tying an incident back to Groupe Lafarge.

For example, Jean Luc's driver had told him his sister-in-law had come across some unusual banking transactions. Jean Luc had called Paul and that was the end of Jeannette Bois. Then there was that photographer who had managed to get pictures of Jean Luc on his yacht with those models. Most of Paul's assignments were overseas, in the murky waters of Jean Luc's unpublicized businesses. The new conspiracy was on a completely different and vastly expanded scale, but it was based on the same principle of applying physical force if it was essential to achieving an objective. Over the long run, violence can be remarkably cost effective.

* * *

"Do you know this man?" Moshe asked politely, holding out a photograph of Paul Rennard. It showed him as he had been four or five years ago in his mercenary days, with his hair almost completely shaved and his eyes squinting against the African sun.

The South African flickered his eyes briefly over the photograph and flipped them away. His tiny office was oppressively hot and there was a rip in one of the fly screens.

"No, I don't."

"I will pay you five grand US for this information. His name may be Paul Rennard. Look him up in your records."

The mercenary contractor stared up at his visitor; scrawny, ugly, untidy, and looking completely exhausted. His floppy linen jacket could be hiding a weapon, but somehow the man seemed too weak and too mild for that. He wondered who the hell he was, and concluded that he was a policeman of some sort. Still, five thousand dollars is five thousand dollars. He glanced at his phone and then made a show of opening into his ancient brass-bound safe and riffling through a few papers. He grunted as if finding an unexpected trove of information.

"He never worked for us, but he's on our professional contact list as a freelancer."

"Who did he work for?"

"He's an independent—could have been anyone."

"Who knows him locally?" Moshe asked, maintaining his polite demeanor.

"I haven't the faintest idea. All I can tell you is that he was available a few years ago."

He appeared to consult his piece of paper.

"He wasn't with Executive Results or Sandline. He was just a freelancer looking for action up on the Coast. I have a local contact number, but it's probably years out of date."

"Sir," said Moshe quietly. "I don't want to be difficult, but I represent an organization that you absolutely do *not* want to fuck with. I have information that you know him, that you handled his account."

The South African closed the file, spun the lock, and turned to face Moshe.

"I don't scare easily. Who the hell are you?"

"I'm a doctor, and I'm afraid I have some bad news. You have very little time left to live if I don't get this information."

There are many organizations that the South African could guess Moshe represented. Some were private, but most were governmental. Moshe's English was good, but it was unaccented, and therefore probably not his native tongue. Rennard came from France, but Moshe did not seem French. That left a range of unattractive possibilities.

He had a gun in his drawer and returned to his desk casually. His visitor looked pretty weak, but it was always best to be on the safe side.

"Five thousand US, you said?"

"Yes, and double that if the information is current."

The South African reached a decision. This guy was government, which meant he had a substantial force behind him. On the other hand, it also meant he had substantial cash, and times had been a mite lean of late. Besides, he didn't owe Rennard anything.

He shrugged and said, "Okay, okay. I saw him three weeks ago."

"What was he doing?"

"Passing through. He was on his way up north and then he was leaving again."

"Where from and where to?"

"That's another five grand."

Moshe did not pause to negotiate.

"Okay, where?"

"He said he was going to Central East Africa and when he came back he was on his way to Canada."

"CEA where the poisoned food scandal just happened?"

The South African's eyes grew opaque.

"Sure," he said.

"Where in Canada did he say he was going?" Moshe asked.

"I think he said Montreal."

"Why did he see you? Did he want anything?"

"I sold him a couple of weapons. These days it's impossible to fly commercially if you're carrying."

Moshe opened his money belt and pulled out a sheaf of five one hundred dollar bills. The South African selected one at random and held it up to the light from the window to examine it with a magnifying glass.

"Okay," he said.

Moshe counted out the balance and handed the money to the mercenary who reopened his safe, tossed the money in, and relocked it. They regarded each other for a second or two and Moshe left.

He waited in the corridor for a minute and re-entered the office. The South African was punching numbers into his telephone, glancing back and forth at a number written on a business card. Moshe shot him between the eyes. He put the business card in his pocket—the first number was 33, the code for France—and looked at the telephone, guessing that the number printed on it was not the telephone number, but the combination to the safe. He had seen the man glance that way before opening it. Evidently, the South African had had a terrible memory for numbers.

Moshe opened the safe—his guess was correct—and retrieved the money, which was covered with his fingerprints. After a moment of indecision, he removed the remaining contents. He wiped the combination dial clean, left the safe open, glanced at the body slumped on the desk in a spreading pool of blood, and quietly closed the office door behind him. The flies were ecstatic.

Le Mans is a sleepy country market town for fifty weeks of the year. For the remaining two weeks in June, it suddenly turns into a mecca for the motor racing world, and then just as abruptly it reverts to pastoral torpor. During the two weeks leading up to the race every hotel, auberge and pension is filled to overflowing at stratospheric prices. Vast tent encampments spring up in the muddy fields, and fairgrounds appear as if by magic.

Hundreds of thousands converge: men who drive family sedans but are suddenly automobile experts; women in tight jeans wishing they had had the discipline to lose another ten or fifteen pounds; children in strollers determined to ruin the pleasures of their parents. In the distance, one can hear the siren song which brought this mass of humanity to this overcrowded and marginally sanitary place: the screams of high performance engines at 9000 rmp.

As the decades rolled by from the inception of the race, various marques rose to dominate for a brief span of years. The brutal Bentleys and the elegant Alfa Romeos of the prewar years, and then, when the race resumed after World War II, the beautiful Jaguars and Ferraris achieved dominance, occasionally challenged by Matra-Simca.

These glorious years were marred by the tragic accident of 1955, when a Mercedes 300 leapt from the track and exploded in the packed grandstand.

Ford arrived with a roar in 1966. Its ugly Mark II with a massive seven-liter engine ended the era of European elegance and amateurism forever, although as late as 1968 a humble one point three liter Austin Healey Sprite could still finish fifteenth overall, even though its top speed was almost one hundred miles per hour slower than the winning Ford. Then in came the long reign of Porsche, first the 917s and then the 956s. Such was their dominance that in 1983 the top eight finishers were Porsches, and the next year the top seven.

But the magic of Le Mans, and the skill of the ACO, is that no one can dominate forever. In came Peugeot and back came Jaguar and then in came Audi, and then, to mark the new millennium with a salute to all that history and tradition, back came Bentley.

The track has shrunk from its original seventeen kilometers to a mere thirteen, and the famous four mile Mulsanne straight now has kinks in it to slow the cars, but the fans in the grandstand still strain their eyes to see the cars bursting out of the chicane at Maison Blanche, and then shrieking past them or diving into the pits for a frenetic refueling stop, or to change tires if it has started raining; and they still open their ears to the howl of the cars downshifting again and again and again from the Dunlop Bridge to the tortuous twists of the Esses, and then shifting up and up and up as they turn sharp right and Mulsanne opens up before them.

The cars go twice as fast as the early cars, and twice as far, averaging well over one hundred and forty miles per hour for twenty-four hours on end, in spite of all the twists and turns and pit stops and eight hours of darkness, traveling more than three thousand miles from noon to noon. But Lagache and Leonard, who drove their boxy four cylinder, three liter Chenard and Walcker Sport to victory in 1928, would still be able to sniff the tang of high octane fuel in the air, watch the speeding headlights in the night, see the weary triumph on the faces of the winners, and recognize that this is still the same Le Mans.

The hastily renamed Sassal-France-Audi team had entered three turbo-charged V8 Audi R8s with competent drivers, and had a good chance of a couple of top ten places and an outside chance of victory. The Sassal pit was *the* place to be. Maria made sure there were nubile Sassal models on hand at all times, which attracted the cameramen, which attracted valuable airtime for the brand.

The drivers and pit crews were one big family; inter-team rivalries were fierce, but good-natured and did not interfere with the objective of having a good time. Each sunset there was an open house and Sassal GT flowed freely. A lanky American from the Viper team shouldered his way through the crowd. The man was blond, obviously extremely fit, and handsome.

"Hey, babe," he said to Maria, ogling her frankly. "I'm a winner. You got some Sassal for me?"

"One moment, sir," responded Maria coldly in English. "Let me get a fresh bottle so I can ram it up your arse."

Jean Luc, standing nearby in the act of drinking, almost choked in his amusement.

"Whoa, sweetheart! No offense! Can't we play nicely?"

Clearly the man had mistaken Maria for one of the models. Jean Luc could see Maria mastering her fury. An ugly scene would not do the brand image any good.

"Okay, no offense," she smiled. "You're with the Vipers?"

"Yep, and we aim to win."

Almost all the cars in the race were turbocharged V6s and V8s with engines less than four liters. The American Chrysler Vipers were vast eight liter V10s; massively overpowered, like throwbacks to the age of dinosaurs. The Viper team man extolled the glories of his machine, and he and Maria bantered back and forth about American brute force versus European subtlety. It would have been amusing if Jean Luc had not known Maria hated America, and he could see her patience wearing thin.

She led the American over to point out some features of the Sassal-Audi's engine, and Jean Luc lost track of them in the crowd. She rejoined him a few minutes later.

"Ugh," was all she said.

The girl had way too much to drink. Rue Universite in Montreal is not a steep hill, but tonight it seemed like Mount Everest. When a man stepped in front of her and slapped her, she wasn't entirely sure it had really happened. When he pushed her into the car, squeezed in beside her and drove off, her principle concern was a wave of nausea. When he stopped on a quiet side street and showed her a photograph she had difficulty focusing.

"You know Robert?" she asked stupidly, and threw up.

He showed her a second photograph.

"You know Jassim as well?"

The man put a plastic bag over her head, which was definitely a bad thing, but she was too intent on vomiting to realize the full implications until it was too late.

Maria watched as three former cover girls from *Sports Illustrated* arranged themselves so that the Sassal-France-Audi hid their nakedness while leaving it perfectly clear to the camera that they were indeed naked. The handsome young actor playing the part of the driver leaned against the car and read the newspaper, ignoring the girls completely. Maria had often been offered modeling jobs and she thanked God she had never gone for the supposedly easy money. The girls were shivering in the early morning cold. Their humanity had been stripped away with their clothes and they were simply objects. The director held a light meter against their chests and frowned at the results.

"This is crap!" he yelled.

Maria tuned out. She *had* to make some decisions. So far, apart from a couple of vague hints, she had nothing on Jean Luc. He had mentioned the President of France would be coming for dinner on the night of the race, and Maria had asked Captain Sandler from the embassy, in his Viper team disguise, to get her a small bugging device. She wasn't sure whether anything secret would occur at dinner, but she planned to wear a bug so the entire conversation could be recorded.

Michel Leclerc was not coming to visit. He had been traveling and Maria had not seen him since their conversation in Paris. She was reaching the reluctant conclusion that she should let him seduce her, even though Jean Luc would be merciless if he found out. But she had to take risks. She had to get results. She also considered seducing Paul, who was clearly more than just a driver, and might even be the man who killed Hans; however, she doubted Paul would betray Jean Luc for mere sex.

She would try to get whatever she could out of Jean Luc, crank up her anti-American thing big time, bug the President at dinner, and do whatever she could with Michel. Then she'd leave. Either she would have broken through to the truth, or decided there was no hidden truth to find. One way or the other, the race would be the end of the operation, at least as far as she was concerned.

She had one other motivation. Life with Jean Luc was incredibly pleasant—the luxuries, the endless self indulgence, the opportunity to play with Team Sassal, the sense of having the entire world at her command, as if she were almost another Princess Di, without the paparazzi and the mother-in-law to contend with, or Jackie O with that Greek billionaire: the comparison didn't seem too extreme.

Jean Luc clearly had great plans for her professionally and was already bringing her into marketing issues involving his other companies. Her self-disgust at seducing him was fading, and now it would be very easy to be seduced herself into accepting Jean Luc at face value. She had to get out *soon* or buy the fairytale wholesale.

🍁 🍁 🍁

The President of the United States put down his daily intelligence briefing with a mixture of alarm and resignation. Perhaps the media were right. Perhaps he was a guy who just simply wasn't up to the job of leading the country and the free world. He had jawboned the Israelis into relaxing their security checkpoints and opening up their borders as a gesture to somehow get past the fallout from the Syrian raid. The Israelis would soon announce 'Fresh Start Day' in which Palestinians could move freely throughout the West Bank and Gaza, and reduce restrictions at the border crossings into Israel.

The deal would be that, if there were no suicide attacks, the checkpoints would remain open. There was even talk of easing the restrictions on Yasir Arafat, who was still confined to his compound in Ramallah, if the Palestinians forewent terrorism. Perhaps that would ease the pervasive European and Arab condemnations of Israel, and of America for insisting on its right to exist. If the situation settled down, he'd be able to approve delivery of the next batch of F-16Is.

He had worked the phones with the few remaining European governments who were reliably pro-American to get them to come out against the 'c'est possible' movement. Whether one supported American policy or not, a celebration of mass civilian murder struck at the very basis of civilized society, and simply encouraged further terrorism. The results had not been particularly encouraging.

He had ordered a Presidential Commission into the health effects of genetically altered foodstuffs, but that was a disaster before it started. The opposition was insisting on full access to all executive branch documentation, raising the whole executive privilege issue. In addition, the UN Secretary General had said that an American commission would not be credible, and had announced a competing UN commission, chaired by that global agricultural powerhouse, Cuba, and featuring centers horticultural expertise like North Korea and Iran.

"Shit," he said to himself, and realized he said very little else these days.

CHAPTER 12

Everyone cheats at everything.

—Jean Luc Lafarge

"So, it looks like Rennard has been an extremely bad guy," Moshe concluded. He shook his head to brush off the cobwebs of jet lag. He looked as if he'd worn the same clothes for several days, and looks were not deceiving.

"Why did you kill the girl in Montreal?" Daniel asked. "The South African I can understand."

"I ran her through the computers and she was on our 'dead or alive' list for some very nasty things. That's how I identified her as a possible contact in the first place. Her father was Mohammed Alawassi and her lover was Jassim Marzook. They did the Israeli embassy bombing in Turkey. She was eighteen carat shit."

He returned to the point at hand.

"Let me ask you, Daniel: Is there any basis on which Rennard could have been doing this without Lafarge? Is there any basis for believing he was not doing it *for* Lafarge?"

Daniel did not answer the question. Instead he asked, "What are you guys going to do?"

Moshe was the man he admired most. They were ill-suited. Daniel was prodding and methodical, while Moshe relied on intuition. Daniel was conventionally handsome, although lack of exercise and a gastronomic wife were now adding layers to his frame, while Moshe was, well, weird looking. Yet at college, the pretty girls always went for Moshe first, while Daniel slipstreamed behind him picking up the discards in Moshe's wake.

His professional relationship with Moshe was technically illegal, although mutual information trading was commonplace among the intelligence services. In fact, his career had gone nowhere ever since the UN aid money investigation had been cancelled from on high and he relied on the occasional goodies Moshe brought him to earn his keep.

Now Moshe had not only come to brief him on his journeys, but had brought his boss along. That made the contact official, and Daniel should have brought his own boss in. Instead of helping a friend, Daniel felt he was being pulled into a Mossad operation.

Moshe's boss answered. "We screwed up. We have to make nice to the Syrians, and we have to placate world opinion. The prime minister's going to go with the old 'Fresh Start Day' strategy."

"There'll be a massacre!" Moshe objected.

"He feels like he has no choice."

"I don't think I should be part of this conversation," said Daniel, uncomfortably. "My question was what are you going to do about Rennard?"

"We want to play him for a while," said Moshe's boss. "See if we can prove Lafarge is pulling the strings. Then we'll take him out. And we'd like your help, Daniel."

"Number one, I can't sanction an operation by a foreign intelligence service in France. Number two, I have to report this. Number three, as I've told Moshe several times, Lafarge is basically untouchable. Number four, we don't have helping Israel or the US as our top priorities around here, in case you haven't noticed. Number five, if I help you I will probably go to jail for the rest of my life, and thoroughly deserve to; and, last and not least, if you touch these guys on French territory I will personally shoot you."

"You know, I like you," responded Moshe's boss. "Now, I want to tell you something and I want to tell you before you decide what to do."

He pushed a list of names and numbers across to Daniel.

"The first two names are Haitian security guys. The next is a customs guy in Algeria who imports the merchandise from Haiti and re-exports it to his buddy in French customs in Bordeaux. The last two names are the guys who run the whole thing from here in France.

"Now, as you know, conventional wisdom has it that most opium coming out of Afghanistan goes north through Russia and into Europe. But that route's been under tremendous pressure. So now it's going south and then by sea to Panama and on to Haiti, where you can also buy a full selection of Columbian and Peruvian offerings as well."

He glanced down at the paper which lay between them.

"The account numbers are the clearing accounts in Luxembourg where the whole thing is put together from a financial perspective. I know you're the expert in that sort of thing. But the really interesting question is what happens to the money the drugs bring in? I've included a Dubai account you may find interesting. Anyway, what you do with this is up to you."

Daniel did not pick up the gold mine of intelligence he had been offered.

"I don't want to have anything to do with this. I mean it."

"Okay," said Moshe, unconcerned. "But keep the intel anyway—you'll probably get the Legion of Honor—third class, of course, but that's better than a kick in the head. We'll stay in touch."

"*Shit!*" said Daniel several times and with increasing intensity.

"Listen, it's okay," said Moshe. "You're a bureaucrat, and bureaucrats don't do moral dilemmas. We understand."

"Daniel," Moshe's boss added, "Here's another proposal: You will have full access and we won't take any action without your prior knowledge and approval."

Daniel rolled his eyes to heaven. "God, why did I have to be born Jewish?"

"So that manipulative bastards like Moshe and me could lay guilt trips on you," replied Moshe's boss.

Paul sat on a pile of tires in the corner of the pit, idly watching the crew at work. Maria was walking around with her fingers forming a square, squinting through them as if they were a camera lens. She was figuring out camera angles. She wanted about fifteen seconds of footage featuring the pit crew refueling a car and changing the tires, demonstrating professional skill and teamwork, which would be followed in the commercial by four eager models approaching them with Sassal GT bottles. If the concept worked, it might open up a blue collar angle for the Sassal for Winners campaign.

The trouble was there was no good angle in the cramped quarters of the pits to show the men at work together. It would have to be broken into a series of shots showing each individual at his work, but they still had to come together as a team when the girls approached them. She glanced up the track to make sure she was safe and stepped back to consider a longer view. She crouched down to peer through her imaginary camera and Paul heard one of the pit crew make a complimentary comment about her cleavage. A man wearing oily orange overalls approached Maria from the track. She glanced up.

"Miss Menendez," he said, pointing across to the far side of the track, so that she involuntarily stared in that direction as he continued to speak. "Let me be extremely brief. I know you work for the CIA."

She turned back abruptly to stare at him.

"I have strong evidence that Lafarge is plotting to severely damage the United States."

He pointed again. "Please think about this and I'll contact you again. I have just told you that the Sassal film truck has broken down over there." He nodded and strolled away.

"Who the hell was that?" Paul asked, walking over.

"He said the Sassal video truck's broken down." She reached for her walkie-talkie. "Sassal truck, Claude, are you guys okay?"

"No, we're fucking well *not*. The fucking truck's stalled."

"Okay, I'll send a mechanic over."

Paul glanced at the retreating orange back. He shrugged. Like everybody else, Paul had originally assumed Maria was simply a gold digger trying to sink her teeth into Jean Luc's bank accounts, but she didn't seem to act like one.

She had two personalities: The cool exterior she wore like a defensive shield against strangers and the endless stream of men she attracted, and beneath that the 'real Maria', cheerful and friendly, a woman who obviously loved her work on the Sassal campaign, and showed genuine affection toward Jean Luc. Paul was concluding that she had had one or more disastrous affairs, which had made her cautious about men, and she saw Jean Luc as a safe haven.

Jean Luc, of course, being Jean Luc, could never trust anyone and was showing an obsessive jealousy of any man who came near her. So Paul had become both her guardian and Jean Luc's spy.

* * *

The President waved the flag and the race was on. First there was the earsplitting cacophony of all eighty cars pouring down the track like traffic on a high speed highway. Then there were three minutes of silence until the cars reappeared. They howled by, nose to tail, like a multicolored snake, and were gone again.

Gradually the cars ceased to be an endless stream and sorted themselves into clumps. As the afternoon wore on, the field began the slow process of erosion as contenders began to fall out. There was the drama of an ugly shunt away on the Mulsanne straight, but thank God no one was injured.

By evening the race had sorted itself into a pattern. The new Porsches were beginning to dominate, with the Vipers and a surprising Ferrari still in contention. The Sassal-Audis were running well, but not in the leading bunch. The crowds began to think about dinner.

A tiny minority of the tens of thousands who flock to Le Mans live in splendor in spacious rented country houses, and wear IDs around their necks which magically propel them to the best seats in the grandstand, and give them access to the elegantly catered restricted cafeterias and to the pits. Jean Luc's party had taken a small chateau on the river in the town of Chateau de Loir, at a rental so high that Jean Luc briefly considered purchasing the property instead. It was in these surroundings of decaying grandeur that he entertained the President to dinner. Professor Diderot was there, and so was one of the President's aides.

Jean Luc had excluded Maria. Earlier in the day, in acute embarrassment, he had said he wanted to talk politics to the President. He wanted to get a commitment on restructuring corporate taxes, and he was sure the President would be more open to persuasion if there were no outsiders present. He told Maria he trusted her at least five times. He insisted she should be present for cocktails before dinner and return for dessert. He just needed the President to himself for an hour or so. She cheerfully accepted her exclusion. Taxes were inherently boring, she said, the worst part of the real estate business. She would run over to the track, which was inherently fun.

The President arrived and greeted Jean Luc fulsomely before passing on to Maria.

"Ah, yes, Señorita. How nice to see you again."

After a few minutes of casual conversation about the race, Maria excused herself.

"You're not joining us?" the President asked Maria.

"I have to run over to the track—I want to see how everything's going. I'll be back later."

"Be sure you do, you're much more fun than Jean Luc."

She offered her cheek to Maria, who touched it to her own, gently placing her hands on the President's shoulders.

Paul was not going with her. For once Maria would not have a chaperone. Presumably Jean Luc was keeping him close at hand even though the house was full of the President's security guards. She left, hoping the tiny bug would stay hidden where she had placed it beneath the President's collar. It was a huge risk, but she had no alternatives.

Jean Luc gave Diderot the lead as they ate a superbly prepared cold salmon plate. The old house had a decaying feeling to it and smelt musty. Jean Luc had had the dining room repainted just for this occasion. The evening was warm and the French windows were open, offering a superb view of the Loir river below.

"The problem with being reflexively anti-American, if I may say so, Madame President, is that ultimately one must defend whatever it is that the United States is attacking." Diderot smiled, and lied cheerfully to remove all possibility that the notoriously prickly French President might take offense. "You, of course, have never fallen into this trap."

The President nodded to acknowledge her own wisdom and Diderot continued. He always found it useful to make the same point two or three times to make sure politicians grasped it.

"Thus, for example, it's hard to argue against the invasion of Iraq without, eventually, being forced into a defense of Saddam Hussein. It's hard to attack Israel without eventually condoning Palestinian terrorism.

"At the international level, it's hard to insist that all important actions must be channeled through the UN while preventing the UN from taking any decisive action. And so forth and so on."

Diderot paused to make sure his point had been taken.

"In order to avoid this trap, one must offer a valid alternative."

"Yes, I saw your interview. Very good, very persuasive."

"Thank you, Madame."

There was a moment of silence while they all reflected on the difficulties of living with one overwhelmingly powerful nation.

Jean Luc said cautiously, "Some of us think there's a possible way forward, Charlotte."

Jean Luc knew the President had two objectives in life. One was to remain, or, in truth become, a major player on the international scene; and the second was to stay in a public office which ensured her immunity from prosecution. Her predecessor's giddy moments of French obstructionist power before the Iraq invasion were now in the past, and time would inexorably bring this President's term to a close. She needed a plan.

"First, Charlotte, the Security Council is a bit of an anachronism," Jean Luc continued. "The permanent members with vetoes are an odd bunch, certainly not suited for coordinated action. China does its own thing. It doesn't have any global ambitions—yet. Russia's a complete basket case. And Britain and France are, with due respect, complete pigmies. The US is the only world power. In these circumstances you may want to consider giving up France's seat."

"What? That's absurd!"

The President was shocked. France's veto in the Security Council was its only basis for international power and influence.

"Bear with me, Ma'am. We give it up by converting it to a *European* seat. In return, we get a French veto on the appointment. In effect, the French President alone gets to pick Europe's representative, and therefore controls Europe's foreign policy. You might want to consider appointing yourself at the end of your term, for example."

He could see the wheels beginning to turn in the President's mind.

"Instead of being one of the three dwarfs on the Security Council, along with Britain and Russia, Charlotte," he continued, "We would become Europe's sole representative, and therefore one of three giants: the US, China, and Europe under our control. And at some point we can propose a threshold for veto power, some minimum size level of population or gross national product, and thereby squeeze out the British and the Russians."

The President was thoughtful. The result would be perfect, if it could be achieved. She'd have to do some skillful maneuvering to get European support for the idea, but she was a master at manipulating EU politics.

In addition, she felt the weight of history on her shoulders. As the first woman in history to rise to her office, she felt she had to make an indelible impression. She loathed everything that Margaret Thatcher stood for, but she deeply admired the woman herself. Not only had Thatcher been the first female prime minister of Britain, she had also been one of the most important British leaders in the twentieth century. She had crushed her domestic and international opponents, rammed through her far-reaching reforms and made them stick, and held her own with the American Presidents of her era, to become known forever, in love or hate, as 'the iron lady'.

The President was a highly-skilled politician, and she was still only forty-four, but she had risen to power through adroit political tactics rather than by articulating a clear sense of vision. And now her rivals were not French party hacks, but the hard-charging leaders of the other European nations, who were at least as ambitious as she. That American idiot, the elder Bush, had said he lacked the 'vision thing', and in the privacy of her own mind she knew she lacked it also.

As if reading her mind, Jean Luc continued, "But we also need a policy, Charlotte. Something that can get the world excited, something that will get them solidly behind us, so this doesn't look like a simple power grab. We have to seize the initiative.

"As for the other UN members, if we don't intrude on Chinese interests they'll let us go ahead. The British are so far up America's arse they have no credibility, if I may say so, and we'll send the Russians some money. And as for the Americans, they're simply not smart enough to keep up."

"What sort of policy, Jean Luc?"

"We say the world is a mess, Charlotte, and, frankly it's America's fault, but let's forgive and forget, because there's a way out. We floated the Diderot Doctrine to see if the general idea had any legs, and, as you know, it's been very successful. Not just 'Let's all hate America', but 'Let's all welcome America back into the fold'. Our reading of American opinion polls suggests that this President, or if not him his successor, will jump right in, because Americans don't like to be hated."

The President realized this was something Jean Luc had been preparing for a long time. World opinion was strongly against the US, and therefore the timing was perfect. America's cumulative difficulties, like the Israeli situation, and the genetic foods scandal, and the 'c'est possible' movement, had all coincided to create this opportunity.

Jean Luc must have been prescient to anticipate a series of diplomatic disasters for the US. In fact, so prescient that perhaps it wasn't simply a coincidence. She needed time to think, but Jean Luc was pressing on.

"We propose a general international reconciliation, a *Rapprochement Generale*. We amend the charter of the UN to specifically exclude preemptive wars, with an automatic sanction clause, and we extend the International Criminal Court to cover that. Therefore any unilateral military action brings automatic economic sanctions and criminal charges. That may not stop the US completely, but it will certainly slow them down. We'll define Chechnya and Taiwan as internal domestic issues, so Russia and China won't object."

The President was already into the horse trading details.

"We'd also better make sure the Russians still have a free hand in the rest of their periphery, particularly the Caucasus," she said. "And we'll have to make sure we speak for the Middle East as well. Perhaps we can arrange something with the Gulf Cooperation Council."

"Excellent point, Charlotte. Later on, if you think it's doable, we can consider leapfrogging the entire nuclear proliferation debate by proposing all military nukes be transferred to the Security Council, with a general amnesty for all past sins and intrusive inspections going forward. Everyone will cheat, of course, but everyone always cheats at everything.

"The point is that it shifts the balance in the Middle East by potentially disarming Israel, and it destroys the rationale for the US anti-missile program. How could they justify a system to defend themselves against the UN? And the Chinese will love it because Taiwan and Japan will be defenseless."

"Very intriguing," the President said, cautiously.

Jean Luc wondered how far her ambition extended. There was no harm in pushing on, he decided.

"Finally, when the timing is right, in a year or two, we'll propose that all permanent members must put one third of their military forces under the UN, or lose their vote, in order to create a muscular Security Council. That costs Europe little, it saves the Russians a bundle of money, and the Chinese will agree with absolutely no intention of honoring the agreement.

"In the meantime, at a single stroke, the UN has almost as much military power as the US, and we have created a huge conflict in the US command structure. Whether or not the US goes for it immediately, we have influential friends in America who can push public opinion a long way."

The President was entranced, but it was all a bit too neat, somehow.

"You think all this is possible, Jean Luc?"

"Oh yes, Charlotte, c'est possible!"

The plan would give the President more than she had dreamed was possible, but she had not survived in politics for so long without understanding that everything had a price. Always read the fine print.

"And for you, Jean Luc, what does this bring for you?"

"Would you excuse us for one minute?" he asked, and Diderot and the president's aide disappeared as if by magic.

"Simply a restoration of the glory of France, Madame President," he said when they were alone. "That's all I hope for."

He paused, both for emphasis and to savor the moment.

"Besides, I am not the sole author of these ideas. Francois Diderot has been invaluable in giving me his perspective, and, of course, a researcher called Jeannette Bois—she gave me some of her papers to review."

The President finally understood. The warm glow, the excitement generated by Jean Luc's proposals was now replaced by a horrid empty feeling in the pit of her stomach.

How could Jean Luc have possibly found out about the Bois woman? Could he have been behind the bank clerk's death? It all seemed a long time ago, and in these circumstances it really didn't matter. Her mind skidded away from those memories, yet she knew, very clearly, that with those papers in Jean Luc's hands this man had absolute control over her.

The President would stride the world stage like a giant, and Jean Luc would pull the strings…unless she could somehow reverse the roles and manipulate the puppet master. Beneath his smooth and civilized exterior, she knew Jean Luc was as tough a son-of-a-bitch as walked the planet. On the other hand, beneath her own smooth exterior she could be pure bitch herself. Lafarge was not completely invulnerable, and she had sources of intelligence of her own.

Maria pulled out her tiny earplug. She had it! She actually had it! The tiny transmitter she had attached to the back of the President's collar when they embraced had actually worked! And there in her lap was the recording tape that proved the conspiracy. She strolled down to the Viper pit trying to contain her excitement and looking for Captain Sandler, but they hadn't seen him. It was his rest period and they were far too busy to pay her any further attention.

She glanced at her watch and headed over to the rest area. She just had time to give him the tape and then get back to the chateau before the President left, so she could remove the microphone from her back. She knocked on the door of the Viper trailer and opened it. Captain Sandler lay sprawled on the floor and there was no life in his staring eyes. She closed the door again and walked away in a fog of horror and confusion. She had no idea how he had died, and now she had no one to whom she could deliver the tape.

First Hans, and now him. Who was *doing* this? Jean Luc? The image of the strange mechanic in orange overalls jumped into her mind.

She drove back to the chateau on autopilot. The grounds were crawling with security men. She was all alone in a dangerous world.

The President and Jean Luc seemed in excellent spirits. Maria paused behind the President's chair.

"Excuse me, Ma'am, you have a thread on your dress."

She removed the tiny microphone and transmitter, and held up a long silk thread.

"Even my job has limits," laughed the President. "If I can't find a reliable dressmaker, who can?"

CHAPTER 13

Secrets are so revealing.

—Jean Luc Lafarge

It takes very little to change the complete complexion of a sporting event. The weather had been threatening showers since dawn, and at nine in the morning the clouds opened, a squall drenched the circuit, and the track turned into a greasy skating rink. The cars threw up spectacular rooster tails of spray, and it was amazing how fast the drivers kept going under the difficult conditions. The downpour lasted less than ten minutes and then, just as abruptly, the sun returned and the glistening wet track began to steam.

At 9.37 am the leading Porsche spun out coming into Maison Blanche, and just clipped the front left bumper of his teammate, who was less than a car length behind with a Viper on his tail. The two Porsches began a stately pirouette along the slick surface as the Viper miraculously evaded them and slipped by, leaving the Porsches sliding to an ignominious ending locked inescapably together in the mud beside the track. Suddenly the two remaining Vipers were in the lead, with the Sassals running in third to fifth positions behind them.

The Vipers had done much better than anyone expected. Conventional wisdom had it they would overheat, or their enormous torque would simply be too much for the transmissions to handle hour in and hour out, but there they were, several laps in the lead, with less than three hours to go. It was beginning to look as if this would be one of the rare occasions on which an American car would win. Elation was beginning to bubble up in the Viper pit, counteracting the pall cast by Sandler's sudden death from overdosing. Who would have ever thought he was a poppy head?

At 11.24 the Vipers blew up. In racing terminology 'blowing up' means catastrophic engine failure, and when word first flashed around that the Vipers had blown up, everyone assumed that those huge eight-liter engines had finally succumbed to the heat, vibration and abrasion of their mechanical torture. After all, in twenty-three hours each engine had turned almost eight million times, and the V10s had sustained the violence of almost eighty million piston strokes.

But everyone was wrong. The two cars had been running some twelve seconds apart on the Mulsanne at approximately two hundred and twenty miles per hour when they had literally exploded.

Paul dropped the transmitter he had used to detonate the explosives into an overflowing garbage pail and made his way back through the crowds, pulling off his gloves. It might have been more spectacular to destroy the cars in front of the grandstands, but he had been concerned that the race would be halted. They might even have crashed into the Sassal pit. At least the plastic explosive he had slipped under the driving seats during a Viper open house had worked.

As it was, there were a few minutes of confusion out on the far side of the track as the remaining cars braked and zigzagged to avoid the scattered wreckage, and the rescue crews rushed to clear the track and move the smoldering hulks. All that most of the crowds could see were two plumes of oily smoke. It was a miracle how few spectators were injured. The race continued while the ACO officials tried to figure out what had happened, and Team Sassal occupied the three leading positions.

At 11.58 the three Sassal-France-Audis formed up in line-astern and entered their final lap. At 12.01 they emerged from the Maison Blanche chicane in perfect formation and roared down to the checkered flag, while the stands erupted in joy and all across France people paused to enjoy the moment and, in gratifyingly large numbers, order Sassal GTs to drink a victory toast.

Maria leaned back against the headrest and closed her eyes as Jean Luc's jet crossed the Mediterranean coastline en route for the villa in Sicily. He was giddy with excitement over the Sassal victory and was making phone call after phone call. Opposite them, Paul was slumped in his seat with a mask over his eyes. There was absolutely no question in her mind Jean Luc had ordered the disaster to the Vipers, and Paul had carried it out.

Her handbag lay casually at her feet, filled as usual with the oddments of daily living and half a dozen of her little dictation tapes, including the recording of the dinner conversation. What in God's name could she do with that tape? She had Jean Luc strategizing with the President to humiliate the United States diplomatically, but she had nothing technically illegal. She wondered who the hell Jeannette Bois was. That name had never come up, but it seemed to be of great importance.

Her mind shifted feverishly. Who knew she was CIA? The intel guy at the embassy knew, and the rock-like Jake Stone, and her boss Frank, but who else could have told Orange Overalls? Some drone-like clerk in Langley with access to Rosebud intel and a willingness to commit treason? The guys who had briefed her on Jean Luc's possible arms smuggling and illegal oil deals before she played herself in? Did Jean Luc suspect her? Had she made a mistake? Thank God she even played her cover in conversations with Be-Be in case he had tapped her phone. Who had killed Captain Sandler? Paul? Orange Overalls? Who *was* Orange Overalls?

Way back when, when she was first asked to transfer to the CIA, they'd found an identity for her in Spain, a woman with the right age and background who had been killed in a car accident, whose name was also Maria Menendez. It had made the substitution much easier—that's why the CIA had asked for her—but she'd often wondered if someone might stumble over the coincidence and discover her true identity. Had someone done that?

She had planned to get the tape and get out, but now she was up shit creek without a paddle. They should have called it Operation 'Cluster Fuck' instead of 'Rosebud'.

She sensed Jean Luc leaning over her, and opened her eyes to see him reaching for her bag. He smiled and continued, sorting through the contents, making a little pile of pens and lip glosses and recording tapes on the armrest, taking out her purse and her recorder, while she watched helplessly. Paul had taken off his mask and was staring at her.

"All your secrets, my dear," he said. "Do you whisper wicked things about me into your recorder?"

He pushed the playback button playfully, but it was the unrecorded end of the President's tape. The air conditioning was very cold.

"One day I'll have to listen to them all. Secrets are so revealing!"

Finally, Jean Luc turned off the empty hiss of the recorder, pulled some tissues out of her bag and returned the rest of the contents. He blew his nose loudly several times and settled back. Cabin pressure always played havoc with his sinuses and blocked his ears.

* * *

"Now what the hell do we do, Moshe?" Daniel asked. The world was celebrating the French victory at Le Mans, crowing over the defeat of the Americans.

"Rennard—or Kamal, as I still think of him—is in Sicily," Moshe responded. "He obviously blew up the Vipers and I assume he killed that Marine. Those are both assaults on American interests rather than French or Israeli interests, so we ought to be bringing in the CIA. But that's a bit weird because the CIA already has that woman in place."

"This happened in France, of course, and Rennard is a Frenchman, but this is criminal rather than security," Daniel said. "We should let the police run with this."

"Daniel, you've got to shit or get off the pot. You really do have to face the fact that Lafarge is out to fuck the United States, and he's doing a pretty good job of it. And he and the President are so tight it's a wonder the scandal sheets are forging photos of them on deserted beaches."

"I can't get political, Moshe, for God's sake! Fucking the United States is the most popular sport in Europe, and it's certainly not illegal."

Moshe spoke with absolute certainty. "Well, where I come from, fucking Israel *is* illegal, even if we're only collateral damage on this occasion, and we're going to take them down, with you or without you."

"*Shit.* This will cost me my job."

"Daniel, you have to reach down, deep down, and decide who you really want to run the entire world."

"Could it be me?"

"No, and Elvis Presley is not on the list either. If you proceed, you have to assume the chain of command above you is compromised. That means you have a significant threat of detection, and it also means that we, I mean the Mossad, is going to take all the executive action. It also means you really *may* need asylum."

"*Shit!*"

"I'll take that for a 'yes,'" said Moshe.

"Now," he continued before Daniel could respond, "Should we contact the CIA woman? She seems to be doing squat, or she may have been turned. Either way we lose. On the other hand, she may be sitting on a gold mine."

"What's the play?" asked Daniel reluctantly, knowing he was effectively stepping into no-man's-land in which he was virtually a stateless person.

It must be great to be American—you had absolute moral certainty that God was on your side: manifest destiny, or something. It must be great to be Israeli—decisions come easily when all your neighbors are committed to destroying you. But when you're French—what then? What are you fighting for? Decaying echoes of past glories? The alienable right of unelected bureaucrats in Brussels to tell you how to live?

"We'll grab Rennard and sweat him," said Moshe decisively. "That will tie in Jean Luc Lafarge. That's my job. You take charge of the financial side. We'll give you as many of our accounting guys as you need. We'll hack whatever Lafarge accounts we can, and we'll see what we have on your President. We'll reopen that UN investigation of yours, and see if it has significance in this case. In the meantime, we'll re-contact the CIA woman and see if she wants to play too."

"I'm not going to sit in my office wondering what the hell is going on while you guys rampage all over Europe and screw up all my banking access."

"Agreed. We run this together," Moshe said. "You have full access. I've already cleared that with my boss and his boss. If you're concerned, you can meet with our prime minister one-on-one."

He paused awkwardly. "One other point: It might be best if Lucille and the kids take a vacation in Israel, and her mother too, just to be on the safe side."

It was a horrible thing to contemplate, but Moshe was right. The course of action he was embarking on was sufficiently dangerous that his family should be someplace safe. Some important people would get extremely upset with him.

"*SHIT!*"

* * *

"I must say, my dear Maria," Michel said approvingly. "That's a remarkably small bikini. Tell me, why do you go to the bother of putting it on at all?"

"My dear Michel," replied Maria with a dazzling smile, "Because Jean Luc would kill me if I didn't."

Maria lay stretched in a chaise beside the pool, while Michel sat in the shade of a huge beach umbrella. Her conversations with Michel had advanced—or descended, depending on one's viewpoint—into a level of raunchy repartee. In almost any company Michel was a man of immense standing. He had acquired enormous wealth, and his investments in the fashion and movie industries kept him prominently in the gossip columns. His pet projects, such as his endowments and donations to efforts to preserve France's architectural heritage, had made him widely admired and popular.

It was only beside his friend Jean Luc that his stature was diminished, but even then his reputation for making money from unanticipated opportunities was considered to be equal even to Jean Luc's. He had seen the upside in the US Internet opportunity before almost anyone else, and had convinced Jean Luc to enter that market. Five years later, Jean Luc had sensed the bubble was about to burst, and they had gotten out just in time.

She knew he could be interesting and amusing on any number of subjects, but when they were alone he behaved liked a horny fifteen-year-old.

"How was your trip? Jean Luc said you were in China," Maria asked to change the subject.

He continued to stare at her figure unabashed.

"Yes, China and a couple of other places. It was just some business meetings; all very tedious."

"Did you get what you wanted?"

"Yes, I think so. I think we'll see some interesting changes in the next few weeks."

"What kinds of changes?"

"Oh, you'll have to let me preserve a little scrap or two of mystery, just like your costume! Or can we trade revelations?"

"Don't start that again, Michel, please." She changed positions, but the bikini had not been designed for modesty. "Will you be going back?"

"No, I don't think so. My money, and Jean Luc's, will speak for us."

"I've never been to China. In fact, I've never been to that part of the world. Which is your favorite country?"

"I like countries where money still talks. It makes things so much more straight forward."

"Like where?" Maria asked idly, rearranging herself on the chaise as Michel watched closely. "Which is your favorite?"

"North Korea," he said without thinking. "People think of it as the last bastion of Stalinism, but, in truth, it's the last bastion of true entrepreneurial capitalism. Money can buy *anything*."

"Isn't it too cold and remote?" She stretched languorously. "I like the sun. Could you press the buzzer, Michel? I want something to drink."

Michel wondered if it had been a mistake to mention North Korea. He had no real idea what Jean Luc had confided in her. On the other hand, she hadn't reacted in any way.

* * *

The town square was dozing in the heat, bleaching out the paint on the ancient buildings which surrounded it, and reducing life to a crawl. A large dog walked slowly from one patch of cool shadow to the next. A priest in a linen jacket sat down at a café table next to Paul and Maria, fanning his face with his straw Panama hat in a futile effort to combat the fierce sunshine.

"Careful, Paul," Maria whispered. "I think he's got an Uzi under that jacket."

"Right," said Paul sarcastically. "And a rocket launcher up his leg."

The priest glanced around idly and smiled vaguely at them, and ordered lemonade. He did so everyday about this time. Paul and Maria had come to recognize the regulars at the café in Aci Costello at the foot of Mount Etna, and had given them pet names. From henceforth the priest would be 'Father Uzi'.

Paul stirred. "I have to get the new battery for the boat."

"You have to go down to the dock?"

"No, just the garage. It's a regular twelve volt car battery."

"We can pick it up on the way back."

"It's in the wrong direction, I'll go now. It'll only take ten minutes."

Paul had been sufficiently dulled by the pleasant monotony of vacation life, the heat of the sun, and the complete absence of anything remotely resembling a threat, to leave Maria alone for ten minutes. Besides, inactivity drove him crazy. He ambled off to the car.

"Señorita," said the priest softly when Paul had driven off. "I am a colleague of the mechanic who spoke to you at Le Mans."

Maria jumped as if he had poured his glass of iced lemonade down her back.

"Who the hell are you?"

"I am a member of the French security services. The man you spoke to at Le Mans holds a similar position in Israel. He and I are cooperating on a joint investigation. It seems that all our three governments have a common interest in Jean Luc Lafarge. We suggest you join forces with us."

Maria glanced around hurriedly. Paul was out of sight and the other customers were out of earshot.

"I have absolutely no idea what you are talking about," she hissed.

"You are a member of the Rosebud team. If you wish, I can give you your USMC serial number. Please, let's not waste valuable time on denials."

She was still trying to absorb the fact that her operation and her cover had been blown wide open when he continued, speaking carefully as he gazed up at the smoldering heights of Etna.

"Anyway, as far as we can tell, Lafarge has not penetrated Rosebud, if you're worried about that. It would seem that Hans Blucher and James Sandler were killed for other reasons. But even so, we believe the net result is that you are temporarily out of contact with Langley. If we join forces, you would have our resources at your disposal, and we can put you back in contact with Rosebud through alternative channels."

"I still don't know what..." Maria began.

"Our researches are complementary," the priest interrupted. "My Israeli colleague has been tracking Jean Luc Lafarge's physical program—his terror and propaganda campaign. I have been attacking the issue from a financial perspective—illegal sources and uses of funds. But we have no one on the inside. If we work together, we can assemble the three pieces of the puzzle."

"Are you sure that's lemonade, Father—or is it something stronger?"

"I very much regret to inform you that a friend of yours named Bernardo has also been killed, if you didn't know that already."

"*What?*" Maria jumped again.

"It was last night, in Milan. Yet another tragic 'accident'."

The priest rose slowly to his feet and fumbled for a few euros to leave on the table.

"Let me leave before your watchdog returns. I shall be here every day, at this time in the mornings and at five in the afternoons."

He nodded and walked slowly across the square, looking up automatically, as everyone does, at the towering slopes of Mount Etna.

Garston Danbury III—he had survived his school years in spite of that name—savored his last mouthful of the splendid Bordeaux.

"That's really good, Pierre," he said appreciatively, "Very good indeed."

"Another bottle, Garstie?" his dinner companion responded, "If it's to your taste? Or there's another year you might enjoy even more."

"I'd love to, but I really can't. They're getting super-picky about personal expenses back in Foggy Bottom."

"Nonsense, I'll buy it. The French Foreign Ministry is always happy to entertain the Department of State."

He flicked his fingers imperiously to the waiter, and ordered a third bottle. In any case, he thought, Jean Luc Lafarge never quibbled about expenses.

"So what's new at State?" Pierre Truffaud asked, as they watched the new bottle being ceremoniously decanted.

"Oh, the usual crap. Frankly, I'd much rather be here in Paris than back there trying to follow the current line of policy—if I dignify it with the word 'policy'. A bull in a china shop is a better way of describing it, if that's not too unfair to bulls."

"Are you still letting the Pentagon run foreign policy? When's the Secretary going to push back? Cheers, incidentally, and how do you like this vintage in comparison to the other one?"

"Wow, this is superb! The Secretary does push back, you know, he really does, but with the VP squarely against us and the CIA spoon feeding the White House whatever they want to hear, and Miss Smarty-Pants trying to prove she's cleverer than the rest of us, he's got an uphill battle."

"Anything new coming up?"

Garston sighed. "Just the same old same old. At least we haven't invaded Korea yet—as far as I know, because the State Department would be the last to hear. Our side is hanging in, but the talks, of course, are going nowhere fast. The Secretary's flying over next week to try to get something going."

"Pity you chaps can't achieve a breakthrough—diplomacy triumphs over saber rattling, that sort of thing. A big one for Foggy Bottom, take the Pentagon down peg or two."

"It's not going to happen, Pierre, I'm afraid, not on the current watch. The White House is adamant that they won't agree to anything which doesn't include verifiable disarmament, so the Secretary's hands are tied. Plus, they're insisting on a complete cessation of arms exports. So what can we do?"

"You can't get it into the UN, where we could help?"

"Once again, I'm afraid, Pierre, the Oval Office and everyone within a hundred feet of it is adamant."

Garston let his frustration show. After all, Pierre was a good friend.

"No deals that let them off the hook; no deals that let them keep their weapons programs."

Pierre had made sure the American drank most of the wine, but even he was beginning to feel the effect.

"It's such a pity Saddam never announced he'd got a nuke," he found himself saying. "He'd have saved himself and the world would be a lot safer."

"True, and Israel would have had to make concessions—the ones that really count; giving up all the settlements, settling for the Green Line, that sort of thing. Damn, this stuff is good!"

"Saddam was such an idiot. He kept insisting he didn't have weapons of mass destruction—he should have announced he did. Then the White House would have had to back off. We tried, you know, but he wouldn't see reason. He kept insisting that the US wouldn't take the risk, but he didn't realize he was dealing with a close-minded bigot out to avenge his father…."

"Ain't that the truth! You know, I must admit that it still amazes me, after all this time, that no WMDs were found, at least in significant numbers."

"Well, let's just say that some of us made sure of it," Pierre said obliquely. "What couldn't be found never existed, right?"

This might be too much, Pierre realized. Franco-Iraqi cooperation on nuclear efforts dated back to the 1970s, when Chirac and Saddam had cooperated on the Tammuz power station, embarrassingly bombed by Israel in September, 1980. Pierre switched tracks abruptly to the main purpose of the evening.

"Listen, Garstie, there are a few of us who really want to help. Have you met Francois Diderot?"

"Yes I have, at some conference last year, and I like the line he's been taking recently: the Doctrot Didetrine. The Diderot Doctrine, I mean."

Pierre leaned forward conspiratorially.

"It would be helpful to us, and by 'us' I mean all the people who are trying to hold the world together in the face of your shoot-first administration, if we had some idea of what was coming down the pike from the Oval Office. We could give things a shove in the right direction."

"What sort of things?"

"Well, take Korea for example. We could help sort that out before your VP starts World War III."

"As I said, we can push, but if the President won't listen…."

"If matters were taken out of his hands—I'm speaking hypothetically—he'd be forced to listen. I just hate to see you chaps taking all this criticism."

"Over Korea?"

"Korea is just one example, Garstie. I see Korea as a global issue, and it would be nice to see a global solution."

"It would certainly take the wind out of the unilateralists' sails."

"Exactly. So, if we knew what the Secretary's position was before his trip, we might be able to help. We both have the same objective—to stop war and foster peace. We're both on the same side."

"Well, if you put it that way...."

"I do, Garstie, I do put it that way. *Someone* has to do the right thing, even if your government won't. It's a basic service to humanity."

"Well, I've seen a copy of the position paper...."

"That would be helpful. Someone's got to rebuild the Atlantic alliance. Here, let's finish the bottle."

CHAPTER 14

There's no such thing as an honest reporter.

—Jean Luc Lafarge

"I think we should go with the legal stage, Jean Luc," said Francois Diderot. "Everything is ready. The American administration still seems to think it can ignore us. We need to apply just a little more pressure before the Korean meetings."

The meetings of Jean Luc's group had become more open as their successes had grown and the men around the table began to believe that success was possible in spite of the odds. One of the most pleasing results of the campaign had been the rash of copy-cat grenade attacks across the globe. They were now an almost daily event in Israel, and had been carried out successfully in six eastern European countries whose governments were still in the pro-American camp.

It was a pity that groups like the IRA, ETA, and the Red Brigades had reemerged since the Spanish election results, but they had all taken on an anti-US and anti-Israel flavor. The most recent ETA bombings in Toledo in Spain, for example, had been a 'protest against the illegal occupation of Palestine'.

"I suggest we implement the Washington March for Peace and the Alien Tort initiatives, and let the Harvard professor get cracking," Diderot continued. "They're all set up, the court case filings have all been done, the judge and the professor have been paid, and we have nothing to lose if the initiatives don't work. We can do all three at once, bang, bang, bang!"

"Has the interviewer been paid? You didn't mention him."

"No, he refused. He gets compensated on the basis of his ratings and he said he'd get paid that way."

Jean Luc frowned. "Send the money anyway, Francois. We need a hold on him."

"He's too smart for that. In any case, the peacenik took the money."

"Oh, very well, Francois, I don't see why not. Let's proceed, if everyone else agrees?"

Everyone else agreed. The US President's balls were exactly where they wanted them and Jean Luc was on a roll. Pierre Truffaud's success at suborning a senior member of the Department of State also contributed to their growing confidence.

Jean Luc did not like the idea that the American TV interviewer had refused payment, but there was a solution. Paul would have to make another trip. In fact, that might make it work out even better.

His mind shifted to Maria, as it always did, even at the most unlikely moments. If only she knew! If only she understood what he was doing! Why couldn't he bring himself to trust her? She was loving and loyal. Her importance to him was eclipsing even the extraordinary power that this enterprise was bringing him. She hadn't gone after him when they first met—quite the contrary—he had gone after her. She showed no signs of being unfaithful, and he knew from her cell phone intercepts that she was telling her friend Be-Be she wanted to get pregnant.

A computer expert had taken a copy of her laptop hard drive, and had found nothing unusual or questionable. He had passed it on to a second expert just to be on the safe side; Jean Luc was certain he'd find nothing. Why not trust her with this ultimate revelation? Why shouldn't she be sitting here with the others? There was no question of her deep hostility to all things American. Her flair for marketing could be extremely useful in some of the PR initiatives.

It must all be some strange defense mechanism, he thought, that since he felt completely in her power at least he could hold back this last secret, or some such psychological rubbish.

* * *

"Listen, Jerry," said the TV talk show host into his phone, "I'm not going to put you on my show just to talk about a pro-peace 'c'est possible' rally. I thought you guys were going to wait for 9/11? Wasn't that the whole point? Frankly, there are a lot of people who find the whole idea offensive, and I'd have to question you on that. The sponsors want the Sunday morning shows to have at least the appearance of political balance."

"That's exactly the point of this preliminary march, Kevin, you know that," replied the rally organizer urgently. "We're losing a lot of public support to that 'c'est sick' counterattack on talk radio. We need the exposure to emphasize that 9/11 was brought about by US policies, not by terrorists."

"Yes, I understand that, but I need something fresh. I can't give you fifteen minutes just to rehash old arguments. People will tune out."

"Well, Kevin, what would it take?"

The TV interviewer considered.

"I don't know…if the police attacked your rally, for example, then we could focus on that and skirt the 9/11 issue itself. The *police* would be the story, and you could get your pitch in."

"Yeah, well, how do we get that to happen?"

"I don't know, Jerry. I report the news, not create it."

"What if we attacked a policeman, and they retaliated?"

"That would be good. If you could get someone to claim they started it, then we could go with excessive use of force. You'll have to provoke them, though, in some way the cameras won't pick up. Maybe spray one of them with mace, or something."

"Okay, on that basis you'll put me on your show?"

"Yes, provided you give me an exclusive."

"Next Sunday?"

"Yeah, okay—I don't have much good stuff for it—all I've got so far is the Attorney General, and he's *booorrring!* Wait, actually, have the fight occur on Saturday afternoon to catch the evening news cycle, and then we'll do the interview on Sunday morning while it's still hot."

In his excitement, the interviewer was crouched over his phone as the idea took shape in his mind.

"I'll have the AG there and we can do a whole brutality routine: 'peaceful protest against international brutality encounters domestic brutality'. Like a paradigm for all that's wrong with current American policies—don't you say that, I'll say that, it's a good line. I'll get the *New York World Journal* to put a photograph of a protester being beaten up on their front page as well. Make sure your guys get some video of the police attacking the demonstrators and we'll play it to the AG. We'll catch him off guard. That will make a great show!"

"Okay, it's a deal."

"Er, listen Jerry, one thing. I do not support or condone violence against the police, okay? I'm talking hypothetically, here, not reality. I am not encouraging you. In fact, if I had any foreknowledge I'd report it immediately. There is no conspiracy."

"I read you, Kevin."

"Oh, and one thing more, Jerry."

"What?"

"If you came to the interview with a black eye, or something, it would add drama."

"How the *hell* did this slip under the radar screen? And what the *hell* can we do to stop it?"

The President held up a copy of the *New York World Journal* with the headlines '$ Trillion Case Against the US' and the subhead 'Government sponsored wrongful death asserted'.

"Mr. President..." the Attorney General began, but the Chief of Staff interrupted him.

"I'm not interested in your opinion. Frankly, after that *cluster fuck* of an interview yesterday morning, I assume your sole reason for attending this meeting is to tender your resignation."

The Attorney General had gone to the interview prepared to attack the increasingly unpopular 'c'est possible' movement, only to encounter an antagonistic barrage of questions about Saturday's march. The AG had been fully briefed for hostile questioning, but the unannounced inclusion of a beaten protestor had thrown him completely off his stride.

"Is this the face of American justice, Mr. Attorney General?" the interviewer had demanded. "Is this the image you wish to project around the world?"

"No, of course not, I...."

"If this kind of brutality happens in broad daylight on the streets of Washington, what happens in the dark of night behind the razor fences of Guantanamo?"

"That's got nothing to do with...."

"Is that an admission that it *does* happen? Is this why you won't let anyone in? After everything that's happened in Iraq?"

"I...."

"In the name of justice, the department that you are ironically supposed to head, I challenge you to prove that. Either let me and my crew into Guantanamo with unfettered access, or we'll draw the obvious conclusion."

The camera held the interviewer's face tightly and the director was ready and waiting to cut off the AG's microphone so that his response about International Red Cross inspections was inaudible to the audience.

"We'll be right back after these messages."

That had been more than enough to give the Attorney General a very bad Sunday, and now this *New York World Journal* article was threatening to make Monday even worse.

"Whoa," said the President. "Let's all try to stay calm. I'd like to hear from the Solicitor General."

The Solicitor General, the number two person in the Department of Justice, with responsibility for preparing and arguing all government cases, was widely known and respected for his legal skills and his objectivity.

"Sir, a US District Court judge sitting in Massachusetts found that she had subject matter jurisdiction in the case of Al Zabar et al., v. Rayan et al., under the Alien Tort Claims Act of 1793. As you may know, sir, that's an old statute which has recently been interpreted to permit overseas human rights violations to be tried in US courts."

"How the *fuck* can we oppose that International Criminal Court with that on our books for two hundred years?" asked the Chief of Staff.

He was loyal to the President, but he had just about decided, with his wife's support, to resign in protest to the President's policies before the popularity of the administration declined any further. He had his future to think about. A resignation would not only preserve his reputation in the history books, but boost the sales of his forthcoming autobiography.

After all, 'A Trust Betrayed,' or some such, was a damned better title than 'Inside a White House Under Siege'. He just had to make sure he had legitimate quotes, like 'I tried to change our position on the ICC, but no one close to the President would listen.'

"That's a good question," the SG replied. "Anyway, sir, the judge cited two precedents, Filártiga v. Peña-Irala in 1980, which had to do with state torture in South America, and Kadic v. Karadzic in 1993, which had to do with war crimes in Serbia.

"In this new case, Ms. Al Zabar, a citizen of the sovereign state of Central East Africa, has alleged that she and her son were given food by a US government employee named Rayan, and that she fell sick and her son died."

"You can't sue the US government for...."

"Excuse me for interrupting. The law is very hazy on all this. What the judge has done is ruled that she will *hear* the case, that's all. The allegations are wrongful death and violation of her human rights. These are civil charges."

He paused for breath. "We can appeal on jurisdiction, we can appeal whether this is a qualified class action, we can appeal on private versus public actions, we can appeal on Ms. Zabar's standing, and we can appeal on the facts. We can, if we choose, jump it straight up to the Supreme Court. The trillion dollars is simply a number her lawyer came up with, just pulled out of the air."

"But, in the meantime, it puts the whole thing back on the front pages, and us on the defensive," said the President. "And as of yesterday, Guantanamo is back on the front pages as well."

"Jesus, anyone would think the French are masterminding this entire thing," muttered the Vice President.

"Right, with that guy Diderot with his so-called doctrine and his UN architecture for peace," the President grunted. "Anything else, Mr. Solicitor General?"

"Well, sir, there may be trouble brewing in Harvard."

Last Sunday's show had been a smash hit. This Sunday's, if handled correctly, could be even better. The interviewer was at the top of his form; 'in the zone' as great athletes described the way they felt during their best performances. He knew he was being watched by many members of Congress as well as the administration, and he would also be attracting a good audience in Europe.

"Kevin," his guest was saying, "I think too much attention is being paid to the actions of the United States which are illegal under the UN Charter, particularly Article 2, Sections 2 and 3, and we should instead...."

"Excuse me, Professor; our audience may not be familiar with the exact wording."

Professor Thomas Grant of Harvard looked just a tad exasperated, as if the audience should have read up on various aspects of international law before watching the interview.

"Oh, really? Then let me quote, if I may: 'All Members shall settle their international disputes by *peaceful* means in such a manner that international peace and security, and justice, are not endangered. That's Section 2, and Section 3 is: 'All Members shall refrain in their international relations from the *threat or use of force* against the territorial integrity or political independence of any state, or in any other manner inconsistent with the Purposes of the United Nations.'"

"I don't see any exceptions or provisos on that," the interviewer commented.

"No, it's absolute. The whole idea of so-called preemption is, of course, a threat of force and therefore completely illegal. You will notice that there is no primacy, or indeed mention, of a right of self-defense, as the United States has been claiming. There is no basis for preemption. None. But that's not the point, which is…."

"Excuse me, Professor, for interrupting again, but I had always thought the UN charter allowed you to defend yourself if you were invaded?"

"Absolutely not," said the professor categorically, "That's a common and basic misunderstanding. The use of force is permitted, but only on a multilateral basis. I quote the preamble which states that the purpose of the UN is: 'To ensure, by the acceptance of principles and the institution of methods, that armed force shall *not* be used, *save in the common interest*'.

"Thus the very notion that the United States can attack other countries in the so-called 'war on terror' is fallacious. Armed force can be used only in the *common interest*, as defined by the United Nations."

"But surely, and I don't want to appear argumentative, the whole point of NATO…."

"There we go again!"

The professor allowed his annoyance to show through. Kevin was delighted, because the professor's attitude was shielding the interview from accusations of bias.

"I just wish people bothered to read the words that we're supposed to be committed to," he continued. "In the case of NATO, Article 1 compels the members to 'refrain in their international relations from the *threat or use of force* in any manner inconsistent with the purposes of the United Nations.'

"NATO Article 5, the so-called right of self-defense, explicitly references Article 51 of the UN Charter as its justification, and when we look at that, *if we bother to look at that,* 51 states: 'Measures taken by Members in the exercise of this right of self-defense shall be *immediately* reported to the Security Council and shall not in any way affect the *authority and responsibility* of the Security Council under the present Charter to take at any time such action as it deems necessary in order to maintain or restore international peace and security.'"

He sat back as if the whole thing was self-explanatory to anyone with an ounce of intelligence.

"Which means, Professor?"

"That any military action taken by the United States is subject to the authority of the United Nations. It really cannot be simpler."

"Geez, perhaps I should read the Charter, Professor. I apologize for interrupting."

"More to the point, Kevin, perhaps the President of the United States should read it. It's a well-established principle that ignorance of the law is no defense, which gets me back to the point I'm trying to make."

"Which is, Professor?"

"People tend to think of the United States constitution as our defining legal document, which of course does speak of a common defense. But the constitution is based on the Declaration of Independence. You can only have a constitution if you're independent, and you can't have a constitution which is at variance with the underlying principals on which your independence is based."

"I see."

"Let me quote again: 'When in the course of human events it becomes necessary for one people to dissolve the political bands which have connected them with another and to assume among the powers of the earth, the separate and equal station to which the Laws of Nature and of Nature's God entitle them, a decent respect to the opinions of mankind requires that they should declare the causes which impel them to the separation.'"

"Yes, we all studied that in school." The guy would soon be losing the audience if he kept up this legal crap much longer.

"Studying and comprehending are, unfortunately, two different things," replied the professor tartly. "Notice that the preamble does not assert a unique status for the US. It asserts the right of a separate and equal status *among the powers of the earth*. That is an associative or normative statement, not an absolute statement."

"Associative?" He had better keep breaking up the flow.

"The US is independent in the context of other independent nations, *not* in and of itself. Note also that the founding fathers recognize the absolute need for 'a decent respect to the opinions of mankind.'"

"In other words?"

"In other words, the Declaration of Independent places us in a *class* of nations, with *class* rights, and *only* in the context of the opinions of mankind. Simply put, the constitution forbids us to take action without global approval."

"So, the invasion of Iraq, for example, was not only illegal under the rules of the UN, but unconstitutional under our own laws?"

"Exactly. Many think Congress can declare war, as the constitution says, and indeed it can; but only *after* such action has been approved by the Security Council."

"I must admit I didn't realize that, Professor. I've learned something today!"

"I only wish the White House would learn also."

The 'priest' came to the café every day. Maria's problem was how to contact him with Paul sitting beside her. She considered finding out which church he was 'attached' to—surely his cover extended that far—and going to make confession, but that would be completely out of character. If she sent Paul off on an errand, he might be suspicious. She considered simply disappearing and returning to the States, but that would not be easy from the island of Sicily. She had two pieces of intelligence, one hard and one soft: the tape of Jean Luc's conversation with the President; and the fact that Michel, presumably on behalf of Jean Luc, had had recent business dealings with North Korea.

She had no reliable means of contacting the Agency without going to the US Consular Agency in Palermo, but that was just a branch of the consulate in Naples, which was subordinate to Rome, and God knows how much insecure bureaucratic fussing around it would take to actually get her into contact with Langley.

In the meantime, Father Uzi and Orange Overalls seemed to know all about her, not only about Rosebud, but even about her relationship with Bernardo, who was not even connected to her mission. She felt useless and trapped.

Her current working assumption was that Lafarge was systematically killing every man she spoke to. Her first assumption had been that Hans and Sandler had been killed because of her mission, to keep her isolated, but if he had also killed Bernardo (as she assumed) his motive was simple jealousy. Perhaps he intended to kill every man she had ever slept with. That, she grinned to herself, would keep Paul busy for quite some time. The only person in the whole wide world who knew about Bernardo was Be-Be, which meant that someone knew what Be-Be knew, presumably from the intercepts on her cell phone.

And there she was, stuck in a gilded cage, without a lifeline and with no real confidence that Jean Luc would reveal anything more. The whole pillow talk strategy was a crock. And that brought her full circle back to Father Uzi, who was sitting in his usual chair at the table next to theirs, boring Paul with the geological obscurities of Mount Etna.

Paul had enormous operational patience. He was prepared to lie on a damp jungle floor for two days being bitten by God-alone-knew-what insects, waiting to spring an ambush, or hold meaningless conversations with endless idiotic Palestinian teenagers before deciding which one was best suited to be a decoy. But guarding Maria, however pleasant, didn't seem like an operation and he was itching for action. He was bored to tears.

"The eruption of 1669, you say, Father?" said Paul, suppressing a yawn. "Perhaps I'll run over to the bookstore and pick up a copy."

He jumped up and started across the square. Anything to get away from Father Uzi's polite, pleasant, well-meaning, and infinitely boring monolog!

"Have you reached a conclusion, Miss Menendez?" the 'priest' asked as soon as Paul had gone. "Can you give me anything?"

Shit! She had to make a decision right now.

"*You* give *me* something first."

"Okay. Paul Rennard is the grenade bomber who conducted those attacks in Israel. He also poisoned US famine supplies in Africa to create the genetic food scare. Now you give me something."

She crossed a bridge. "Michel Leclerc went to China to meet some North Koreans two weeks ago and made a deal—I don't know what—but he expects a dramatic announcement soon. Your turn."

"Lafarge had a banking clerk named Jeannette Bois killed two years ago, presumably because she discovered illegal money transfers. Do you know anything about it?"

"Lafarge used that name less than a week ago with the French President as if it was a threat or a basis for blackmail."

"Shit! The *President?* Are you sure? I shouldn't say this, of course, but I always think the Hellenistic myths are much more interesting than the Christian ones, Vulcan's smithy, for example. Ah, you're back. Did you find it, Paul?"

"Yes, thank you, Father. And now, Maria, I think we'd better get going. There're guests for lunch."

* * *

Jean Luc flew to Paris to have lunch with the President. She had sent him a motorcade of three cars, preceded and followed by police cars and motorcycle outriders. It was a service that even his billions could not buy. How very pleasant it was to see the traffic halted as they swept through the Place D'Etoile.

"The money has been transferred, Charlotte, following Michel's successful meeting. He's agreed to the deal."

"May I ask what it is?"

Jean Luc permitted himself to luxuriate in the moment. The President of the Republic of France was asking him if she could be told what France's foreign policy was.

"Certainly, Charlotte. Kim gets fifty million dollars in cash just for seeing you, and another fifty for agreeing to the terms, payable when they're announced on Korean TV; and he has to provide an authentic simulcast in English. Then he gets a final fifty if he doesn't renege publicly for twelve months.

"We're also paying him five million to be videotaped with you in a working session, and another five for saying in an interview that he trusts you, but he doesn't trust the US President. That's the cash component—a hundred sixty million all together."

"That's a lot of money."

"Yes, it is, but it's not an issue considering where it came from in the first place. I'm sure Saddam Hussein would approve of how we're putting his money to use. Then, in addition, Kim gets a hundred million in jet fuel for his air force and another hundred million in military equipment. That will come into Vladivostok and then through Russia, and we have to pay the Russians ten million to look the other way.

"That ten million, incidentally, also covers your flights through Russian airspace to and fro. All of that is taken care of. Finally, he gets food and civilian fuel oil worth a hundred million a year for five years. That's the piece of the tab you'll have to pick up, because that's the visible deal. However, I think you should be able to squeeze most of that out of other countries."

"What kind of military equipment, Jean Luc?"

"Advanced mine detection and destruction robots. He can use them to open up access routes across the demilitarized zone which separates North and South Korea, the DMZ, if, or probably when, he invades the south. Like the jet fuel, that's strictly illegal. That's why we're using a Russian route."

"And what's he giving in return, Jean Luc?"

"He's letting the inspectors back in, but only in principle. He's agreed they can 'find' some highly-enriched uranium that we're sending over, and confiscate it. The inspectors will be told that's all there is and they'll probably swallow the story. After all, the UN swallowed everyone else's lies, why not Kim's as well?"

Jean Luc was thoroughly enjoying himself.

"He's also agreeing in public to withdraw his army a hundred miles from the DMZ provided the Americans pull out of the south. That's unlikely, but it's the offer that counts. He's agreed—and this is the big one—to disarm provided the UN guarantees his safety against the US."

"We'd never get that through the Security Council—you know that, Jean Luc."

"He wants a NATO-type Article 5 provision—an attack on North Korea is automatically an attack on the UN."

"That will never work, and no one wants to attack North Korea, for God's sake."

"It's not meant to be practical, Charlotte. It's just meant to make the US look like they're the aggressors and the UN is the avenue for peace."

Really, the woman was a bit dense. Thank God French foreign policy was now safely in his hands.

"Kim will say that he only developed nukes to defend himself against the US, and he'll give them up if the UN guarantees his safety. Since the US has no intention to invade North Korea, they'll be hard put to explain why they oppose a UN anti-invasion safeguard. Anyway, you pull this rabbit out of the hat, the US is caught flatfooted, and we carry the momentum into the G8."

"I'm not sure," the President said, hesitatingly. "There're a lot of risks…."

"Charlotte, let me put it this way," said Jean Luc firmly, "I am presenting this to you on a plate. Jimmy Carter got a Nobel Prize for a vastly inferior deal. You will be practically guaranteed. *You* will be the person in the world's headlines; *you* will be the most prominent person at the G8. *You* will be, how shall I say it, the Margaret Thatcher of the hour."

"What about the South Koreans? Won't they be upset? Won't they be concerned that a million soldiers or a million refugees will come south?"

"Probably, but that's not your problem. The US has thirty-seven thousand troops there. Let them sweat a little. You're just advancing the cause of peace."

"Well, if it gets me into the G8 on a high note," the President said doubtfully. "Is there anything else I need to know?"

"Just a couple of cosmetic details. You have to wear flat shoes, for example, because he's so short and otherwise he won't agree to photographs. A few odds and ends like that."

CHAPTER 15

One day soon the Stars and Stripes will be hauled down and a white flag of surrender will replace it.

—Jean Luc Lafarge

The British Deputy Foreign Secretary tossed his reading glasses theatrically onto the conference table.

"Ladies and gentlemen," he said in considerable exasperation, "We must be able to agree on *something.* We can't have a G8 meeting without a joint communiqué."

The G8 was originally founded in 1975 as an informal forum to address macroeconomic issues, such as exchange rates, and includes the US, Japan, France, Russia, the UK, Germany, Italy and Canada. It operates at two levels. There are quarterly meetings of finance ministers and central bankers, who really do discuss economic and monetary issues, and there is an annual summit of heads of state, who discuss whatever they wish.

The G8 (and its predecessor, the G7) is often described as a meeting of the leaders of the world's leading economies, and that is true for the US, Germany, and Japan, although the inclusion of Russia, which has a GDP smaller than Portugal's, emphasizes the essentially political nature of the group. Like all exclusive clubs, everyone wants to join, and so the IMF and the European Commission participate and others circulate on the fringes. This gives the G8 a decidedly Euro-centric nature, and the opportunity for photo-ops in which the US President is seen surrounded by many European equals, and the Japanese premier, always seems to be wondering exactly what he is doing at this European party.

Like all international summits, the result is negotiated and decided *before* the meeting takes place, lest the world form the opinion that the group is not in total agreement about everything, or, God forbid, that it is a waste of time and taxpayers' money.

"Let me run through the agenda one more time and see what we've got agreement on," said the senior British official, replacing his glasses and consulting his notes. "Let me see. Exchange rate stability: Yes, but no suggestion that the euro, the yen, or the dollar, are either too weak or too strong. We support free currency markets, but with appropriate intervention.

"The Middle East: No. We can't agree that we should condemn violence on both sides. African hunger and AIDS relief: Yes. Reorganization of the IMF: Yes, but only as a non-binding study group, and with no suggestion that nations currently in default should actually have to pay their loans back.

"Genetic foods: No agreement so it's out. Land mines: No. Intellectual property: No. War on terror: No. Global warming: Of course not. Nuclear proliferation: Yes, provided individual violators are not mentioned by name and there's no implication of displeasure with Korea. That's about it.... Oh, and a plan for a global disaster relief organization, but we can't agree that the International Red Cross should run it."

He repeated his gesture with his glasses.

"We've got a statement that says economic stability is good; nuclear arms proliferation, AIDS and earthquakes are bad; and the IMF needs to be studied. That, if I may say so and strictly off the record, is pretty bloody pathetic."

"If our American colleagues would just..." began Pierre Truffaud, but the Englishman cut him off.

"Please, Pierre, let's not get into that again. Let's make the best of a bad lot. Let's see if we can put a little more emphasis on disaster relief, for example. That at least has the advantage of being a fresh subject."

Jean Luc returned from his meeting with the French President in high spirits. He had advised prime ministers and presidents on many occasions, but he had never actually *told* one what to do. He thought of the great powers behind the throne in history—Richelieu in France, Bismarck in Germany, even Eleanor Roosevelt; and the men who had changed the course of history through the sheer power of their personalities, like Churchill and Napoleon. Now he, too, knew how they must have felt, and it was a stupendous feeling. He could not wait to share his victory with Maria. He could not savor his triumph fully if he could not share it with her.

"How was your meeting, Jean Luc?"

She was reclining on their bed, surrounded by Sassal sales reports and dictating into her little machine, when he burst into the room.

"It was *wonderful*," he crowed. "It was *spectacular!* She swallowed every word I had to say. It's working. It's actually damned well working!"

He danced a few inexpert steps and twirled an imaginary cane.

Maria laughed. "I'm pleased that you're pleased, about whatever it is, Jean Luc."

"Let's have some champagne! Then the most powerful man in France, no, in Europe, will make love to you. I am Napoleon, and you are my Josephine, my empress!"

"Why, have you conquered all Europe?"

"No, much more. I've conquered America. Your nemesis is about to find it has feet of clay, Josephine!"

"Are you serious?"

"Never more so!"

He continued to dance.

"I have conquered America, by way of Korea, and a few other stations along the way. One day soon the Stars and Stripes will be hauled down and a white flag of surrender will replace it."

"You conquered America? What did you do, buy General Electric or Microsoft, or both?"

"No, I bought North Korea, and that will get me the G8, and that in turn will get me the UN."

She laughed gaily again. "Jean Luc, you're not making any sense."

He threw himself onto the bed beside her. "Are you a CIA spy?"

"Jean Luc, how much champagne did you drink on the plane?"

"Are you a spy? Do you have anything to hide?"

He playfully lifted her nightgown.

"No, I don't think you are. CIA spies always have the stars and stripes tattooed over their hearts."

"Please, Jean Luc, I really don't understand anything you're trying to tell me."

"Then let me explain."

And somewhere in the mess of papers on the bed, or in the sheets, or perhaps by his elbow as he propped himself comfortably to explain, someplace she couldn't see and didn't dare look, the reels of her little recorder were still turning.

The President stood before a lectern. The Korean leader stood to her right, speaking interminably in Korean. She looked at him with a fixed smile. She was not wearing headphones for a simultaneous translation because that might spoil her hair, which had enough spray on it to secure the foundations of the Eiffel Tower. Beyond him she could see an interpreter, who was nodding to indicate that the Korean was sticking to the agreed text. Whenever she thought her smile might appear to be getting too fixed, she glanced down to his feet. He was standing on a footrest which increased his height by six inches.

Finally it was her turn to speak.

"I am pleased to announce that the leader of the Democratic People's Republic of Korea has agreed to re-admit the United Nations' weapons inspectors," said the French President. "In these circumstances, we shall be bringing in immediate supplies of fuel oil and humanitarian aid, and we will be urging the UN to take a broader responsibility for re-opening global relationships with Korea. In the coming weeks, the exact terms of the inspection regime will be agreed. The relief effort will commence immediately, under UN supervision."

Her opening remarks had been delivered deadpan. Now she paused for effect and glanced around the room. It created the impression that she was leaving her prepared remarks to speak unscripted from her heart.

"Many have said that full engagement would only be possible if the nuclear issue was solved. *It has been solved!* Creative diplomacy is always superior to destructive threats and the use of force! Many have said that Korea's economy has been ruined by its huge military budget, which accounts for more than a third of the GDP."

She permitted her voice to become more strident, as Margaret Thatcher used to do. It was unattractive, but it conveyed steely conviction.

"This imbalance can also be solved at the stroke of a pen if and when the prevailing mood of international threats against the People's Republic is replaced by one of openness and respect for Korea's sovereignty and traditions.

Korea should not be forced to spend its hard-earned money defending against aggression!"

Now it was time for a moment of intimacy, to bring the listener into the conference room and share her experience.

"I have had the pleasure of working on these difficult issues with Kim Chong-Il personally during the past few days in Pyongyang. I have come to know him as a man of peace and honor. I call upon the global community to accept the hand of friendship he is offering."

The Secretary of State was pole-axed. He had spent an exhausting six days shuttling between Moscow, Tokyo, Seoul, and Beijing trying to keep the six-party talks going in the face of North Korean belligerence and intransigence. His partners, as usual, had shrugged off his calls for unity and a firm hand with diplomatic pabulum. He saw the news announcement in Moscow, following a series of meetings after which the Russians had described the American position as 'too inflexible'.

Now France had secretly walked into the middle of the North Korean situation and cut a deal. The fact that North Korea had repeatedly broken every single promise it had ever made seemed irrelevant. The fact it was the world's bargain basement for WMDs seemed unimportant.

France had 'solved' the problem with which the United States had struggled for a decade, ever since the disastrous Jimmy Carter 'Framework' deal in 1994. The cumbersome apparatus of six-party talks had been bypassed and now lay on the trash heap of history. The lesson being conveyed to the world was clear: even when the US tried a multilateral approach, it got all screwed up. Only a pragmatic European approach, or specifically a French approach, offered a way forward.

How could she *do* this, the Secretary wondered? With the G8 fast approaching, the United States was becoming more isolated than ever. The 'c'est possible' campaign, which had been losing ground as people began to have second thoughts about publicly celebrating a terrorist act involving the deaths of more than three thousand people, and governments began to wonder if it was really a good idea to stand aside while political violence was praised, had gotten a second wind after the march in Washington.

Korea had been the only undisputed multilateral effort in which the United States had been engaged, the only all-diplomacy no-force initiative to which he could point. Now she had outmaneuvered the whole damn thing. He wondered if the Russians and the Chinese had been tipped off, and he didn't like the probable answer.

The Israeli and the Syrian strolled along the promenade in Beirut a second time. This was the first high level contact between the two governments since the global tide of disapproval had swept across Israel for its attack on Syria. On the occasion of that meeting, the Mediterranean had had a sullen look, and the chill wind seemed like a commentary on the discussion, but today the sea was a classic blue, the sun was shining brightly, and the damage of decades of civil war seemed less prominent.

"Certain additional facts have now come into our possession, and I wish to share them with you."

"So? What are you going to threaten us with now?"

The Syrian was coldly angry. His fury arose not so much from the action itself, which he secretly thought had been quite reasonable, but from the way it had emphasized Syria's weakness, its inability to defend itself.

"First," the Israeli said, "We now know that Syria itself, and groups hosted by Syria, had nothing to do with the ricin attacks. The sites we destroyed did contain our enemies, but not the particular ones we were looking for. We wish to make reparations, some public, and some private."

"What kinds of reparations?" the Syrian demanded bluntly, careful not to show his surprise at this admission.

"We will state publicly that we regret the incident, and we will provide a victims' fund of five million US dollars. We will not admit culpability, merely regret, and we will not bring charges against those involved. You may issue a new statement condemning us, you may threaten retaliation, but you will also state publicly that you do not wish the ICC process to go forward. You may give as your reason that you fear we will retaliate if the ICC continues. That's on the top."

"That's not much. You put yourselves in a stupid position, and now you're asking us to let you off the hook for five million dollars. That's almost insulting! What's underneath?"

"Wait—we will also announce a Fresh Start Day—you remember the idea of opening all the checkpoints to the Palestinians so they can move around freely? The idea is that we will suspend our controls, and keep them suspended provided the Palestinians respond by refraining from more suicide attacks. It's a gesture at returning to normalcy, even though we're taking a huge risk. You can claim it was all your idea, and you pushed us into it, but we'd appreciate it if you could restrain Hezbollah."

"None of that helps Syria. I repeat, what else are you proposing to do for us?"

"We will not publish itemized details of illegal oil shipments of Iraqi oil through Syria," said the Israeli. "And we will destroy the information identifying the Syrian recipients of cash payments from the former regime."

"That's useful, I agree, but a lot of it is deniable, and it's fast becoming ancient history." Police states are not easily embarrassed. "The whole invasion of Iraq is so discredited that it won't cause much of a stir. I remain unimpressed."

"It will save you the difficulty of explaining why you were accepting large cash and oil payments while sitting on the Security Council. Finally, we will also give you the names of certain individuals who have concluded, shall I say, that your President is not the right leader for Syria."

The Syrian stopped dead in his tracks.

"Are you serious?"

"We'd rather deal with the devil we know, to use the old phrase," replied the Israeli. "Obviously this offer is time-sensitive, since you will want to take action before those individuals do. In fact, while you still can. Perhaps you'd like to make a phone call?"

Without waiting for a response, the former prime minister strolled off, while his Syrian contact pulled out his cell phone. A Syrian bodyguard came up carrying a portable CD player and started breaking Lebanese noise pollution regulations—a significant challenge in its own right. The Israeli wondered if anyone would be able to intercept the call. God knows, the Mossad had an army of electronic specialists trying to do just that! The phone call lasted about ten minutes.

"Do you have the list of names?"

The Israeli pulled out several folded sheets of paper.

"These are the names and some e-mails between the conspirators as evidence, which will give your interrogators a place to start. The conspirators were foolish enough to use the Internet. Deal?"

"Deal."

The Israeli handed over the sheaf of papers.

"There's one other thing.... I need your help. I need access to certain recent banking transactions through Syrian banks. Not the old UN oil rip-offs, but new ones."

The Syrian stared at him in astonishment. "You actually have the chutzpah to ask for my help?"

"I do. This may be an issue of survival for us, and it will not damage Syria in any way. If you do this we will owe you one."

"Why should I worry about Israeli survival? Is there an 'or else'?"

"No, not in this case. No threats—I just need your help. Will you do it?"

The Syrian thought. He already had the list of the names of the men plotting to overthrow his President, so this request for intelligence was not part of that deal. Perhaps it was the underlying reason for Israel offering reparations in the first place. If so, it must be critically important. What banking transactions could be of such urgent interest to Israel?

"Why did you admit you were wrong about the ricin attacks?" he asked finally.

"It sounds ridiculous, but you have to be able to trust us."

"*Trust* you?"

"Well, I said it sounded ridiculous."

"There's no harm to Syria in this banking intelligence?"

"None at all."

The Syrian made up his mind. "Very well. As you said, you owe us one."

"The details of the transactions we need are on the last sheet. I appreciate your help."

The Israeli nodded and strolled away. The Syrian studied the sheets and then hurried off. He had a lot to arrange.

Paul was glad to be away from the mind-numbing boredom of Sicily, where his biggest problems were balky scuba valves and trying to avoid staring at Maria's figure too obviously. It was a pity that Jean Luc had chosen America as his target, because Paul liked America. If the truth were known, he would have emigrated if he hadn't gotten a job at Genitaire and so met Jean Luc. Still, mercenaries do not question their employer's causes and therefore Paul was here in a parking lot in rural Virginia, waiting for his victim.

The talk radio pundit emerged from the back of the decrepit building which housed the radio station and crossed the lot slowly, avoiding one of the steel guy lines which supported the mast. He was bald, smoking, and substantially overweight. He paused to summon the energy necessary to pull himself into his pickup truck when Paul stepped up quietly behind him and struck him in the nape of his neck. It was a tactical error, for now Paul had to strain himself to drag his unconscious carcass to the back of the truck and heave him onto the cargo bed. For several minutes he thought he would be unable to achieve it.

He bound the man's arms lightly behind his back, using duct tape outside his clothing because he wanted to minimize the chance of bruising. He tied the man's shoelaces together, rolled him onto his back, and covered the cargo bed with a thin insulated tarpaulin. Paul figured the man was so corpulent that he would not be able to escape.

He took the pundit's cell phone. He turned the truck's radio up loudly to overcome the man's cries for help. He couldn't risk gagging him, in part because of leaving marks and in part for fear the man would suffocate.

It took two hours to drive through the early evening into Washington. Paul called a number in the suburbs of Washington every fifteen or twenty minutes, getting an answering machine every time. He stopped once to make sure the pundit was still securely bound. The man stared up at him in terror.

"Not quite yet, my friend," Paul told him. "You still have a couple of hours to live."

The Sunday morning TV political news anchor lived in a pretentious suburban villa. All the lights were out. Paul parked a little down the street and waited, continuing his periodic unanswered phone calls. He did not want to risk entering the house in case it had an alarm system that he could not disable.

Finally at ten o'clock a limousine turned into the circular driveway and the anchor emerged. Paul waited until the limo had left and then rang the doorbell, hoping the anchor would assume it was the driver with something he had left in the car. The door opened and Paul stepped forcefully into the hallway, pushing the anchor back.

"What the hell—" the anchor started, and Paul shot him three times, once in the shoulder, once in the stomach, and once through his right ear, to create the impression he had been attacked by an inexpert assailant. The anchor staggered backward across the hall and collapsed at the foot of the stairs. Paul ran quickly through the house to make sure no one was home, and then searched more carefully until he found a revolver in a bedside table.

The anchor was unconscious and breathing shallowly; he had only minutes to live. A variety of liquids was seeping from his abdomen.

Paul went back to retrieve the truck, and half-carried the radio pundit into the house, pausing to push the man's finger against the doorbell, and dumped him unceremoniously on the hall floor. Paul knelt and undid the man's bonds and assisted him to his feet.

"That's, that's—" he began, staring at the body of the anchor, and Paul stepped back and shot him with the anchor's revolver, one shot through the chest. He dropped the anchor's gun beside his body, and fitted his own into the radio pundit's hand. He checked the scene carefully—as if he were a detective—the angle of the shots and the distance between the two men. He had shot each of them from the position where their bodies lay.

He could see nothing to suggest that the radio pundit had not arrived at the anchor's house in a deranged state of mind, after repeatedly calling the house, as his cell phone would show. The pundit had begun a violent argument. The anchor had taken the precaution of arming himself before answering the door at that late hour. The pundit had started shooting wildly and the anchor had been able to kill him before succumbing to his own wounds.

Finally, Paul dusted each man's right hand with microscopic gunpowder just in case the police went to the trouble of checking if they had actually fired the weapons. He had brought four types because he couldn't be sure what type of weapon the anchor would have. Paul checked that the anchor was now indeed dead, and left, leaving the front door ajar and the truck parked outside with the driver's door open.

He left through the backyard and through two neighboring properties to the next street, emerging where he had left his car earlier that afternoon. He stopped at a phone outside a drugstore and dialed 911.

"Shots, I hear shots, Carlshorten Crescent, very bad, very bad, shots, bang, bang," he said rapidly, in what he imagined might be an Indian accent. He dropped the receiver, hearing the operator's voice asking his name and location, and drove off, removing his latex gloves. The police would be able to trace the call, check Carlshorten Crescent, and discover the bodies.

PART III

Break

CHAPTER 16

There is no distinction between business and pleasure.

—Jean Luc Lafarge

"Listen, just between us, what the hell are we going to do, Mr. President?" asked the National Security Advisor.

With the abrupt and unexpected resignation of the Chief of Staff, and the endless and disruptive battles between the Secretaries of State and Defense, the President's inner brains trust was down to two—the NSA and the Vice President.

"We're going to stay the course, that's what we're going to do," he responded. "From a domestic perspective, thank God the ANWAR/CAFÉ deal is finally bearing fruit. That's keeping the economy going as much as anything is, and, when all is said and done, people vote on the economy. Bill Clinton had that exactly right. The current numbers are respectable and the way our energy independence is gradually increasing is building confidence."

He sounded more assured than he felt.

"Jim's resignation doesn't help, I admit—the idea that rats are leaving the sinking ship, and all that—but no one outside the beltway gives a shit."

"I was talking internationally, sir."

"Oh, as far as all the rest is concerned, the global stuff, well, ultimately, I don't dare. My job is to keep the country as safe as possible, and I think we're doing that. Nobody is actually in *favor* of terrorism, and nobody believes they can project force against terrorists if and when it becomes necessary, without our help. Intel cooperation is still as solid as it ever has been, even from Germany and France. No one's going to repeat the Spanish mistake. So the anti-American bullshit is ninety percent window dressing and jealousy."

He arranged his boots in the center of his blotter.

"As far as this latest Korea fiasco is concerned, we will do whatever it takes to defend South Korea and Japan, and we will only talk about normalization if they *really* abandon their nukes. It's that simple."

"Listen, Mr. President," said the NSA urgently. "Someone has to crap on the Europeans. Someone *has* to. If we don't argue back, sooner or later we'll be judged guilty just because we didn't offer a defense. Jim's resignation just adds fuel to the fire. Please let me do it."

"I agree," said the Vice President. "She can carry the intellectual battle to them for a change. Ultimately, they're too biased against you and me to even listen to either of us at this point."

"I don't like sending other people to fight my battles."

"That's not the point. The point is to fire back at that Diderot guy and the Harvard UN guy and all the rest. You stick to what you do best; working the crowds of Middle America. Every state you visit we get a positive lift in the polls. Keep pushing the positive economic news. Stay above the fray with the Europeans. Just keep talking brotherly love and ignoring the barbs."

"Listen," said the President awkwardly. "Don't get me wrong, but if you debate this Diderot guy, can you beat him?"

"No problem, sir," responded the NSA with finality.

"Why?"

"I've read his stuff—he's incredibly intellectually arrogant. That's his weakness."

Disaster struck Marseilles in the evening hours, when people drew power to cook their dinners and to light and cool their homes. The torrid summer heat had been stretching electrical supply capacity for weeks, and finally, something somewhere simply snapped. It was one of those complicated multipoint failures in the long distance power transmission systems which just seem to happen every few years, as occurred in the northeastern United States and in Italy in 2003.

All electromechanical systems are subject to periodic failure, and transmission grids are sufficiently complex and lacking in adequate redundancy, that failure is inevitable. In addition, the route from generator to kitchen stove often runs through many jurisdictions, and electrical power distribution is subject to endless bureaucratic bickering.

During the first few hours, as much effort was devoted to mutual recriminations among the various entities involved as to actually fixing the problem, and the fix required difficult repair work to remote and inaccessible transmission lines in rugged territory, and a complex restart procedure as various generators, which had shut down automatically to protect themselves from surges, were brought back online.

After twelve hours, power had been restored to twenty-five percent of the city, but then an insufficiently planned reconnection sequence caused further damage and the entire system crashed again, sparking other scattered failures throughout Provence.

The city lacked sufficient emergency power systems and critical public services were curtailed or completely unavailable. There was also great concern that elderly people living alone might be isolated in their apartments, and the government feared a repeat of the humiliating death toll of the Paris heat wave of 2003. A serious fire broke out in a crowded neighborhood and there was insufficient pressure in the waterlines to contain it fully.

Task Force 60 of the US Navy Sixth Fleet was undertaking exercises in the Mediterranean approximately a hundred miles south of Marseille. When it became apparent it would take several days for power to be restored, the navy proposed that the *USS Ronald Reagan* should sail into Marseille and provide auxiliary power. The nuclear powered *Reagan* has four, one hundred ninety four megawatt shafts and was only four hours away. It was, in effect, a massive floating power station.

The notion of TV programs showing a huge American aircraft carrier coming to the rescue of a major French city was unacceptable to the French President, and she dismissed it out of hand. Had the carrier been named the *Lincoln*, or the *Washington*, or the *Eisenhower*, she might have considered it, but not a ship named for that cheerfully militaristic B-movie idiot.

The underlying concept was a good one; however, and the nuclear powered French aircraft carrier *Charles de Gaulle* was also fairly close by, off the Mediterranean coast of Spain. The President ordered her to turn for Marseille and declined the US offer. Never mind that the *Charles de Gaulle* was farther away than the *Reagan*, slower, less than a third of the size, and with only a quarter of the *Reagan's* power. Frenchmen would come to the aid of Frenchmen.

There was a superb live TV shot from a circling news helicopter of the *Charles de Gaulle* passing the *Reagan* at flank speed, battering through the steep Mediterranean swell. Somehow the *Reagan* seemed fat and ponderous and ungainly, and the F/A18 Hornets on its flight deck reminded everyone of its menacing mission of projecting unilateral US military power. As the two ships passed, the French admiral ordered a colorful set of signal flags to be displayed, and the following morning his jaunty message dominated the front page of every newspaper in the world. '*Merci mais non merci*'—'Thanks, but no thanks'.

"Unfortunately, the United States just doesn't get it," said Professor Diderot during an interview that evening. "If America had taken the money it spent on aircraft carriers and used it to support the Kyoto treaty and the fight against global warming, it is possible that the tragedy striking Provence would never had happened in the first place."

"Perfect!" grinned the French President, almost hugging herself in glee as she watched the program. Diderot's point was excellent. The problem was not a European power failure, but American environmental obstructionism. The G8 meeting was only a few days away, and this symbolism reinforced her case perfectly. She needed a punchy applause line for the third paragraph of her G8 speech, and she rolled the words on her tongue, '*Merci mais non merci*'.

Maria spent most of her days on the telephone and at her laptop, fine tuning the extraordinary success of the Sassal GT campaign. Jean Luc was similarly engaged in his many enterprises.

"Isn't this silly," he commented to her on one occasion. "We come down to Sicily to relax, and spend the whole time on the phone. I often think there is no distinction between business and pleasure."

She set aside her laptop.

"That's not true of every form of pleasure," she smiled. "And I can think of one of them right now."

She and Paul left the house every day for coffee in Aci Costello, or to take drives to remote beaches. Sometimes she would go out and scuba dive in the warm waters, exploring barnacle encrusted wrecks and submarine grottos formed by eons of lava flows.

Paul still drove her everywhere and seldom let her out of his sight, unless he was on a special mission for Jean Luc, when another bodyguard took over. Paul was still vigilant, suspicious of every person they encountered, but even he could not translate every villager into a would-be assassin or every tourist into a possible CIA spy.

Maria treated him in a very friendly manner although Jean Luc's proprietary shadow always fell between them. Paul had his own diversions and was perfectly satisfied with her amiable manner and the occasional glimpses offered by her skimpy attire.

They were driving along a narrow track by the sea early one morning.

"Jesus, that looks *so* inviting," said Maria. "Stop the car, would you please, Paul?"

Maria bounded down the sandy beach and splashed among the tiny breakers running up on the sand. Paul parked the car and got out. It was already hot and sweat prickled beneath his shirt. He lit a cigarette and watched Maria playing at the water's edge like a child. A bigger wave surprised her and she squealed in delight as she tried to back away from it, tripped over her own feet and sat down with a splash. Paul grinned. The lower part of her skirt was drenched. She glanced around. The beach was deserted. As Paul watched from the car, she pulled off her clothes and plunged into the breakers, splashing deliciously. He grinned wolfishly and automatically looked up and down the road, but there was no traffic.

When she emerged from the sea, she looked uncertainly at her pile of discarded clothes. There were beach towels by the dozen in the trunk, but Paul waited to see what she would decide to do. After a few moments of indecision, she evidently concluded that it was best for the sun to dry her, for she flapped her limbs energetically and then lifted her arms high in the air and rotated slowly. Paul sensed movement behind him, but his eyes remained locked on Maria.

There was a sharp pain in the back of his head and darkness fell abruptly.

Moshe knelt to give Paul an injection and then struggled to pull his limp body into the car. Maria ran up to help him. When Paul's body was finally lying on the floor in the rear of the car, Moshe climbed in behind the wheel and Maria started to get in beside him.

"You'd better get dressed," Moshe said, and she pulled on her wet clothes as they drove off.

Two miles down the road an ambulance was waiting. Two medics emerged and transferred Paul's limp body to a stretcher. One of them placed an oxygen mask over his face. The driver of a passing car drew up.

"What happened? Do you need help?"

"No, thank you for stopping, it's a mild heart attack. He'll be okay if we're quick."

Maria called the villa an hour later.

"Jean Luc? Did you send Paul somewhere?"

"No, why?"

"He left me at the café and went down to the boat to get a broken scuba valve or something. That was two hours ago."

"That's strange.... Did you try his cell? I'll send another car. In fact I'll come myself."

The little twenty-two foot outboard they used as a diving platform was missing from the docks, and was found two days later washed up on a remote beach. One of the scuba sets was missing. Paul must have decided to go diving—perhaps to check the faulty valve—and run into difficulties.

For Jean Luc it was annoying, rather than tragic. He wondered if he could somehow get access to Paul's Swiss bank account It would be a pity to let all the money he had paid Paul over the year's just lie there. He ordered the senior manservant to find a temporary driver.

In the meantime, everything else was going splendidly. Maria was awed—no lesser word would do—by the breadth and success of the conspiracy. Now she looked at Jean Luc with genuine respect in her eyes, and the balance between them was now a delightful partnership of equals. The President was completely in hand, and indeed she was contributing some useful ideas—if she had really thought of 'Thanks, but no thanks'—he had to compliment her.

Paul's latest trip to America was paying unexpected dividends, in addition to silencing the TV host. The amusing news item that a deranged conservative radio pundit had shot a TV personality in an apparent political dispute, thus reaffirming the Neanderthal characteristics of the unilateralists, had produced its own media firestorm of outrage. The term 'right wing terrorism' was gaining currency, and a German newspaper had suggested that White House, or the Israelis, or perhaps both, were bringing the practice of political assassination to domestic American politics. It was a final touch of pleasure, like pepper in vodka.

* * *

The phone rang, and the President picked it up in high spirits. She was practicing her G8 speech, polishing the cadence of her sentences and deciding the exact timing of her dramatic pauses. It would be a great speech.

The Defense Minister was on the phone.

"Ma'am, the *Charles de Gaulle* has broken down."

"Shit!"

"She cracked a propeller blade—the same thing happened when she was first commissioned—and she's scarcely moving in the water. The seas are running high and there's a storm warning. Our nearest salvage ship that's big enough is thirty-six hours away."

"Shit!"

"However, there's an American ocean going naval tug on the scene which could take her in tow."

"Never! That's completely out of the question," she snapped. "They'll have to wait for a French tug."

"Ma'am, I already told the captain that, but he says his top priority is the safety of his crew and his ship. She can maneuver without using that propeller, but things could get dangerous if the seas get worse."

"Shit, shit, *shit!*"

"We need a decision, Madame President."

"They just cracked a blade? Is that enough to stop them? Why can't they continue?"

"The blade's unbalanced, and if they continue to use it they'll get violent vibrations which will wreck the entire engine system. You have to decide, Madame President."

The image of an American naval tug towing the crippled *Charles de Gaulle* into Marseille would be even worse than the *Reagan* supplying emergency power generation, and it would rob her of her punch line.

"They'll have to wait. No American assistance of any kind. And I want nothing in the press."

"Ma'am, with respect, I disagree." He was unusual in that he had been chosen for his competence rather than his political leverage.

"They'll manage. Tell the captain it's a direct order. And remember, no distress signals and no press. This is a military secret. We'll say the ship is going through nuclear safety drills, or something, before coming into a civilian port."

Of course word would get out, but hopefully not until after the G8 summit. When it did, she'd plant a whisper that the US had refused to help, and the docile press would run with it.

Paul woke up. There was an American movie about a man who kept waking up on the same day and having to repeat it over and over again. He felt as if he were trapped in a similar movie. He had no idea how long he had been here. Sometimes it seemed as little as three or four days, and sometimes it seemed like three or four months.

He was in a cell made of clear plastic about an inch thick. The ceiling and the floor was made of the same material. The cell was fifteen feet square, and eight feet high. The whole structure was raised about a foot off the floor. Near the top of the walls was a line of circular drill holes about an inch in diameter to permit fresh air to circulate. Set into one wall was a sliding drawer arrangement which permitted food trays and other objects to be passed back and forth without anyone having to enter the cell. A squat toilet was set into the floor in one corner, and high above that was a showerhead.

The cell stood in the center of a large featureless room, like a warehouse, with white cinderblock walls and air conditioning ducts and neon lighting fixtures hanging from the roof. Four small TV cameras with microphones stood mounted on tripods about ten feet from each wall.

One of the air holes contained a pipe leading to three small anonymous tanks of gas mounted on a rack near one of the cameras. Paul assumed this was to render him helpless or unconscious if necessary.

Paul's days were well organized. In the 'morning' (the lights were never dimmed) he awoke to the strident tones of a Klaxon horn honking until he stood up. At first he had been confused by the Klaxon, but he had learned by trial and error what he was supposed to do. He went to the toilet and relieved himself and continued to stand beneath the showerhead. The shower turned itself on and he had two minutes to wash himself down. He was not provided with soap.

He remembered his first day, when it had taken him four hours, with the Klaxon blaring endlessly, before he had tried standing in various parts of his cell, and finally he had stood on the toilet and the Klaxon had stopped.

After his shower, he waved his arms and legs vigorously to dry himself, as he had once seen Maria do, and then went to stand by the wall opposite the drawer. A door opened in the warehouse wall (it always opened toward him so he couldn't see around it) and a wheeled robot mechanism rolled in. The robot would bring him his food and retrieve his empty trays. It would pass a toothbrush through the drawer and wait for him to return it.

At other times of the day it would circulate slowly around the warehouse vacuuming the floors and walls, and performing necessary household functions such as changing lighting tubes. At 'night' it would bring him a cheap air mattress that he inflated to sleep on.

Paul spent a great deal of time trying to figure out whether it really was a robot with some level of built-in intelligence, or whether it was entirely radio controlled. It always seemed cautious and almost tentative. A robot without any self esteem.

The warehouse was silent except for the occasional, shockingly loud blaring of the Klaxon, and the whisper of the air conditioning. The temperature was quite cool, too cool for Paul's taste, and he was naked. At 'night' he was given no bedclothes.

After a 'week' he had learned the routine. In addition to the tasks of everyday living and keeping his cell neat and tidy, there were permitted activities, such as exercise and calisthenics; and forbidden activities, such as talking to himself or masturbating, or sleeping during the 'day', or attempting to scratch marks on the cell walls to record the passage of time. A forbidden activity would cause the Klaxon to sound until he stopped.

He had racked his brain to figure out a way of committing suicide, but the only one which seemed feasible was starvation, and he had not tried that yet. He simply did not know if you could kill yourself by beating your head against the wall, and they would use the gas tanks in any case.

In the meantime, the robot seemed anxious to preserve him in good health. From time to time it would bring him a blood pressure cuff to put on, or a little cup to urinate into, or a thermometer, and painstakingly hold up whichever instrument it was to read the results with its TV camera eyes.

Paul knew all about interrogation techniques and had applied them in his mercenary days. He knew that the constant light and the absence of any measurement of time was a basic disorientation technique designed to weaken his resistance. Sometimes, for example, he could swear the robot brought him his mattress for the 'night' only an hour after it had collected it in the 'morning'. On the other hand, he knew he was capable of daydreaming for hours, and since the meals were always the same wholesome but unidentifiable slop, even they did not form a point of reference. He wondered what drugs were being mixed into his food. The length of his hair and nails were no help either, because the Klaxon would insist he shave completely and trim his nails with safety clippers every 'day'.

He knew eventually his interrogators would appear, and do a 'good cop, bad cop' routine. One would be sympathetic and suggest he would be rewarded if he confessed. The other would make threats. Eventually the 'good cop' would come alone and beg him to give him something, because the 'bad cop' was winning an argument with their bosses about whether to torture him. Paul knew the 'good cop' would become his sole lifeline to humanity, and that, in the end, he would confess. The problem was that no interrogators had appeared, whether good or bad. There was only the cautious robot.

Maria's aunt suffered a mild stroke and was rushed to a hospital in Barcelona. Maria received the news on her cell phone.

"I have to leave immediately. Even though they say it's not life and death, thank God, I'm her only living relative."

"Of course, my dear. Take the plane. In fact, I'll come with you."

"No, no, that's sweet of you, but you've got lots of work to do. I shouldn't be gone more than two or three days. I'll just throw some things into a bag and take off."

Lafarge's personal assistant entered the room.

"Excuse me, Monsieur, but the President's office is on the line again. Can I tell them you're available?"

Jean Luc shook his head ruefully and shrugged his shoulders.

"Damn the woman. She can't blow her nose these days without calling me first. Are you sure you'll be all right?"

"I'll see you on Friday or Saturday, sweetheart," said Maria, blowing him a kiss, and hurried from the room.

Later Jean Luc called the hospital. The old lady was resting comfortably and could not be disturbed. Her niece had called to say she'd be there in three more hours. The hospital regretted it could give him no further details because he was not a relative, but assured him the chances of a full recovery, without any lasting physical impairment, were very good in cases such as these.

Maria called with the same information. She was still in the air and would call him from the hospital. Jean Luc toyed with the idea of sending someone to watch her, but with Paul gone it was not obvious who he should send. The pilot was loyal and tough, but he had no security training beyond anti-hijacking procedures. He called Be-Be's number but there was no answer. His own phone rang again and he turned to other matters.

CHAPTER 17

Never, ever, trust anyone.

—Jean Luc Lafarge

"Monsieur?" Jean Luc's computer security expert stood before him, absurdly overdressed for the hot Mediterranean afternoon.

Jean Luc glanced up from a business report.

"Monsieur Lafarge," said the man nervously. "My associate checked the C drive files you gave me and found something unusual—something I must admit I missed completely. It was in the telephone directory in her Outlook folders. He checked all the telephone numbers by actually calling them. They're all correct except for three; two are simple number transpositions and the other doesn't exist."

Jean Luc experienced a sinking feeling, a sense that a chill sea breeze had suddenly swept across the patio.

"Which one doesn't exist?"

"The US number, 746 362 5379. There's no such area code. Actually, she had erased it, but a lot of people don't realize that erasing something doesn't actually get rid of it, if you know where to look."

"Whose number is it?"

"It was in her directory for a woman called 'Rose B'. A lot of the names are truncated. Like the name 'Hans B' for 'Hans Blucher', or 'Jean Luc L' for you, sir."

"She's never mentioned a Rose someone."

"Anyway, I checked with all our contacts to see if anyone knows a Rose with a last name starting with B, with an American phone number. There are dozens of Roses with a last name of B. There are also lots of flower names: 'rose this', or 'xyz rose'."

"Can you get to the point?" Jean Luc asked him, impatiently.

"Sorry, Monsieur, I'm trying to explain, if I may. Anyway, our Russian connection came up with an unusual Rose B—a CIA security ID called 'rosebud' on the American consulate secure network."

"Surely that's a coincidence?"

"I would have thought so too, but they put the number through a cryptographic deciphering program and came up with a telephone keypad substitution match. In self-defense, Monsieur, those ex-KGB guys are better equipped for this kind of analysis than we are. That's why we pay them.

"Anyway, it's not the number itself, it's the letters on a telephone keypad: 746 362 5379 could be 'Rimena Kery', for example. It also stands for 'shoemaker9', and that's a valid password for the secure system ID 'rosebud', Monsieur. It's a CIA messaging access gateway."

"CIA?"

The chill sea breeze became an Arctic hurricane, freezing the blood in his veins. Never, *ever*, trust anyone. He had broken his most basic rule. He called the pilot.

"No, Monsieur Lafarge, negative, we landed twenty minutes ago. She's just gotten into the limo; I can see her driving off."

He listened intently for fifteen seconds.

"Roger that, Monsieur."

Maria hurried along the Carrer Provenca toward the Passeig de Gracia in the bustling center of Barcelona. It was lunchtime and the streets were crowded. She was almost half an hour late. She glanced back at the traffic to cross the street and as she did so saw Jean Luc's pilot about twenty paces behind her. He stopped in mid stride. There was no point in pretending she had not seen him, and he saw no point in pretending he wasn't following her.

They stared at each other as if frozen into a tableau, and then he started toward her, reaching into his jacket. She turned abruptly into the closest doorway behind her and ran. She was in a courtyard. Someone seemed to be asking her for a ticket or to buy a ticket. Ahead was an elevator, crowded with people and with the door closing. She bolted into it and the doors closed. The pilot almost reached the elevator, but not quite. She looked at the elevator operator.

"He's such a *pig!*" she said.

The elevator operator smiled and they ascended. She exited onto a vaguely familiar passageway and started down it. Where the hell was she? Then she realized this was the weird Casa Mila, designed by the architect Antoni Gaudi in the 1920s, the most famous, or most bizarre, or most beautiful apartment building ever built, depending on one's perspective, and known as La Pedrera—the Rock Pile.

Maria knew the pilot would be pounding up one of the staircases in pursuit, and she could not risk going down in case she guessed wrongly and met him. She ran upward to the roof, a crazy multilevel quilt of turrets and oversized chimneys and walkways surrounding the shaft of the central courtyard.

Moshe had seen her turn and run with the pilot hard on her heels. He was almost hit by a taxi crossing the street as he took off after them.

Maria ran along the little walkways and up and down the steps which connected the different levels and areas of the rooftop. It was much more cluttered with architectural oddities and twists and turns than she had remembered, and there were tourists with cameras at every turn. It had been a mistake to come up here. She paused briefly to scan the rooftop for the pilot, but he was not in sight. She would pick the next set of stairs she came to and take her chances. Hopefully, the pilot was lost somewhere in the maze.

Then she was shoved violently from behind and the force flipped her over the guardrail onto a sloping facade. The street was six stories below her.

She was slipping down the slope, clawing at the ceramic mosaic that covered it. She watched a fingernail break and she skidded a little further. The pilot was leaning over the guardrail above her, pretending to try to save her, yelling for help in English. Her feet went over the edge of the parapet into thin air. Her belt had caught temporarily on some knobby extension. A female tourist was screaming in horror. The pilot's hand reached for hers, trying to break her hold on the smooth tiles, grabbing one wrist while pushing it toward the void.

The edge of the parapet was beneath her thighs. If she slipped another six inches, the balance of her weight would be over the side of the building and she would fall to her death. She could feel the shapes of her two precious recording tapes pressing sharply into her stomach; she had taped them there beneath her panties. If the tapes were ripped off and fell they would be lost forever.

Moshe's hand appeared beside the pilot's. The pilot let go and she grabbed Moshe's hand as her belt gave way. The pilot toppled slowly down on top of her until she was bearing half his weight also. Their faces were close together and there was terror in his eyes. Blood was dribbling out of the corner of his mouth. Moshe's hand was clamped like a vice around her wrist and the pilot's extra weight was pulling her shoulder out of its socket.

She had no way to push the pilot away. She was defenseless. She kicked with one dangling knee and found his groin. His reflexes took over and he blinked and recoiled and dropped slowly over the edge. She heard his screaming as he fell.

She dare not move again for fear of breaking Moshe's grip. He must have one hand wrapped around the guardrail stanchion and the other around her wrist. She realized he was gripping her watch strap as much as her wrist itself. It was a big, heavy diving watch, with a sturdy rubberized strap, but how much strain could it take?

She had been subconsciously aware of sirens for some time. She sensed rather than saw a big fire ladder rising toward her. Someone was a few feet beneath her saying, "Hang on, I'm almost there." Heads of firefighters and police officers appeared beside Moshe, and a firefighter's hand reached down to haul her to safety.

Her watch strap broke. She fell.

She bounced off the top of the fire ladder and began to fall headfirst past it. A massive hand gripped her ankle. The ladder retracted slowly toward the ground as she hung headfirst. The street was awash with emergency vehicles. Hands grabbed her and she shook with relief as she felt the pavement beneath her. People were saying things like "You're safe now" and "Just relax."

She was lifted onto a stretcher and it was manhandled into an ambulance. She felt her stomach and the tapes were still in place. A paramedic climbed in beside her and another man jumped in just as the ambulance was taking off. It was Father Uzi. The paramedic began to protest, but Father Uzi knelt and began to pray as the ambulance swayed around a corner, and the paramedic fell silent. He and the driver fell even more silent when Father Uzi pulled out a gun and forced them to stop the vehicle and get out. Father Uzi got behind the wheel and inexpertly drove the vehicle to a marina where he helped her out.

She half walked, half staggered into a hotel beside the marina. He pushed her into an elevator, and her knees gave way.

"Too much to drink, I'm afraid," Father Uzi was saying to the other passengers. "It's so sad in one so young."

He almost carried her along the corridor, and helped her into a room. She collapsed on the bed. A maid appeared in the open doorway, staring at the priest leaning over the disheveled girl.

"Please come back in an hour," Father Uzi said, and closed the door in her face.

Maria lay on the bed shaking. Time passed as Father Uzi made phone calls speaking in a language she didn't understand. She wanted to go to the bathroom, but she didn't have the strength to move.

"What's your real name?" she asked him weakly.

"Daniel."

There was a loud knock on the door. Moshe appeared.

"Okay, Major, rise and shine. We have ass to kick, big time."

By tradition the G8 summit is never held in a capital city. This year Germany was the host, and the meetings would take place in the ornate glories of the Frankfurt opera house. The European Central Bank, just down the road, would be a powerful reminder of Europe's strong position in the world economy.

The French President decided to spring her trap on Friday evening. She would dine privately with the German Chancellor and the Russian President, and the three leaders would emerge for an impromptu press conference, at which they would say they were in complete accord. The American President was flying in from South America, and he would still be in the air. The French President would then give an interview at which she would announce her proposed *Rapprochement Generale*—her General Reconciliation.

It would still be late afternoon in New York, and the Secretary General of the United Nations would hold an interview at which he would endorse the plan strongly. The two interviews would dominate the US evening news and there would be favorable editorial coverage in almost every newspaper the following morning. Her earlier dinner would imply she had the support of Germany and Russia. The American President would land in Frankfurt with the Rapprochement already dominating the discussions. He would have no time for evasive action or to prepare a counter position.

At some point Paul suddenly began to make a confession to the watching TV cameras and their microphones. Nothing had suggested or implied that he should, but it just seemed the right thing to do. Perhaps it was a way of asserting his individuality, his free will, against the whispering of the air conditioning and the hesitant silence of the robot.

The Klaxon did not go off when he began to speak—his voice was cracking and harsh from disuse—and he gave a fairly detailed account of his life up to and including his work as a mercenary. When he was finished, the robot entered the room and passed a warm, moist, freshly baked chocolate chip cookie and a plastic cup of warm milk through the drawer. Paul almost wept with pleasure, holding the cookie tenderly beneath his nose to savor the aroma before nibbling it with tiny bites to prolong the experience.

A 'day' or so later, he told the cameras a fictitious story about going to Afghanistan to help train Al Qaeda volunteers in urban combat. The robot did not bring him a cookie. In the end, he gave a detailed account of his activities in Israel, Central East Africa, and Canada. This produced another cookie. Finally, he gave a detailed account of his relationship with Jean Luc, including specific physical evidence which would link his confession irrefutably to Jean Luc. The robot brought him two cookies.

The Israeli Defense Minister called the American National Security Advisor, an unusual but not unprecedented occurrence.

"I would like you to meet three people. I want you to get this intelligence raw, right from the source. I want it going straight to you and from you to the President."

He was a serious man, a straight shooter, and a former prime minister in the ever-revolving doors of Israeli coalition governments built on fragile factional alliances.

"The subject matter approximates 9/11 in severity."

With that addition the NSA agreed, even when the Israeli stipulated a clandestine meeting on the neutral territory of the Azores Islands on the very next day. This was highly inconvenient, because the NSA was due to join the President in South America and fly on with him to the G8 summit meeting.

She flew across the Atlantic wondering what the *hell* had gone wrong now, punctuated by thoughts of how disastrous the G8 was shaping up to be. She would have six hours in the Azores before Air Force One touched down briefly to pick her up. She was too strung out to sleep.

"Okay, so what have you got?" she asked the odd assortment of people facing her the next day—the gorgeous CIA spy, the plump French bureaucrat, and the ugly young Israeli.

"Okay," began the Israeli, without any preamble, matching her abrupt manner. "We have the intersection of three separate investigations. The first was run by the CIA, who had reason to believe that Jean Luc Lafarge, the French industrialist, was operating an illegal arms business. He has extensive connections in the Russian oil sector, and past connections with Iran and Iraq."

He glanced at the woman and she took up the story.

"I was inserted into his household to try to develop the lead from the inside, while Langley followed the paper trail. What I found was a consortium of ultra-nationalists. Lafarge uses Professor Diderot as a one-man think tank, and meets frequently with the President.

"I concluded that Lafarge was hostile and exerting influence over the President, but I could not find anything illegal, or anything representing a clear and present danger to the United States. However, two of my Langley contacts were killed, one after the other, and I suspected that Lafarge might have compromised my operation. Still, without any hard evidence, I decided to sit tight and wait for developments."

The NSA frowned with impatience. There was little there which surprised her, except for the information that Lafarge might have penetrated the CIA in some fashion. This woman had used the oldest technique in the world and come up with nothing but a bunch of wealthy French Ameriphobes. So what?

Moshe began again. "In the meantime, we were tracking down the perpetrators of the so-called 'Sons of Hebron' campaign. We followed the trail to an employee of Lafarge's company. In addition, we found that this man had been in Africa immediately prior to the genetic foods scandal and in Montreal immediately prior to the start of the 'c'est possible' campaign.

"We connected the dots and concluded that Lafarge was fomenting anti-Americanism by deliberately creating these incidents. His operation would fall well within all accepted definitions of terrorism. But like the CIA probe, we had no concrete evidence."

Now, this was interesting. It had not occurred to the NSA that the recent chain of diplomatic disasters had been deliberately manufactured. It was one thing for the European elites to donate money into conduits which eventually trickled into terrorist hands, but this was on a completely different and more dangerous scale. If it was true, it would easily meet the threshold of 'a clear and present danger to the United States'.

Daniel interrupted the NSA's racing thoughts.

"Some time ago the Gendarmerie Nationale was pursuing an investigation of the UN Oil for Food program in connection with illegal arms shipments and other payoffs. We are, of course, not the only country to have done so. However, we were well positioned, since much of the money flowed through French banks. We found plenty of circumstantial evidence of illegal diversions, including Lafarge, but nothing definitive.

"As a matter of routine, we also tracked bank personnel who had had access to this information, and found that a woman, an accounting clerk, had died under uncertain circumstances. She had a connection to Lafarge through a family relationship, therefore, we could develop a theory, but we had no evidence. I decided to treat it as a murder. At that point; however, my investigation was cancelled abruptly and the information was suppressed. The orders came from the minister who has subsequently become our President. Then separately, and by complete coincidence, Moshe asked me for help in identifying his unknown terrorist, which eventually brought to light its own Lafarge connection."

This was also good stuff. Everyone knew that the UN's Oil for Food program, theoretically a deal whereby Iraq had been allowed to sell oil to buy humanitarian aid for its undernourished population, had become an enormous Saddam slush fund, riddled with corruption. Very good stuff, except that the bureaucrat had no hard evidence.

The ball was passed back to the Israeli.

"We had reason to believe the CIA had installed a hum-int asset into Lafarge's household."

'Reason to believe'? she thought.

That meant this strange looking man was casually admitting to Mossad espionage within the CIA. Langley must be riddled with moles! But he was continuing.

"We went outside channels and contacted her. When we pooled our combined intelligence, the implications became clear. Ms. Menendez obtained a tape in which Lafarge specifies the details of his plan, which he calls Casse-noisette, or Nutcracker. In addition, Ms. Menendez also enabled us to identify and track specific money flows immediately prior to the French President's visit to North Korea."

"*What?*" The NSA was shocked into a response.

"I believe you understood me," said the Mossad man. "We took the suspected terrorist, Lafarge's operative, into custody. He has not only confirmed the Lafarge plot, but he has provided us with additional supporting financial information: hard, verifiable, third party physical evidence. I have our summary of what we've just covered and a copy of the hard evidence on this CD. We would like you to give this information to the President. We think he needs to know it."

"Where is this terrorist now?"

"He's in protective custody."

The NSA rose from the table and stared out the window at the Atlantic rollers breaking on the rocky shores of the Azores. God, these islands are remote! She sifted through the information and sorted it out in her own pedantic, academic way: facts, suppositions, implications, conclusions, possible actions.

Finally she rejoined the ill-matched trio sitting wordlessly at the table.

"Okay, I understand the outlines of the plot. But let me also make sure I understand your own actions."

She stared at Daniel. "You, Monsieur, have gone outside your chain of command because you suspect it is corrupt, and the information would be suppressed."

Her attention shifted to Moshe. "You, sir, found Ms. Menendez because you have undoubtedly penetrated the CIA."

Finally it was Maria's turn. "You, Ms. Menendez, have circumvented the entire CIA structure because you believe it has been penetrated by Lafarge or the French government, let alone the Mossad. I find it troubling that you are prepared to trust foreign intelligence services but not our own. If you doubted the CIA, why didn't you go to State or the Pentagon?"

"Two reasons, ma'am. One, I didn't want to wait two years while the bureaucrats screwed around with it; two, I didn't want to read all about it in the *Washington Post*."

The NSA grunted and looked around the table, marshalling her thoughts.

"Okay, the way I parse it is this. I am approached by three individuals with evidence—purported evidence—of a plot by a respectable businessman to create virulent anti-Americanism, and subvert the policies of the French government toward us."

She turned to Daniel.

"One individual is a member of the French government, which would *love* to see another American intelligence cluster fuck. The Iraq WMD debacle damaged our credibility and another fuckup would destroy us. The preemption doctrine would be dead.

"If I were in the French government, and I wanted to damage the United States, I can't think of a better way to doing it than fabricating a story like this, and delivering it 'unofficially' through a concerned official who says he can't trust his own chain of command. I can't call your bosses for verification How very convenient, and how very typical of your government's recent policies—devious and self-serving. This is the seventh or eighth time in the last few years you've offered us a Trojan horse."

Daniel looked pained, struggled between two or three possible rebuttals, but in the end said nothing. She did have a point.

She looked at Moshe.

"The second individual is a member of Israeli intelligence. The Israeli government is desperate to shore up American support after that cretinous attack on Syria, because, among other things, it is terrified that we'll hold up delivery of the next batch of F-16s. Once again, I couldn't think of a cleverer plot. And, coincidently, our loyal friends and allies mention in passing that they have once again penetrated the CIA. With friends like you, who needs enemies?"

Unlike Daniel, Moshe did not seem the least put out.

Next it was Maria's turn.

"The third individual is the chief suspect's mistress, or one of his call girls. I'm not sure whether your services are exclusive or not."

Maria flinched.

"Either way, it's not a common occupation for a serving officer in the United States Marine Corps. I would have thought that Marines are paid to serve their country on their feet, not on their backs."

Maria suppressed a tear of humiliation which was threatening to trickle down her burning cheek.

"All of this is presented in circumstances of elaborate secrecy," the NSA continued. "It is timed just as the President may be assumed to be grasping for straws in a losing election campaign, with French egg all over his face from the Korean situation, and facing the prospect of an extremely hostile G8 meeting.

"The information is provided to someone known for her fierce loyalty to the President, her distain for multilateral diplomacy, and her urgent need to justify her authorship of a highly unpopular foreign policy. 'Oh, thank you,' you have calculated she will say. 'This proves I was right all along and rescues my boss from a humiliating domestic and international defeat.' I must admit, your sense of timing is superb."

As usual, the group left it to Moshe to respond.

"Ah, yes, but will you tell the President?"

"That's none of your fucking business," she snapped. "As far as I can tell that's about the only communication channel you *haven't* broken into."

CHAPTER 18

There is always a way out of everything.

—Jean Luc Lafarge

Everything went according to plan. The French, German and Russian leaders engaged in a public love fest for the cameras, and the TV interview was a triumph, particularly the ending. The interviewer was almost groveling at the President's feet.

"How would you sum up your vision, if I may say your dream, Madame?"

"I must admit I do have a dream: a dream for a world in which every country is judged not by the size of its economy or the power of its military, but the content of its character."

She seemed to be wrapped in a mantle of benevolent wisdom.

"Each nation is precious to me, and each is equal. As it says in Isaiah Chapter 2: 'They shall beat their swords into plowshares and their spears into pruning hooks. Nation shall not lift up sword against nation.'"

"Do you really think it's possible that the United States will beat its swords in plowshares?" The questioner was almost whispering, as if he were having a religious experience.

"Oh yes, c'est possible."

The President switched on the TV in her limo as she was driven back to the hotel.

"In an interview which is already being compared with Roosevelt's and Churchill's finest speeches, the French President has called for a new world order in which the United Nations will have absolute say over all matters of peace and war."

She flipped channels.

"In a gesture of remarkable generosity, France will give its seat in the Security Council to Europe. The French President announced her plan in an historic interview, saying that some things must be done, and I quote, 'Not because they are easy, but because they are right'."

She flipped again, and frowned.

This news announcer was saying, "I repeat, early reports are confusing, but clearly there has been an enormous eruption or explosion at Mount Etna in Sicily."

* * *

Mount Etna is a large volcano on the island of Sicily, part of a chain that stretches all along the Mediterranean. The tectonic plate upon which Africa stands, is in infinitely slow collision with Europe, and the resulting stresses create earthquakes and eruptions. The Alps are the result of this titanic continental pile up, or convergent boundary, as scientists would describe it.

Etna is highly active, but the complex geology of fractures and fissures in the strata beneath it, combined with the intermediate viscosity and silica content of its andesitic magma, permit the subterranean pressures to be relieved by constant minor eruptions. It is only every few hundred years that the pressure builds up sufficiently for a major eruption to occur, as happened last in the year 1669.

The mythological forge of Vulcan and the home of the Cyclops, Etna stands almost eleven thousand feet above the coastal town of Catania, on the eastern shores of Sicily. The local population considers the mountain to be a major source of tourist income rather than as a threat to their lives and property. There are frequent tours which permit hardy enthusiasts to venture close to the spectacular lava fountains and flows.

The pyrotechnics are particularly impressive at night, and it was on one such evening tour, just as a local volconologist was explaining Etna's inherent stability and quiet personality, that the upper two thousand feet of the mountain, consisting of more than a quarter of a cubic mile of cumulative pyroclastic materials, exploded.

The energy released by the eruption was equal to three times the first atom bomb which exploded at Hiroshima. The top of the mountain disintegrated, releasing thousands of tons of molten lava with a temperature approaching one thousand degrees centigrade. The event was analogous to a cork being popped from a bottle of champagne, but on a vastly greater scale and with catastrophic results.

There were five principal causes of death: falling rocks and debris, including blocks weighing a hundred tons or more which crashed down for distances of up to twenty miles; entrapment by lava flows, which flowed unusually far and fast due to their enormous volume and the exceptional pressures that propelled them; widespread building collapses caused by the associated earth tremors and aftershocks; and, to a lesser extent, tidal waves which turned Catania harbor into a churning caldron and spread out across the Mediterranean.

The final cause of death was simply terror, in the form of heart attacks, unnecessary road accidents caused by frightened and distracted drivers, and all the other mistakes produced by extreme stress and gut-wrenching fear.

Air Force One was climbing above the Azores in route for the G8 summit when the President received the news. He set aside a transcript of the French President's interview, which he had just begun reading, and called the Italian prime minister. The Italian had abruptly left the conference on hearing the news and the President caught him on his way to the airport by helicopter.

"I can send men and equipment from Wiesbaden in Germany," the President offered. "And I can send the *Reagan* to Catania."

"That's very generous of you, Mr. President. We can use all the help we can get."

They discussed logistics for a few minutes. The Etna region was effectively cut off from the rest of Sicily, and most help would reach the stricken area by air or sea.

The Italian premier finally changed the subject. "Incidentally, Joe, did you hear about Charlotte's interview?"

"I just got a transcript, but I haven't read it yet. Is it good or bad?"

"From your perspective it's pretty bad."

"Well, thanks for the warning," the president grunted, and then continued as another thought struck him. "As a matter of fact, would you object if I divert to the local airport? Fontanarossa? I have a complete operating theater here on board, among other things. I'd like to help if I can."

"That's very generous once again. I'll see you there in a few hours. But excuse me, I have to hang up and get on my plane."

"Good luck and God bless Italy."

❧ ❧ ❧

The American President came down the hill with a little girl in his arms. Her arms and legs were wrapped around him and her head drooped on his chest in exhausted sleep. Like every one and every thing around them, the President was gray with ash, and his unruly hair was ruffled by the fitful wind.

A reporter saw him and screamed into her microphone, "I've got the President live! Get me on the air!"

She raced across the broken ground toward the President. This would be an exclusive! This could make her career! He always tried to avoid interviews and now she had nailed the bastard one-on-one! The President slowed and a little knot of onlookers gathered around them, attracted like moths to the TV lights. Two Secret Service men were trying to form a barrier, but in the circumstances it was not possible. The cameraman positioned himself for an uphill angle, with the President coming down toward the camera and the red fire of Etna behind him. It made a great shot. The cameraman loved natural disasters. They were so *visual.*

The reporter jumped in.

"Mr. President, Carla Thompson of the *New York World Journal* Television Service. What are your reactions to the French President's proposals last night?"

"What, Ms. Thompson? I must admit I know she made a speech, but I don't know what she said."

"She's called for a sweeping reform of the United Nations and, in effect, the establishment of a new world order which will eliminate all acts of aggression."

"Well, as I said, I haven't heard about it, but she's a good friend and a good leader and I'm sure that…."

"Her proposals finally solve the nuclear proliferation issue, Mr. President."

"Er, anything in that direction will certainly be welcome."

"Is that an endorsement? She solved your problem with Korea for you and now she's solved the broader issue as well. Do you endorse her plans or will you obstruct them?"

"Well, I'd need to consult with…."

"Then, with respect, shouldn't you be at the conference addressing these issues, Mr. President, instead of coming here unilaterally without authorization?"

The President seemed genuinely startled. "Without authorization? The Italian government…."

"The Secretary General of the United Nations has appointed the International Red Cross to coordinate international relief efforts, and the IRC has said it does not want foreign military forces involved. Are you claiming you didn't know that either, sir?"

A US military helicopter flew low across the mountainside in the background, black against the red glow of Etna, as if to punctuate the point. The open doors were crowded with evacuees sitting in a line with their legs dangling down.

"No, I didn't. The Italian government appealed…."

"And yet, sir, you sent an armed aircraft carrier into European territorial waters without UN authorization which, regardless of what you claim your intentions were, is clearly an act of war."

"We've been kind of busy…."

"In her speech the French President very generously proposed a general amnesty for America's actions over the past twenty years, the Secretary General endorsed it, and yet you have immediately violated it, Mr. President.

"Twelve hundred American soldiers have already been flown in from Germany, and there are five thousand more heavily armed personnel on the *USS Reagan*. Some are beginning to describe this as more of an invasion than a relief effort. Shouldn't you withdraw your forces before you make matters worse?"

This is wonderful stuff, exulted the reporter to herself. I've actually nailed the bastard! On live TV with no wiggle room!

"There's still a lot of people missing and buried under the rubble."

Clearly the President would have scratched his head in confusion if he had not been burdened by the sleeping child in his arms.

"Shouldn't your first priority be to ensure that the global community is governed on humanitarian principles? Isn't that your job?"

He looked down at her, and she wished she'd stood a little farther uphill so he didn't look taller to the camera. On the other hand, her current angle often came across sympathetically, the brave press resolutely attacking and exposing the bastions of power, like David looking up at Goliath. It appeared he was going to make a speech, which was bad, but from a professional perspective, she had to let him start a reply before she could interrupt him again.

"No, as a matter of fact, it isn't, Ms. Thompson. My first priority is to find this little girl a nice clean bed to sleep in. She's had kind of a busy night. And my second priority is to help find the rest of her family back up there under the ruins."

It was time to interrupt, but he spoke too quickly. "Here, can you look after her and I'll get back up the hill?"

He prepared to hand the child to the reporter, but she jumped back.

"I'm from the *New York World Journal*," she said. "I have an obligation to report events objectively, not interfere in them."

"Ah, of course," said the President sadly, and one of the onlookers stepped forward.

"Here, Mr. President, let me take her."

The President gently transferred the little girl to her safekeeping.

"Thank you. I'll check in on her later, if I may. And you are?"

"Major Maria Menendez, United States Marine Corps, sir."

"Thank you, Major."

The President sketched a salute and turned wearily back up the hill toward the glowing lava flow, framed between the Marine cradling the baby and the reporter clutching her microphone, and the Secret Service men scrambling to follow him.

The studio cut away to the G8 conference, coming in on the French President's morning speech.

"Only through the correct and appropriate modalities and structures," she was saying, "Can we, as a global community, bring effective help to the suffering. Good intentions are not enough. We must establish the mechanisms and procedures through which good intentions can be translated into good deeds.

"As you know, I have already urged the Secretary General of the United Nations to establish an Etna Relief Task Force, and its representative balance of members will ensure not only a fair apportionment of relief funds to suppliers throughout the world, under the supervision of the WTO, but also a swift and timely coordinated response under the direction of the IRC and the WHO, consistent with the policy objectives and general oversight of the UN.

"To the people of Sicily in their hour of tragedy I say: Be of good cheer—help will soon be on its way!"

Jean Luc stared at the television as if he had seen a vision of his own death. It was not the cruel juxtaposition of the tousled American President covered with ashes, actively bringing relief to the afflicted, while the elegant French President waffled on about meaningless bureaucratic mumbo-jumbo; it was the sight of Maria taking that baby from the President's arms.

"Major Maria Menendez, United States Marine Corps, sir."

The implications crept slowly into his mind like wraiths of toxic chemicals seeping into the room. She was only ten miles away, up on the mountain, but she might as well have been on a different planet. His pilot had never reported in from Barcelona, for reasons that were now all too obvious. He had been on tenterhooks for twenty-four hours and then the eruption forced all other thoughts from his mind. The villa was knee-deep in ash, but did not seem to be damaged structurally. Fuck it, he'd sell it, just like every other place she had ever stepped into!

Finally, he pulled himself together and rose abruptly to his feet.

"I'm leaving now!"

"But the airport is still closed to everyone except relief aircraft, Monsieur, I checked again just a minute ago."

"I'm going anyway."

He strode from the room and ran down the long flight of stairs.

"Major Maria Menendez, United States Marine Corps, sir." It was simply incredible.

His car was waiting in the forecourt, covered in ash like everything and everybody, and he gestured urgently to the driver.

"They assigned me to drive you today, Monsieur."

"Major Maria Menendez, United States Marine Corps, sir." He simply could not get his mind around it.

"What?"

He scarcely broke his stride. He had completely forgotten about Paul's disappearance.

"Well, drive me to the airport as fast as possible."

"Major Maria Menendez, United States Marine Corps, sir." Good God! What had he told her? Or, more to the point, what *hadn't* he told her?

"Yes, Monsieur, immediately," said Moshe, closing the car door carefully behind him.

It was all very confusing. Jean Luc's car had followed a winding path to the airport, for many of the streets were damaged and those in the best condition were reserved for rescue operations. Eventually, the driver stopped and consulted a police officer, who advised him to drive right down to the docks and follow the back road to the airport from there.

"Just about everything else is blocked to civilian traffic," he said, and seemed inclined to discuss the disaster at some length. Jean Luc yelled at the driver to hurry up and they drove on.

The docks were full of American sailors unloading supplies and loading the wounded and other evacuees into small boats, for the *Reagan* had become a vast floating hospital ward and homeless shelter. A massive naval policeman with white cross-webbing and a huge 'SP' on one arm stopped the car and ordered them out. It became clear the idiotic sailor had mistaken them for relatives of casualties and he led them to a waiting boat, half filled with victims from the catastrophe.

Jean Luc objected vehemently, but the Neanderthal policeman kept saying in English, "Don't worry, sir, if your family is among the wounded I'm sure you'll find them. Please hurry, now, there are a lot more people waiting."

He took Jean Luc by the arm to assist him down. Jean Luc almost lost his balance and the driver grabbed at him to save him, half-caught him, and they both almost fell into the boat. Before he could protest the boat cast off and headed for the aircraft carrier.

"This is *ridiculous!*" Jean Luc screamed to the driver. "That man is an *idiot!*"

"We'll just have to come back on the next boat. It looks as if they're shuttling back and forth like ferries, Monsieur."

The ride took less than five minutes. The bizarre misunderstanding had temporarily driven all thoughts of Maria from his mind.

The *Reagan* was vast—*vast!* It was hard to believe that the huge ship was actually floating. It had squeezed into the bay, dwarfing the town and making the Lido di Plaia look like a sandbox.

A flight of hanging steps led to massive double doors halfway up the side. Jean Luc tried to protest once more, but the clattering of a hovering helicopter made communication impossible and the sailors in charge of the boat smiled and shrugged to indicate they couldn't hear him. They clearly thought he was afraid of stepping from the boat to the dangling companion way. A huge grinning sailor picked him up like a doll and placed him carefully on the steps, pointing upward with encouraging gestures.

"Nothing to it, sir," he yelled. "I was scared shitless myself my first time."

Others were already jostling him as they tried to climb from the boat. It was obvious he would have to go up and explain the misunderstanding before he could go down. He climbed the steps and entered a gigantic hangar, full of aircraft with folded wings, impromptu dressing stations and soup kitchens, huddles of exhausted evacuees, and the casual, but disciplined bustle of the absurdly young-looking crew.

"I must see an officer *immediately*," he said in careful English to a sailor at the top of the stairs, who wore a complex badge signifying some senior rank.

"Right away, sir. That would be the Civilian Liaison Officer. Just follow me."

At least this man seemed to have some basic intelligence. They crossed the hangar, stepping over snaking hoses and cables, walking around piles of crates in cargo nets, and pausing to let a forklift growl by with a portable power generator. They came to a small door and entered a rabbit warren of starkly lit gray corridors. Eventually the petty officer opened a door and stood aside to let him enter.

"Civilian Liaison Officer, sir," he told Jean Luc by way of explanation.

Jean Luc strode into the cabin with the driver at his heels. The petty officer closed the door behind them. Two people sat at the table. Jean Luc stopped in his tracks. The driver stepped around him and gestured to a chair.

"Please sit down, Monsieur Lafarge."

Jean Luc's brain seemed to have stopped working and he obeyed mindlessly.

"My name is Moshe Bechman," Moshe told him. "I am an employee of the government of Israel. This gentleman is with the Gendarmerie Nationale, and you already know Major Menendez."

He glanced at a side table.

"Great! Fresh coffee," Moshe said. "Would you like some, Monsieur?"

Jean Luc did not reply, and Moshe helped himself before sitting down.

"Now, sir, let me explain the situation," said Moshe. He seemed bizarrely friendly and enthusiastic.

"First of all, you need to know that Paul Rennard is in our custody. Second, the question of jurisdiction is a little foggy, to put it mildly, but you have committed several serious crimes against each of our countries, as well as others. There is no question you will face life imprisonment without parole, wherever you wind up. So, there is no real basis for a plea bargain—a reduced sentence if you confess.

"And, third and finally, there is absolutely no question but that you will make a confession: none at all."

Moshe paused to sip his coffee while Jean Luc struggled desperately to pull his thoughts together. Maria and the French policeman seemed happy to let Moshe take the lead.

It was completely inconceivable to Jean Luc that this woman dressed in military fatigues could actually be his Maria. 'It isn't just about sex', his mind screamed at her, 'It's everything about you, the very idea of you.'

Grasping for some kind of control of himself he considered demanding a lawyer, but that seemed implausible. The man from the GN seemed unlikely to come to his defense on the basis of Jean Luc's French nationality.

"I think, Monsieur Lafarge," Moshe finally continued. "That the important thing from your perspective is to get this settled before the Central East African Republic demands jurisdiction for the murder of their citizens by poisoning. There, as you may know, serial amputation is a fairly common sentence in cases like this."

He took another sip of coffee while Jean Luc struggled against panic. There *had* to be a way out of this—there was always a way out of everything.

"Now, sir, let's jump over the whole Casse-noisette conspiracy. That was damned well thought out, incidentally—although in my opinion you definitely overpaid the North Koreans. Anyway, let's start with Jeannette Bois."

CHAPTER 19

Always attack; never retreat.

—Jean Luc Lafarge

The motion for the Great Debate was taken from Lord Acton's famous quotation, 'Power tends to corrupt, and absolute power corrupts absolutely'. Professor Diderot and the NSA sat at a large round table flanking the moderator.

He explained to the television audience that his job was to make sure each side received approximately equal time, but that he hoped this would be a conversation or exchange of views rather than alternating prepared statements. Each participant could not speak for more than five minutes at one time. Each side would have the opportunity to make a brief opening statement.

"I have studied history all my life," said the Professor. "We stand at a moment of crisis. History teaches us that excessive power is corrupting. The United States *must* understand that the world will no longer tolerate a situation in which one country, with a mere five percent of the world's population, consumes thirty percent of the world's resources, and spends more than the next ten countries *combined* on its military.

"This kind of power creates hubris and arrogance. This kind of power creates fundamental imbalances. This kind of power *corrupts*. This has been true throughout history. We in Europe stand ready to lead the United States back toward a more civilized form of behavior. The United States is, shall we say, intoxicated by its own power. Just like a doctor in a drug rehabilitation center, we can *help* before it is too *late*."

The moderator nodded, and turned to the NSA.

"I believe there is much more that unites us than divides us," said the NSA. "I hope we'll be able to spend time talking about how we can work together. Rather than debating the past, and revisiting old disagreements, I hope we can concentrate on working together in the future."

She sat back.

The moderator gave the floor to the professor, who spoke for some fifteen minutes. His essential message was that the world demands balance, that an excessive concentration of power in one state is inherently dangerous and indeed immoral. A civilized society demands a sense of equity, and the United Nations is the only legitimate authority which can monitor the excesses and aggressions of the powerful.

"There is much to admire in America," the Professor concluded. "But the world needs the civilizing hand of Europe on the tiller, in partnership and as a counterbalance. We understand power; we know how to control it. Thus, we must remember Lord Acton's famous dictum, 'Power tends to corrupt, and absolute power corrupts absolutely'."

He would have continued in this vein for the entire program, but eventually the moderator felt obliged to turn to the NSA.

"Well, Doctor, the Professor presents a compelling case. How can one argue with that?"

"There can be no doubt," she replied, "That throughout most of history, nations with disproportionate military and economic strength have sought to dominate the world..."

"Then you agree with me, Doctor?" interrupted the Professor. He smiled. "Goodness me. There is perhaps hope for us after all! You acknowledge the essential correctness of the European perspective?"

"I agree with you completely, Professor," she responded. "The Europeans in particular have good reason to fear that strength creates an overwhelming impulse toward aggression, domination, and repression."

The moderator could scarcely believe it. Perhaps his show would witness a major shift in global policy. This could be even better than the French President's interview. He turned to Diderot, who could not restrain the smile playing around his lips.

"Perhaps, then, Professor, if we are agreed, we could ask you what practical steps need to be made to bring the United States back into the fold of civilized society?"

"Well, if we can begin with..." the Professor began.

"Now, now, Claude," said the NSA playfully, patting the moderator on the arm. "Could you not give me a couple of minutes to explain *why* I agree with the Professor?"

He had little choice. He could not be too openly biased, and, since she had already conceded the point, there was no harm in letting her dig her own grave a little deeper.

"Of course," he smiled back.

"The history of Europe teaches us the very point that the professor has been making. For more than two thousand years there were constant wars of aggression, as each country sought to conquer and exploit its neighbors. French history, from William the Conqueror to Louis XIV to Napoleon, a span of almost eight hundred years, is a good example. It's not surprising that the Europeans fear power, since they have always turned it upon their neighbors."

The moderator began to interrupt, but she tapped his arm again.

"Now, now, Claude, you can only interrupt me if you or the Professor can give me a ten year period between the years 945 and 1945 in which a European country didn't start a war," she chuckled, and paused long enough for his face to register shock before continuing.

"And it's not only the Europeans that have cause to fear, of course, because that urge to conquer and exploit was also turned outward toward the rest of the world, in the form of colonial exploitation."

The moderator turned to the Professor, but he did not seem to have an instant rebuttal. He was searching for a ten year window, and he was already well back into the nineteenth century.

"The last one hundred years saw the final great paroxysms of that process in two terrible world wars, until at last, after a millennium of unfettered European power, this poor old continent lay crushed beneath the rubble of its own self destruction, and millions lay dead across the globe."

This was *not* what the moderator had planned. The professor stirred himself, but the NSA swept on.

"But the good news—the great news—is that since then three great things have happened. The European Union has emerged as a great powerhouse for good, a true turning point in history; the threat of communist totalitarianism as a global menace has been beaten; and, for the first time in history, in America we have a nation of unparalleled military power without the desire to enslave even one square inch of someone else's territory."

She sat back and smiled sweetly. The moderator stirred himself.

"You dispute Lord Acton—you expect us to believe the US is a power for good and not evil? That it is not inherently corrupt?"

"The professor is the expert in European history, and so I stand to be corrected. I think the evidence shows Acton was right. He made that statement, if I recall correctly, in 1887, at the height of European power. He had only the history of what Europe had done with its economic and military might to use as a basis. Naturally he concluded that power corrupts. In 1887 he could have no concept of a non-aggressive power like the United States, because he only had Europe's use of power to evaluate. So I do agree."

She shook her head.

"But, if I may, I'd much rather talk about the things that unite us rather than the things which divide us. I read several of the professor's books when I was in college and I've been so looking forward to this opportunity to meet him. For example, Professor, what can we do to avoid the mistakes of the League of Nations in the 1930s? What can we do to make the United Nations live up to its obligations? Can we, in the spirit of cooperation, focus on our joint strengths instead of focusing on our separate weaknesses?"

* * *

It had not been a good ten days for the French President. Her G8 proposals had been drowned out by the twenty-four-seven coverage of the eruption, and her speeches were being compared extremely unfavorably with the US President's prompt humanitarian intervention. The *USS Reagan* and its sailors were getting worldwide approval, while, after several days of denials and contradictory statements by the French navy, the story broke in the Spanish press, of all places, that the *Charles de Gaulle* had broken down and refused American help, and was now stuck ignominiously on a sandbar. Power had still not been fully restored in Marseille; ugly questions were percolating in the press about the wisdom of refusing help to save French lives.

South Korea had complained to the Security Council about the French President's deal with the North Koreans demanding she send forty thousand troops to defend their country if the US pulled out. Apart from anything else, this shed an embarrassing light on the fact that France didn't have remotely forty thousand combat troops in the first place.

Jean Luc was not returning her phone calls. Perhaps he had been killed in the eruption.

That idiot Diderot had made a fool of himself on that TV show with the American woman. Although the media had done its best to suppress her views, enough people had seen the show to start a debate questioning European moral infallibility.

The Italians, always fickle, had suddenly fallen in love with all things American and were leading a revolt against her policies from inside the EU, with the support of Britain and Poland. The Chinese and the Russians had gone back to being enigmatic on the UN restructuring issue, and the Secretary General was backpedaling on his endorsement of the Rapprochement Generale.

Student mobs had stormed into American war cemeteries in Normandy and desecrated them. 'No American soldiers in France—alive or dead' had been their motto, but somehow the public's reflexive anti-Americanism hadn't surfaced on this occasion.

In fact, a movement had sprung up among the older generation under the motto of '*Merci, et merci*—'Thank you, and thank you'—which was threatening to overwhelm the '*Merci, mais non merci*' tag line.

And then, to cap it all, those stupid Palestinians had sent a truck bomb into Tel Aviv on Fresh Start Day. Two hundred people had been killed and even the international press and the pundits couldn't come up with a way to blame Israel.

Nonetheless, there remained a good solid bedrock of global anti-American sentiment and she was seen in many quarters as its champion. She was still a force to be reckoned with. 'Always attack; never retreat'—it was one of Jean Luc's favorite expressions, and perhaps it was best not to let a bad situation fester. She issued an invitation to the American President to visit her in Paris, and, to her amazement, he accepted. The idiot was giving her another chance.

CHAPTER 20

All's fair in love and politics.

—*Jean Luc Lafarge*

The French President staged her meeting with the American President, which she dubbed the 'world summit', at Versailles. She would stand on the steps of the palace as the American President's car drew up, and wait for him to climb the stairs. On TV it would look as if the American President was arriving as a supplicant. Then the two leaders were to take a walk through the splendid gardens talking of world affairs, while the world press watched from a respectful distance out of earshot. In a reversal of the Korean situation, she was wearing three inch heels, which killed her feet but made her calves look good.

She had arranged for the public to be allowed into the massive forecourt of Versailles, thus ensuring that protestors would get prominent TV coverage. The Presidential motorcade would have to squeeze through a narrow lane of hostile onlookers. The Secret Service, which is charged with protecting the US President, objected strenuously, providing the opportunity for the President to be painted in the press as a coward, afraid for his own skin and unwilling to acknowledge democratic opposition to his policies. In a stroke of genius, many of the protestors wore bulletproof vests, claiming they were afraid the Secret Service would start firing indiscriminately into the crowd.

The American President's motorcade rolled into the forecourt in bright sunshine. There was excellent TV coverage of the police fighting to restrain the legitimately enraged citizenry, and the crowd broke into a prolonged chant of

'*Non, non, non*' as he emerged from his car. The roar came to a crescendo as he mounted the steps to shake her hand. They stood together briefly (she was standing one step higher) as the mantra washed down upon them, and then they withdrew through the massive doors of Louis XIV's palace.

In spite of the hostile reception, the American seemed to be in an accommodating mood, and anxious to find a solution to their differences as they strolled across the magnificent terrace in the morning sunshine. The chants of the protestors on the other side of the building died down as the TV lights flickered out, and people started to wonder where the hell they were going to be able to find some place to eat in *this* scrum.

"Mr. President, Joe," she said. "I remain convinced that we can find middle ground."

"I believe that too, Charlotte."

"I'm delighted to hear that, Joe, she responded warmly." I'm not an unreasonable woman. Perhaps the terms of the Rapprochement Generale are a little one-sided—a high opening bid, shall we say?"

She clapped the American President on the shoulder and chuckled.

"I'm sure you don't blame me for trying, eh? 'All's fair in love and war'?"

"Indeed it is, Charlotte, indeed it is," he replied, just as warmly. "Actually, Charlotte, Jean Luc Lafarge said something kind of similar in his confession. 'All's fair in love and politics', or something to that effect. I'll give you a copy of the transcript, if you'd like."

He returned the shoulder clapping gesture for the distant cameras. "Advise me, Charlotte, should I hand him and all the evidence over to the International Criminal Court, or should I simply keep him on ice? What do you suggest? You're so much better at international politics than I am."

The French President again clapped her American counterpart on the shoulder so that the cameras could not see her face. They saw a friendly bear hug which lasted several seconds.

"My God, it's a love fest," commented the reporter from the *New York World Journal* Television Service to her producer.

(She too had had a difficult week, but her bosses had supported her decision not to help the little girl. 'A news service of record cannot get directly involved in events without losing its impartiality' they had intoned. 'But she was just a little girl in need of help!' someone from the rival newspaper had shouted to the *World Journal's* spokesperson. 'She was in the arms of the President, and therefore she was an overt political symbol', he had shot back.)

The French President had managed to compose her features and broke the hug.

"I...I think it would be better if you kept him on ice, Mr. President."

They descended a magnificent flight of stairs and began to stroll along the superb reflecting pool which stretched behind the palace. The press was allowed to follow at a distance. Again, this was a wonderful scene for the cameras. The elegant French President was explaining the diplomatic facts of life to the burly simple-minded American President in his ugly work boots as they walked beside the placid waters, a splendid contrast to the raucous protests broadcast a few minutes before.

"Perhaps the Rapprochement Generale is an idea whose time has not yet come," she was saying. "Or, indeed, an idea whose time will never come."

The American President nodded slowly, and the French President continued rapidly.

"In fact, I have grown very weary of all this silly anti-Americanism. In truth, I have prepared an edict banning the 'c'est possible' demonstrations in France, and I shall urge that as a general EU policy. I find the whole idea revolting!"

Her rejection was clear to the cameras. Again the American President nodded.

"My God," said the reporter to her producer. "She's crapping all over the American!"

She spoke as if she was not an American herself.

The French President had paused as more inspiration struck her. The cameras saw her gesticulating in animation as he listened carefully, his head bowed to catch every word of advice.

"The anniversary of the liberation of Paris is fast approaching, and I intend to attend the ceremonies myself. We will never forget our debt to America: never. I was thinking of quoting Churchill, albeit out of context, 'Never has so much been owed by so many to so few'. Or even in context he said something about 'The new world, with all its power and might, stepping forth to the rescue and liberation of the old', something like that.

"Perhaps you'll come yourself, Joe, and we could hold a banquet in honor of the fallen soldiers, and serve the best American corn-fed beef. There's been such a lot of stupid nonsense about genetic foods. They've never hurt a fly. It will help to set that dreadful graveyard business to rest."

The American President nodded slowly once more.

"I appreciate that Charlotte, I really do. I'll certainly be here. You know, I've been thinking about an idea I got from a woman named Jeannette Bois. I think you're familiar with her work?"

Such was her self-control that she managed not to flinch at his casual mention of that name, but she turned her face away from the cameras as he continued.

"Based on her analysis, I've been thinking that you would make an excellent Secretary General of the UN. As you know, the position will open up in another few months. If you could find your way to resigning from your present position early, you could count on my full support for the office.

"We could work together to reshape the UN, and you would be the first woman Secretary General, in addition to having been the first female President of France. What do you think?"

The French President was flabbergasted. He had her, hook, line, and sinker, but now he was actually offering her a way out! She patted his shoulders again, and the cameras and reporters saw her complete dominance of the conversation.

"That...that would be very attractive, Mr. President."

"Good, then that's settled. But there's one other thing. Lafarge also talked about the Middle East, and I don't speak for the Israelis—nobody speaks for them!"

She stopped and turned to him. In her excruciatingly painful shoes, utterly unsuitable for strolling on gravel, they were the same height.

"Let me speak frankly, Joe. We have had accords and road maps and resolutions and agreements and plans and God knows what else. Nothing has ever worked. Nothing!"

Her gesture of utter rejection of every argument he could make was vividly clear.

"Jesus Christ, did you see that?" asked the TV reporter. "Whatever she's saying she's got him by the balls!"

"We Europeans need a new statement of policy, Joe. We will do whatever we can to help the Palestinians, but the guiding principle must be that Israel deserves to live within secure and peaceful borders: UN Resolution 242 or nothing! If the Palestinians won't disarm their terrorists, then by God we will do it for them! Europe owes that to the Jewish people. We can never forget.

"I shall make it a personal commitment. It will take a few months to line up European support, but I can do that by the fall. I *will* do it by the fall!"

The cameras saw her thump her fist energetically into her other palm, while the American nodded.

"Perhaps you could announce it on Yom Kippur, Charlotte."

"Why Yom Kippur, in particular?"

"It's the Day of Atonement."

He gestured at the press corps waiting in the distance.

"Look, Charlotte, the fourth estate is waiting. Shall we go over and give them the good news?"

Epilogue

"So what the hell did this woman Bois *know*, for God's sake? What was such a big goddamned deal?"

The prime minister's personal representative searched his pockets out of habit until he remembered he'd given up smoking again. The windows were open to the sunny Jerusalem morning.

"It's not what she knew, it was the implications of what she knew," Moshe said. "Daniel, you explain—this is your area."

"She worked at the bank where most of the money for the old UN Iraqi Oil for Food program was handled," Daniel told him. "You remember, when Saddam was under sanctions, and he was allowed to sell oil for humanitarian reasons. The UN, it its wisdom, gave Saddam control over who got the oil exports and who got the import contracts, giving him complete control of the process. You remember when a lot of UN guys and the French and Russians had their fingers in the till, and the Secretary General tried to hush it all up?

"Anyway, the Bois woman could see money coming into her bank from the oil sales, and she could see where it was going. She saw sizable amounts going into a small bank in Switzerland, which she assumed was a mistake. She contacted the Swiss bank and they told her the names of the recipients. But there was no mistake. She had discovered a huge and corrupt diversion of funds."

The prime minister's representative frowned.

"I thought Swiss banks kept their mouths shut?"

"They do, but bank clerks spend their lives trying to sort out mistakes and screw-ups, and information *has* to flow back and forth at the accounting level. Anyway, three names caught her attention in particular. One was A Q Khan, the Pakistani nuclear scientist guy. Another was Kim Chong-Il.

"She guessed, correctly as it turned out, that this money was going in payment for nuclear know-how and equipment. Saddam had failed to build a bomb himself, so he simply bought the raw materials from North Korea and Khan assembled the bombs for him in Pakistan and shipped them over. The third name was a certain French politician who was one of the leaders of the effort to stop the war against Saddam."

"You mean?"

"Yes," Moshe said. "She packaged the deal. She suppressed Daniel's investigation—he was hot on her heels—and when it became inevitable that the US would invade Iraq, she arranged for the bombs to be brought out of Iraq and stored in the French embassy in Damascus for safekeeping. That not only covered everyone's tracks, but also made the US look like morons when no WMDs were found."

"You've got to admit, she's very smart."

"Anyway, to make a long story short, Jeannette Bois took copies of the transactions and the payment details she got from the Swiss bank, and took them home. She told her sister, who told her husband, who happened to be Jean Luc Lafarge's driver. So Jean Luc stumbled into the hottest secret of the new millennium. He has a reputation for being lucky.

"Lafarge had his private hit man, Paul Rennard, kill the woman and get hold of the documentary evidence. He also killed the Swiss bank clerk to be on the safe side. Now Lafarge was in a position to blackmail the French politician. In due course, she moved up the political ladder and he cooked up his Casse-noisette idea, and got the politician to do the diplomatic dirty work."

"None of this was in Jean Luc's confession transcript. I read it myself."

"No, and not surprisingly. Jean Luc's name was on the list also, in connection with Russian deals."

"So how did we find out?"

"Rennard is no fool," said Moshe. "When he killed the Bois woman, he stole the bank records from her apartment and took copies before he gave them to Lafarge, and the same with the Swiss woman. When we got his confession he told us where they were. We're keeping Rennard on ice, just in case we ever need a live witness."

"I had been tracking the money some years ago, but I could never get into the Swiss bank." Daniel continued. "My investigation was shit-canned when the Bois woman was killed. Now we know why. With the additional Swiss information from Rennard I had what I'd been missing. We could see the money coming out of Switzerland and into Syria, and you guys got the details out of the Syrians; first the old Saddam deals, and now the recent flow back to Korea in payment for the nonproliferation deal.

"And of course Maria Menendez got Jean Luc Lafarge on tape tying it all together," Moshe added.

"What's happened to the Menendez woman, incidentally?"

"She's back in the US Marines. She says intel makes her feel dirty, and I know exactly what she means. I believe she's volunteered for Afghanistan."

"So now we're going to get a new UN Secretary General, and the President of the United States has the dirt on her?"

"Yep, and Lafarge is in Guantanamo while his status is determined. I believe they've temporarily classified him as an 'enemy combatant'. I wouldn't be surprised if we see a couple of changes in international politics."

The prime minister's representative pondered.

"And we have Rennard, so we also have her by the balls, metaphorically speaking?"

"Metaphorically speaking," said Moshe.

Paul had been seized by a great anxiety. Now that he had nothing more to give, would they dispose of him? They did not seem to care.

The air whooshed softly in the air conditioners, and the unblinking cameras watched him, and the robot came and went about its duties, and thus the routine continued inexorably, 'day' in and 'day' out.

He fell into a deep depression, overwhelmed by loneliness and boredom and hopelessness, but weeping was not a permitted activity.

0-595-31863-0

Printed in the United States
21293LVS00005B/105

9 780595 318636